Dor Slinkard is an unstoppable storyteller. Be it through writing or voice, her stories will enthral. Inspired by life, especially as a jillaroo in outback Australia and later as a race horse trainer, her imagination thrives. In her lasting marriage to Wade, a jackaroo now horse trainer, they have produced two children and they, in turn, five grandchildren.

DEDICATION

I dedicate this story to Victoria Shaw, an extremely talented Race Caller, who is well known for trail blazing the way to have women recognized among the field of competent race callers.

And to anyone, who has ever experienced, in- justice, for any reason.

ISBN **9780648539179** (Paperback)
ISBN **9780648539117** (E-Book)

First Published (2021)

ACKNOWLEDGEMENTS

Without help from friends and family, this story would not be possible.

Firstly, to my Husband Wade, who encourages me and proofreads with attention to detail. Plus, he is always there to cook dinner. Thank you.

My lifelong friend and Editor Margaret Mooney, I'm certain you were sent from above. My appreciation for your brilliance in helping me achieve my goal, has no end. Thank you.

John and Anne Tapp, for their friendship, and agreeing to proofread. And with that, they helped in correcting dates and significant facts. Thank you both.

Ron Worthy for his brilliant portrayal on canvas, depicting the characters and the era so well. Thank you, Ron.

To all the friends who volunteered to give an appraisal on the story. In particular, Sandy Gray, Marie Mitchell and Jan Dowd. Thank you ladies.

Finally, to my Computer genius's Deborah and Mick Jones of 'Computus Australis.' I cannot thank you enough for keeping me up and running. And to Deborah, who up-loads my stories to, Publishers, 'Ingram Sparks,' with the care of a mother. Bless you both.

By the same author

Henri-etta

For the Love of Trilogy
Book 1 – For the Love of Patrick
Book 2 – For the Love of Freedom
Book 3 – For the Love of Justice

Dor Slinkard

WRONG SIDE OF THE FENCE

CHAPTER 1

Caulfield Racecourse 1940. Victoria, Australia.

At the end of a narrow laneway, an old wooden fence sat precariously, seeming to defy the gale-force winds that sometimes hammered its existence. Still, it managed to separate the outside world from the Caulfield Racecourse. On specific Saturdays and at forty-minute intervals, the racing fraternity would gather in the grandstand to watch the jockeys and their thoroughbred mounts gallop around the track in an exhibition of skill and speed.

Standing on top of a fruit box and watching this spectacle from the wrong side of the fence, was thirteen-year-old Grace Nobel. Her dad, Tom, stood alongside. And her brother Walter sat in a wheelchair watching the races through a gap in the fence, where Tom had removed the customary palings. Walter could have stood on a box too, but he was a bit wobbly and tended to lose balance when excited.

Each time the field flashed by in a swirl of colour and a thunder of hooves, it fuelled Grace's dream of becoming a race caller. A few weeks ago, when she had blown out thirteen candles on her birthday cake, she wished fervently that one day, when the war was over, she would have the chance to make her dream a reality. Grace had inherited her dad's passion for calling races from an early age, and as she grew, so did her desire. Now, with her elbows propped on the fence, binoculars ready and concentration apt, Grace waited for the barriers to spring open and the charge to begin. With her clear speech and precise reckoning, Grace thought she called every race, as well as her dad, did – and he would confirm this by ruffling her hair, a habit which Grace found both annoying and endearing in equal measure.

"What do you reckon, Dad, was my call good?" Grace looked expectantly at Tom. "I could see the trailer was going to make a winning dash in the home straight, so I kept my eye on him, and I was right!"

"Don't get too cocky, Grace. You may miss something important if you only keep your eye on one or two horses. The trick is to train your eye to have a panoramic view."

Walter clapped his hands, repeating, "Pan...pan...panoramic. Great w...word, Dad."

Grace wiped a dribble of saliva from Walter's lips using the piece of cloth that she carried specifically for the job.

"Yep, it is Walter, my boy," Tom said, his blue eyes filled with love as he squeezed his son's shoulder. "Well," Tom continued, checking his pocket watch. "We'd better go before your Mum gets home from shopping." He pushed the fence palings back in place then swung Walter's wheelchair around.

"But Dad," Grace pleaded, "Nelly said she was going to Grandma's first and that means an extra hour. And she said she'd booked in to have her hair done – Nelly will probably do her shopping after so she can show off her new hair style." Grace gathered up her auburn hair and, piling it up on top of her head, struck a pose. "Come on, Dad. Nelly won't be home until at least four o'clock! Can't we stay a bit longer? Please? I want to see my favourite horse win!"

"That old crock?" Tom chuckled.

"He's not a crock," Grace protested, "he just had some time off with an injury. You watch. He will win – this is his first start back and he's in the next race. Please, Dad, stay for one more? Please?" Grace clasped her hands dramatically to her chest.

"Okay - but you'll have to face up to your mother when she sees the lawn hasn't been mowed. Deal?"

"I will, I promise. I'll think of something," Grace assured him happily.

Grace positively glowed when her favourite horse, Singintherain, bolted in, winning by five lengths. She knew her dad disliked boasting, so she refrained from showing her delight at being right – once again – but she couldn't stop smiling as they headed home.

Each Friday night before a race meeting, the trio would sit at the kitchen table studying the jockeys' silks, trying to memorize the numbers, names, and colours of the horses: 7 - Harvey Boy, a grey; 10 - Kingdom Come, a chestnut; 3 - Power Pack, a bay, and so on. However, this ritual was never conducted when Nelly was present. Nelly often denounced horseracing and gambling - not that Tom had ever placed a bet. He simply loved the sport and dreamed of calling races professionally. Luckily, for all concerned, on Friday nights, Nelly played Bridge at a friend's home.

It was never an option for Tom and his children to attend a Caulfield race meeting. Nelly would never allow it. Having been brought up in a God-fearing household, Nelly's principles were set in stone, having been carved there by her mother. "Gambling of any kind is a sin!" Grandma would shout. "Money is the root of all evil," was another of her favourites - and yet, the old hypocrite worshipped the stuff. Of course, Nelly playing cards was never considered gambling.

"Money is never involved. Bridge is purely a game of skill and intellect", Nelly would proclaim righteously, head held high.

Why Tom married Nelly, Grace could never understand. Granted, Nelly had a slim figure and was considered pretty, but Grace had no idea whether this made up for her caustic nature. However, whenever Nelly was happily absorbed in one of her 'romance novels,' Grace would see her mother's stern expression soften, and she would become dreamily preoccupied. Preparing dinner or hanging clothes on the line, Nelly would sing love songs and afterward, she'd hurry back to her novel and sit in her special armchair, the reading lamp with the pink-frilled shade behind. No one else ever dared to sit there.

Grace was happy when her mother read, which was most of the time, and so was Tom. He was her main provider of books and ensured she had an endless supply of Mills and Boon novels or something equally romantic. Whatever he had to do to make Nelly happy, Tom mostly obliged - except for one thing. When Walter had been born with cerebral palsy, Tom had rejected all the well-intentioned advice and adamantly refused to put him in a home. Tom had fought many battles with Nelly and her parents over this issue. They seemed to think Walter's condition was a punishment sent to them from God.

"Bloody idiots," Tom cursed. "God-bothering, hateful bastards! What happened to Christian love and kindness?" Tom had prevailed so far, but not with those words. He had argued more cautiously and had won his case to keep Walter at home. While Tom's ambitions of race calling had been set aside for a job that would provide a more predictable income for his family, he did what he could to encourage his daughter's ambition and protect his son's welfare.

*

Nelly stood on the front veranda, hands-on-hips, glaring at the front lawn. The lawn didn't need mowing - but Nelly was well, Nelly - and everything except her reading Romance Novels ran to a strict timetable.

The sheets she washed every Thursday, the furniture polished, and the carpet vacuumed each Friday. On Mondays, without fail, the clothes she washed in the morning she ironed after dinner, while Tom and the children listened to their favourite radio program, *Dad and Dave*. It was hardly Nelly's favourite. She failed to see the humour in the struggles of *this ill-bred farming family* as she called them, despite the vast majority of Australians loving the endearing and straightforward stories which, for half an hour every night, took their minds off their problems.

"Where have you been, Tom?" Nelly demanded angrily, but not loudly enough that the neighbours might hear. Tom looked to Grace, who swallowed and coughed nervously to buy time before she confronted her mother as she had promised she would.

"Well, it's like this, Nell – uh, Mum. We went for a walk to the shops, and Walter's wheelchair got a flat tyre," Grace wiped her brow for effect, "and you wouldn't believe it, we just couldn't find the right size tube to mend it." She looked squarely at Nelly, who was now tapping her foot, a sure sign she didn't, for an instant, believe Grace. *We're in trouble.* "Well, anyway, Dad thought we'd better just patch it up. And you know what? The garage man had run out of glue, just our luck! So …"

"Enough of your lies, Grace! I know where you lot have been! Mrs. Album saw you standing at the racetrack fence!"

Grace had hidden the binoculars under the rug across Walter's lap, and with an awkward effort, he pulled them out and waved them triumphantly at Nelly, smiling broadly. "You guessed right, Mu…Mum"

"Oh, shit," said Tom quietly. "Now you've done it, mate."

Nelly walked back inside after giving an exaggerated huff.

Grace had lost the battle and, conceding defeat, reluctantly retrieved the mower from the shed and furiously proceeded to push it back and forth across the grass. Walter watched intently from the sidelines. His eagerness in wanting to help Grace had him almost bouncing out of his wheelchair. Grace relaxed and laughed, but then thought, *He can walk, so why not? Just because that chair makes it easier to get him around, it doesn't mean he has to spend all his time in it.*

"Come on, Walter, do you want to have a go?" She moved the mower close and helped him stand. Walter was two and a half years older than Grace and handsome - apart from the fine trickle of saliva that seemed to flow continuously from the corner of his mouth. Tall and lean, he was easy to maneuver. Grace held him close to the mower and Walter grabbed the handles while Grace stood behind, kicking his feet to start him off. Walter got the gist and proceeded to push the mower forward - alone. His eagerness had him sometimes struggling with his center of gravity, though not enough to fall. They laughed all the way around until, both out of breath, they stood to view their efforts.

"Not exactly straight, Walter, but not bad for your first go!" Grace patted him gently on the back.

Tom appeared on the front veranda, a beer in hand and a smile to conquer the world. "Walter, my son, you've mowed the lawn. Why haven't you done it before?" Tom's tone was light-hearted, but his pride in his son's achievement was unmistakable.

Walter let go of the mower handles, gently nudged Grace out of the way, and took three steps towards his dad. "Well, nobody's asked me be...before," Walter said with hardly a stutter - his confidence building. He then wobbled a little before taking another three steps. Tom didn't move - he needed to see how far Walter could walk unaided. It was something Nelly never encouraged for some obscure reason. Tom's face was beaming. He was so proud of his son and always had been.

The front door opened and slammed shut. "You'll fall, you stupid boy!" Nelly hissed. "Get the wheelchair, Grace!"

Tom froze like he'd been knifed in the back. "Leave him be, Nelly," Tom said evenly. "He has to try, or he'll feel like a burden all his life." Raising his voice, he called encouragingly, "Come on, Walter. You won't fall, mate. You can do it!"

Walter looked from his father's smiling face across to his mother's sour expression. She laughed derisively. Walter's confidence evaporated, and he fell.

"Told you so," Nelly said with a sneer. "Now go and pick him up, Tom. He's already given me a bad back, and I'll never be the same. The pain is unbearable." She began massaging her back, hoping for a bit of sympathy.

Tom looked at Nelly, his expression stony. Nelly turned away and crossed her arms.

From across the lawn came the sound of applause. Edward Hobbs lived next door and had been a part of Tom's life since he was a youngster and a part of Nelly's since she had married Tom.

"Well done, Walter," Edward said, smiling over the Photinia

13

hedge. "I've been watching - just thought I'd ask if you wanted a job mowing my lawn? What do you reckon?"

"Yes, please," Walter said with a broad smile. He gently pushed Grace away as she tried to help him stand. To everyone's amazement, he turned on his knees, focused, and lifted himself off the ground. Applause, again from Edward.

"It looks to me like you want the job, Walter. It'll be getting dark soon. How about tomorrow morning, say about ten?"

"Walter goes to Church tomorrow morning, Edward. And you must be joking. He can't mow lawns, don't be stupid!" Nelly said, full of self-righteous indignation.

"I just saw for myself, Nelly. I reckon he did a pretty good job, love."

"Don't call *me* love! And I'm telling you, Walter will not be mowing your lawn, Edward, and that's *that*!" Nelly went inside, slamming the door for effect. Everything Nelly did was for effect.

*

At nine-thirty the following day, Edward knocked on their front door. Grace opened it and smiled. "Come in, Edward." Grace loved the older man as she had his wife Sylvia, who'd died suddenly twelve months before.

"Good luck with getting Mum to agree to Walter mowing your lawn, Edward," Grace whispered, waving her arm in the direction of the kitchen, where her family was gathered. Tom sat reading the newspaper, Walter was eating his breakfast, and Nelly stood at the sink peeling potatoes, moaning about having to cook a roast every Sunday.

Nelly's church hat sat askew, messing up her newly permed curls. She pushed it back to wipe her brow and said over her shoulder:

"Walter *is* going to church Edward. I told you that. Besides, I've dressed him in his Sunday Best."

"Like hell you did," Grace muttered under her breath, "he did it himself."

"What was that Grace?" Nelly asked sharply.

"I said, Mum, that Walter would rather stay home and mow Edward's lawn." She gave Walter a gentle push. "Isn't that right, Walter?"

Walter duly nodded, and grabbing another piece of vegemite toast, shoved it in his mouth and chewed enthusiastically.

"Slow down, Walter. There's plenty of time to mow my lawn."

Edward teased.

Nelly stopped peeling mid-spud and pointed her knife at Edward. "I told you – "

"And I'm telling *you*, Nelly," Edward interrupted her with authority, "Walter would rather do something *useful* than sit in church *all morning* listening to that *piss-weak* preacher."

"How *dare* you speak like that in my home! Edward, please leave now!" Nelly gestured towards the door, swinging around so quickly her hat toppled to the floor, ruining the drama of the moment. *I should use a hat pin*, she thought before tearing off her apron and throwing it at Edward. She made a show of bending to pick up her hat, emitting groans of agony. "Oh, my poor back!" She straightened up in increments and, after dusting off the hat, placed it awkwardly upon her head. She picked up her handbag from the table, gave a loud *harrumph* and marched towards the front door.

Tom folded the newspaper carefully and looked at his children, an unreadable emotion playing over his features. Edward looked at him apologetically. "I'm sorry, Tom, I can't help myself sometimes. Jesus, she'd rile the Good Lord Himself, I reckon. Sorry, mate."

"Don't apologize Edward. Just take Walter with you. Let him mow your lawn. Go out the backdoor." Tom nodded at Grace. "And Gracie, sweetheart - you go with your mother. Tell her I'll be along in a minute."

"Okay, Dad." Grace hurried to catch Nelly, knowing her mother would be talking to herself, fuming. Sometimes Grace felt sorry for Nelly. Having been brought up by Grandma would be any kid's worst nightmare.

You must always do the right thing. God is watching you. God sees everything! Her grandmother would preach through lips as tight as a cat's bum. Doing the *right* thing meant *everything* imaginable. From eating carefully to walking down the street with your head held high. How to behave in public, avoid anyone common, have bad manners, or live on the wrong side of the tracks. Her demands would have stifled even the bravest kid. Grace felt lucky to have her Dad. She could not imagine her life without him; if she thought about losing him, Grace felt like she would crumble and break. That went for Walter, too. She loved him just as much as she loved her Dad. But Nelly? Well, Grace's feelings for her mother were a mix of both love and aversion, not always in equal

15

amounts. Nelly was broken and urgently needed fixing. But the question was, *how*?

Grace jogged until she caught up. "Mum, please don't be angry. Look at it this way. We won't be pestered by all those stickybeak do-gooders asking, *Has there been any improvement in Walter, dear?*" Grace snorted mockingly and went on in her normal voice. "Well, what I mean is, if we don't try and help him do things for himself, he'll never improve." Grace glanced sideways to catch Nelly's expression. "What do you think, Mum? Shouldn't we encourage Walter to do things for himself? Then you can tell everyone, *Yes, Walter is getting better all the time, thank you.*" Grace turned to her mother, waiting for an answer, and was surprised to see a tear trickle down Nelly's cheek.

"I suppose you're right, Grace. It's just that Grandma keeps telling me things, terrible things that I know in my heart aren't true. I'm sure God didn't send Walter as a punishment." Nelly blew her nose with her embroidered handkerchief and sighed with resignation. "I've been a good person; I've never done a bad deed." Nelly's conscience quickly reminded her of the night she'd been overcome with passion and let Tom make love to her – before they were married. They were engaged, well, sort of; Nelly had been sure Tom would ask her to marry him, particularly after she had shown him how much she loved him. But the proposal only came eight weeks later when she tearfully told him she was pregnant.

Tom had felt duty-bound to do the honourable thing and marry Nelly. He had *done the deed*, thinking only of his own satisfaction. Tom had been attracted to Nelly's prettiness, although he had never been *in love* with her. As for Nelly, she had adored Tom. But after they were married, Tom didn't behave like one of the Mills and Boon book heroes, sweeping her off her feet and showering her with compliments. Over time, her heart, like a flower needing rain, withered away until her love had almost died. A little spontaneous show of affection from Tom now and then would have helped revive it. Yes, she had been so sure their love for each other would flourish, if only he could have delivered the romance she so desired.

"I'm sorry, Grace, I know I always seem angry. I don't mean to be. I do love you and Walter." Nelly drew a deep breath and straightened her back. "Come on, Grace, we'll be late for Church." Nelly looked over her shoulder. "Where's your father?"

"He said he'll be along in a minute, Mum." Grace hooked her

arm through Nelly's to show she appreciated her apology – they were rare. As they walked on, Grace asked her mother a question she knew would take her mind off her worries. "What *Mills and Boon* are you reading, Mum? When can I read them? I'm sick of the *Anne of Green Gables books*; they're a bit boring." Grace had just finished reading *National Velvet*, which she had adored, but her mother would have had a pink fit if she had known it was about a girl riding in a famous horserace.

"Grace, I'm shocked! You won't be old enough to read romance until you're at least twenty-one." She squeezed Grace's hand. "But maybe when you're sixteen, I'll let you read the tame ones." Nelly giggled, remembering how her mother had never known she'd read them. Nelly had hidden the books in a box at the bottom of her cupboard. She supposed she'd always been a romantic, but where had it gotten her? Her mood suddenly changed. "It does you no good being a romantic, Grace." Nelly shook a finger. "When things don't turn out like you dream they will, you will lose heart and become bitter."

Grace had never heard her mother speak so honestly. What had gotten into her?

"I might be young, Mum, but I understand. I dream about being a race...." Grace clamped her lips, realizing what she was about to say. No matter how understanding she seemed right then, Nelly would turn into the Devil if Grace confessed her desire.

"What were you about to say, Grace?" Nelly asked, now in a somber mood. Her moods changed like the Melbourne weather.

"Oh, it was just a joke, Mum. I was going to say a racing car driver, but I thought it'd upset you that you wouldn't find it funny..."

"No, not at all. I think it is funny, Grace, because you can't drive. Now, where's your father?" Nelly turned around; her brow furrowed as she looked down the road; there was no sign of Tom. "I hope he's all right."

Geez, she's never said that before. What's got into her? Grace pulled her mother's sleeve, "They'll be along any minute, Mum. Come on. We'll be late."

17

CHAPTER 2

Walter had gone with Edward – he was safe. Grace and Nelly, Tom knew, would be sitting in church; this suited his plan to leave quickly, without personal farewells.

As he began to write, first to Nelly and then to the children, his heart ached so badly he wanted to rip up the paper, torn between his commitment to the Army and his love for his children. He took a deep breath and began to write.

> *Dear Nelly,*
> *I'm sorry to be leaving this way, but I've joined the Army.*
> *I felt the need to join the ranks to help keep my family and this country safe. I know one man cannot do it on his own, but together we will conquer the enemy, I'm sure. My cowardice at not being able to tell you face-to-face is not a good start to a fighting career, I know, but this is the hardest thing I'm sure I will ever have to do.*
> *Please believe me when I tell you, my conscience has struggled with my heart for a long time before making this decision.*
> *Take good care.*
> *Your dutiful husband,*
> *Tom*

At least his letter to Nelly was honest. However, trying to explain his leaving to Grace and Walter was almost more than he could bear. Tom needed to wipe his eyes many times to stop his falling tears from smudging the ink.

> *Darling Walter and Grace,*
> *My heart breaks to leave you both.*
> *I have joined the fight to keep those bloody Nazis from our shores. Your love is what will keep me alive, so please, never stop loving*

18

me. I can hardly bear to leave you, but I must. I know, Grace, you will always be there for Walter. Don't let anyone take him away. Edward will help you; I've asked him to look out for you both, and he's on our side, remember that.

  I believe in you Walter, keep trying to do the things you want to do, son. You can achieve anything mate. I know you can. Grace, you will make the best race caller this country has ever heard. Keep up the fight, believe in yourself, and don't let anyone tell you, you can't because you can. I'm so proud of you both. Stay strong and believe in the power of good.

  Your loving father, Tom.

  P.S. Don't show your mother this letter - hide it or rip it up if you must. I will write as soon as I can.

*

When Grace's tears had finally abated and her heart had healed enough, she did as Tom had asked. She became more assertive and even more protective of Walter's independence. However, it took many more months before she could think of her father without tears.

  Nelly, at first, had collapsed into a hysterical mess, and she was still finding it hard to cope at times. It was several weeks before the first pay cheque arrived from the Australian Army. It was scant compensation for Tom's absence, but at least Tom wrote regularly from his Army training Camp in the Atherton Tablelands, Queensland.

  "Wow, Walter, Dad's learning to fight like Tarzan!" Grace quipped as she finished reading Tom's latest letter.

  Walter laughed and the trickle made its way down his chin. Grace gave him a stern look and Walter wiped it up with much less difficulty than when he'd first begun.

  "I did it, Gra...cie."

  "Yep, you can do anything, Walter. Just like Dad said."

  Grace and Walter had been left alone at home while Nelly attended to what she had told them was 'urgent business' in Melbourne. "It must be special," Grace said to Walter as she watched her mother strut down the path in her best outfit.

  Nelly had been gone for nearly four hours when Grace heard the front door open and her mother call, "Grace! Come here, please."

  Grace, followed by an unaided Walter, walked from her bedroom into the kitchen. Nelly sat at the head of the table in Tom's usual seat. She looked in control, positive – almost.

"Please sit down, children. I have something important to tell you." Nelly's tone was severe. She looked at them before they had a chance to sit, and a flicker of uncertainty crossed her features.

"I know you may not like what I'm about to say, Walter, but we cannot survive on your father's Army pay, so I must go to work. The accounting firm, C. J. Brown, and Co., who employed your father, have been most generous in offering me a position as their receptionist. It was after I had a meeting with the boss today and explained our situation." Nelly paused, drawing a deep breath before continuing. "Therefore, I will not be able to care for you, Walter. I must place you in a home where you will get the care you need. I really need to work and - "

Grace slammed her fist on the table. "He's not a bloody child, Nelly! And haven't you noticed? He can look after himself now!"

"How *dare* you speak to me like that, Grace. I am your *mother*! Go to your room. I will speak with Walter. I'm sure he understands the problem." Nelly smiled sweetly at Walter, whose expression was a mixture of anger and sadness. Yes, he understood.

"*I said*, Walter can look after himself while you're at work and I'm at school, Mum." Grace stood and gripped the back of her chair.

"Go to your room. Now, Grace!" Nelly shrilled, finger-pointing.

Grace charged out of the kitchen, scaled the side fence and zigzagged through Edward's manicured garden, yelling, "Edward! Edward! Are you there?" She hammered loudly on his door before it opened.

Edward knew Grace's distress could only mean one thing. "Grace, what happened? Is it Walter?"

"Yes! Nelly's going to send him to a home! She's got a job and says she can't look after him and we can't survive on Dad's Army pay!" She grabbed Edward's arm. "I'll eat bread and dripping if it keeps Walter at home," Grace pleaded. "What are we going to do?"

Edward scratched his stubbly chin. He thought it a waste of time to shave every day now that Sylvia was no longer alive to kiss him goodnight. "Calm down, Grace. Let me clean up and get dressed, and I'll come over and talk to your mum. I have an idea, okay?" Edward reached out and ruffled her hair, just like her dad used to, *and* Grace trembled, pushing the memory aside.

"Now, go home, Grace, and stay calm. I'll be there in two shakes of a lamb's tail, okay darling?" Edward lifted her chin and placed a kiss on her forehead. "Trust me Grace. I know your mother well. Don't worry."

Yes, Edward did understand Nelly. Apart from wanting to give her a bloody good shake sometimes, he felt sorry for her.

Edward had been a respected lawyer in his working life, and his kindness had often compelled him to take care of those less fortunate, perhaps too often. He'd tell them, *'Don't worry, just pay me when things pick up. I'm glad we won the case.'* In the Depression years, the payouts were almost nothing; everyone was scraping for a living. However, his wife Sylvia had been lucky. Her parents had left her a considerable amount of money, as well as their lovely home in Caulfield. And it had set them up. But Sylvia had also been unlucky; six miscarriages had taken their toll on her health. Nevertheless, she had always been a doting wife to Edward.

Edward had once dealt professionally with Nelly's parents, the Hardy's. Not that he had wanted to; they were almost neighbours, and he knew the law had a way of entangling people. While the Hardy's had all the appearances of being good, God-fearing people, they were ruthless with both money and other people's feelings. They were the owners of a third-generation chain of grocery stores and other diversified commercial interests. Some of Edward's other clients had engaged him to challenge the Hardy's on different occasions. He didn't like the family one little bit, except for Nelly. She was the youngest of the children; the two older brothers had flown the coop as soon as they could. Good on them, Edward had thought at the time. Sadly, Nelly alone had to suffer her mother's critical nature, which she disguised as' a righteous Christian.' The older her mother grew, the more unrighteous she became, and Nelly bore the brunt of it. When young Nelly was away from her parents' influence, Edward would hear reports from those who knew her, saying what a pleasant and caring girl she was—living with a mother who showed her neither compassion nor love always had and still made Edward feel sorry for Nelly.

Once shaved and showered, Edward brushed the lapels of his best suit and smiled into the mirror. The last time he'd worn it was at Sylvia's funeral. He knew she'd be proud of him and what he was about to offer. After all, Walter, and Grace, in a way, had been like their own children.

Edward and Sylvia had always kept an eye out for Walter and Grace while Tom was working late, and Nelly attended her Bible classes or some such thing. *After school care*, Sylvia called it; she loved having them in for afternoon tea. However, if ever Nelly joined them, the conversation would inevitably turn to God, how He was watching over them and how God would punish those who did wrong. Nelly treated these visits as a special occasion. Sometimes Edward thought she'd gone completely dippy, the way she'd arrive wearing a hat, matching gloves, and her best day dress as if she were having tea with the Archbishop.

"All for a bloody cup of tea and a piece of cake. God, that woman riles me, Sylvia," he'd say. "How come I can stay calm in Court, dealing with idiot judges and the biggest crooks, and yet *she* can infuriate me?" Edward would ask this of Sylvia as soon as Nelly had said goodbye and their front door was closed.

Sylvia had been a wise, loving woman with an unexpectedly wicked sense of humour. "Nelly lives in another world, Edward, one you and I are incapable of understanding. Don't worry, dear, just pretend you're listening to one of those dreadful soap operas on the radio. Pretend she's one of those silly, dramatic characters. That's what I do, and it's very entertaining." More seriously, Sylvia added, " But I do admit, it's all a bit sad really, Nelly carrying on like that. Poor girl, she's been through the mill, being brought up the way she was, and I suspect Tom doesn't love her as much as she'd like." Sylvia looked thoughtful. "I suppose her only consolation is to escape into her romance novels. That reminds me, I borrowed three more from the library for her. If it weren't for Tom and me, Nelly would never have anything to read. She'd be too ashamed to buy or borrow them herself. And just think how *terrible* she'd be without them," Sylvia said, smiling.

"I know what you mean, Sylvia. I've seen her go totally off with the fairies when she's reading one of those - what do you call them - *Bills and Moons*?"

Sylvia laughed joyfully and gave her husband a playful poke. "No love, *Mills and Boons*!"

Still smiling from his reminiscence, Edward picked up a stack of borrowed romance novels, a bunch of flowers he'd collected from his garden, and a Violet Crumble that he had been looking forward to after dinner and walked out. "Oh, well. All for a good cause," he muttered. With his hands full, he made his way to Nelly's place.

22

He paused at the front door, mentally rehearsing the case he would put to Nelly. He couldn't quite manage to ring the bell, which was one of those twisty ones, so he kicked the door with his foot. It made him smile, reminding him of a joke he'd heard about a man who'd asked directions on how to get to his friend's house for his birthday party. The friend gave him directions, then he said, '*Just kick the door.*' The man asked. '*Why would I kick your front door?*' and the friend replied, '*Because your hands will be filled with my birthday presents!*'

Grace opened the door. "Why didn't you ring the bell, Edward?"

"Have a look, Grace," Edward inclined his head towards his full hands, "I come bearing gifts for your mum."

"She doesn't deserve them but come in anyway. I hope they help," Grace said, but she didn't feel optimistic as she led the way into the kitchen.

Nelly's anger mollified by the show of gifts, she visibly softened, especially when presented with the heavily scented Gardenias. "Oh, Edward, sometimes you are *lovely*. You *do* understand. I know you do." She sighed dramatically. "Things have been *so* difficult without Tom. I know he's doing the right thing, but it's so awfully hard on me, especially with Walt—"

"That's who I've come to talk about, Nelly." Before Nelly could say another word, Edward continued. "Please hear me out, Nelly. I have an idea that I think will solve both our problems."

He relaxed a little, watching Nelly move gracefully to the sink and arrange the flowers in a vase.

She turned with lowered eyes and a shy smile. "We shouldn't let Gardenias go without water for too long, Edward." Nelly was behaving like a young girl receiving a corsage for her school formal.

Oh, poor bugger - her mind's caught up in one of her romance books! Edward cleared his throat nervously. "Yes, well, as I was saying, Nelly, I'm more than happy to care for Walter while you're at work. It would be my pleasure."

Nelly continued to arrange the flowers. With her back to him, Edward was unable to gauge her reaction.

"I'm afraid, Edward," Nelly said as she turned around, slowly flicked her luxurious auburn hair behind her shoulders, and assumed a pose she had seen in the movies, placing her hands on the bench behind her and leaning back, so her breasts jutted forward. "Actually, my parents

23

have offered to take care of Walter."

"No!" Grace yelled: "No! No, you can't do that!"

Nelly's parents would never, not even in their wildest dreams, have made this offer, but Nelly wanted to hear Edward beg, just like one of those heart-throb *Mills and Boon* heroes she so desperately desired. Edward obliged.

"Please, Nelly, please - don't do that. Please, I'm begging you. Your parents are far too old to look after him. It will put a strain on their health. Please, let me care for Walter. It's only through the day." A winning smile accompanied his raised eyebrows. "I could get your dinner ready, so you won't have to worry about cooking when you get home." He looked expectantly at Nelly.

Grace's initial anger was replaced by desperation. As she sat at the kitchen table, her face on her folded arms, the sound of her muffled sobs filled the silence.

Edward rubbed Grace's back, "Don't worry, Grace, I'm sure your mum and I can work this out."

He smiled at Nelly, noticing how perfectly groomed she was. No doubt the effort had been made for her job interview that morning. "Nelly, you look *so* lovely. How about I take us all out for dinner?"

At this proposal, Nelly stood up straight and preening herself, paraded around the kitchen like a peacock.

"Oh, Edward! I can't *tell* you the last time I dined out." Nelly was clearly excited until her gaze rested on Walter. She drooped visibly. "But what about Wal -"

"Walter will be fine, Nelly. I'm sure we can find him some fancy duds."

"No, I mean...."

"I know what you mean, Nelly. Just trust me, he'll be a gentleman, won't you, Walter?" Edward gave Walter a friendly punch on the arm.

"Ow! Y...yes, I will," Walter said, smiling widely.

"There you go - all settled. Now, buck up, Grace." Edward put his arm around her shoulders and gave her a little cuddle. "Dry your eyes, put your party dress on, and I'll help Walter spruce up a little." He gave Nelly an admiring glance. "Your mother doesn't need to do a thing - she already looks beautiful." Nelly blushed.

*

Sitting opposite Nelly, admiring her by the soft candlelight, Edward's feelings were in a state of confusion. She looked stunning. Her long auburn hair shone, and her emerald eyes sparkled whenever he or Grace made a quip. Nelly's figure was that of a much younger woman, and the red dress she wore clung to her curves and swung about her knees when she walked. Nelly was some fifteen years Edward's junior, and tonight he was acutely aware of it. However, he thought how much more attractive Nelly would be if she would just free herself of her prejudices, especially the ones that had been driven home so hard by her mother.

He shook himself from his thoughts when Walter touched his arm, and in a clear and carrying voice, announced, "Toilet, please."

Edward rose and wheeled Walter to the Gents.

Nelly lowered her eyes, not through embarrassment at Walter's demand, but from the knowledge several men in the restaurant were admiring her. They seemed to be taking every opportunity to look her way. Grace noticed the approving glances; she didn't like it one bit.

"Why did you wear that dress, Mum?" Grace whispered through gritted teeth. "Isn't it the one Dad bought you for your birthday last year? You're not supposed to wear it; it's only for when you and Dad go out *together*. I remember him telling you so." Grace folded her arms in defiance.

"Don't be silly, Grace," Nelly said dismissively, smoothing the silky fabric over her thighs. "Your father would want me to wear it, especially tonight. As I said, it's not often we all go out for dinner." Nelly sat up straight and tilted her chin high. "Besides, I'm wearing it in memory of your father."

"He's not *dead*!" Grace protested angrily. "He won't *die*, and he *will* come back. Don't ever say *in memory of*; it sounds like he's gone forever!" Grace's eyes welled with unshed tears.

Nelly's eyes shot around the restaurant. She plastered a smile on her face and whispered, "Grace, keep your voice down. This is a very exclusive restaurant. Do you want us to be asked to leave?"

"No, I don't - but don't *ever* say that again," Grace whispered back, her heart breaking at the thought of her father never returning.
Edward wheeled Walter back to the table just as their entrées arrived. Walter looked worried.

"I'm sure you can manage oysters, Walter. Just concentrate. You only have to stab them with your fork," Edward encouraged him.

Walter carefully followed Edward's instructions. They all watched

25

as the oyster was speared, carried to Walter's mouth, swallowed, and sent sliding down his throat. He hated the taste, but to his own and everyone else's surprise, he maintained control. He looked at their expectant faces and said simply, "I, d, don't like oysters." Even Nelly laughed good-naturedly. Edward felt relieved that he had helped to breach the wall of frustration and anger, if only for a night, which seemed to keep Nelly and Walter apart.

CHAPTER 3

Saturday morning, Edward knocked on Nelly's door. She appeared dressed in a simple house frock with her hair in rollers, neatly tucked under a scarf.

"Edward, what a surprise. I was coming to see you later." Nelly stroked the scarf and fluttered her eyelashes. "I don't like anyone seeing me like this. You know, about to do the housework."

"Oh, come on, Nelly. I've seen you like that plenty of times. You look lovely whatever you wear." Her girlish giggle made Edward think that perhaps he should back off the flattery. After all, it was just to soften her up so she would come around to the idea of him looking after Walter.

"Thank you, Edward, and thank you again for the lovely evening. I know that restaurant is awfully expensive. Really, you shouldn't have."

Edward shrugged. "Occasionally, it does us good to have a splurge, Nelly. And we never know where this war will take us. I think even simple living will be a lot tougher soon. Rationing is sure to get tighter, so we'll have to be very frugal from now on."

"Yes, I know. I've just used the last of my flour to bake a cake. Would you like to come in and have a piece of apple cake with a cup of tea?" Nelly stepped back from the open doorway.

"Yes, I'd like that. Perhaps we can talk about Walter?"

"Yes, of course," she agreed as she led the way into the kitchen.

"Where are they? Grace and Walter?" Edward asked, looking around.

"They've gone up to the shops; I ran out of milk."

"Good." Edward seated himself at the table. "That gives us time to talk alone."

As Nelly busied herself filling the kettle, cutting the cake, and adding tea to the pot, Edward did his best to convince her he was quite capable of caring for Walter and teaching him to do things for himself. Nelly sat at the table and poured the tea into her best bone China cups.

27

She hadn't spoken as she listened to Edward's plea. She looked up at Edward, her smile accentuating her becoming dimples which had made few appearances until lately. *As a matter of fact*, Edward thought, *I've never seen Nelly smile so much - not since Tom left.* He knew Nelly had cried and thrown tantrums about Tom leaving, but now a certain peace had overcome her in his absence. Edward knew she loved Tom, but maybe they were like many married couples - they loved each other but found it hard to live together. He recalled some of the rows he had heard over the fence. *Maybe? Like hell, I know they found it challenging.*

"So, what do you think, Nelly?" Edward asked with more confidence than he felt. Nelly's eyes lowered while she refilled their cups. When she met Edward's gaze, he saw a new kindness in her eyes.

"I've been thinking about it, Edward, and I must say it is a *very* generous offer. I feel I should pay you, though. I was going to pay the home, no, I mean my parents."

"No, I wouldn't hear of it, Nelly. It would be my pleasure, and it'll help relieve my boredom; now I'm retired. Besides, Walter would be great company, and I don't need to be paid for something that would help me, too."

Nelly reached across the table and placed her hand over Edward's. "I'd appreciate it. I start work this Monday, and I have a lot to organize, so your help would be wonderful."

Edward felt the warmth of her hand. "It's a deal then."

"Yes, it's a deal." Nelly seemed reluctant to let go of Edward's hand, and he had almost to pry it away. Was this the time to ask for another favour?

"Ah…Nelly, you know how I like to go to the races, especially when they're here at Caulfield? I'm a member, you know." Nelly nodded as Edward gave a nervous cough. "Well, I was wondering if you'd let me take Grace and Walter sometimes? Actually, the races are on today." He saw the sudden, frightened look in Nelly's eyes. "Come on, Nelly. What do you think?" Edward swallowed, unsure of what to expect.

It was true. Nelly was frightened; she looked like a stunned mullet, as Tom would have said if he were there. It was Nelly's turn to cough nervously. "I'd say if my parents ever found out, they would disown me!"

Edward felt like telling Nelly she'd be better off without her parents. "But they wouldn't know. Who in their group would ever go to the races? And besides, this is the last meeting they're holding at Caulfield until the war is over. It's going to become an Army Camp." He took a deep breath and plowed on. "Don't you think it's about time you made your own decisions, Nelly? You're a grown woman, not a little girl. You don't have to do what your mother tells you anymore." He went on, his voice gentle. " It's time to follow your *own* heart, your conscience." "Oh, Edward," Nelly said. " I'm not really – "

"Horse racing is a wonderful sport. And I never punt." Edward mentally crossed his fingers to cancel the lie. A little flutter here and there surely didn't count? " And your Grace - did you know Gracie has an amazing talent for calling races? Like her dad, she just loves horses and the sport of racing." T*om could have been a damn good race caller if only you'd given him a chance*, Edward thought, but wisely refrained from saying anything.

Nelly dipped her head as she swept the crumbs off the table into her hand. Edward waited. Nelly dusted the crumbs onto her plate and folded her hands. She looked steadily at Edward.

"Well, if you *promise* me, you won't gamble and that you'll watch them closely. Don't *ever* leave the children on their own - for *any* reason!"

Edward sighed with relief. "Yes, of course. I'll do *exactly* as you say, Nelly. I won't take my eyes off them. They'll be so happy. Thank you." Edward stood, walked around the table, and placed a kiss on Nelly's cheek. She blushed. "I'll take a look outside and see if they're coming." He said, squeezing her shoulder before leaving. "Thanks, Nelly; you certainly can brew a good pot." The cake, as usual, had been a bit dry - but never mind.

Edward stood on the footpath, eyes squinting against the morning sun. In the distance, the glimmer of sunlight reflecting on metal caught his gaze, and his heart raced with the thought of telling Grace that she was finally allowed to go to the races. What a triumph! He waved to Walter, who sat back, hanging onto the arms of his speeding wheelchair, Grace running behind like she was in a battle charge.

"That's the way, Grace! "Edward called out. "We're in a bit of a hurry! I have a surprise for you!"

Grace, breathless, slowed as she reached Edward. "What - is - it - Edward?"

"Wh..what is it, Ed...ward?" Walter parroted.

29

"You won't believe this, but your mum has agreed." Edward placed his hand on Walter's shoulder. "Walter, you and I are going to keep each other company every day from now on." Edward paused for effect. "And…I can take you both to the races!"

Walter hooted, banging the side of his wheelchair, while Grace bounced up and down like she was riding a pogo stick.

"Really and truly? How did you get Nelly to say yes?" Grace asked.

"It wasn't too difficult," Edward said, smiling modestly.

Grace kissed Edward on the cheek and then Walter before saying. "Oh, Walter, I'm so happy for you." Grace turned to Edward, "Thank you, Edward. Now, what should I wear to the races?"

"Wear your prettiest dress, Grace." Edward grasped Walter's hands and looked him in the eye. "And you, young man, I bought you a pair of trousers, a shirt, and a jacket the other day. They were on sale. And as Sylvia used to say, we shouldn't let a bargain go to waste. And I'll give you one of my ties to top it off." Edward had noticed Walter's trousers were always too short, and his sleeves never quite reached his wrists.

Nelly decided the housework could wait until after Church tomorrow. Nervous and excited, she dressed in a stylish blue wool suit with a matching pillbox hat. She had sewn blue netting around the sides, and it sat seductively over her eyes.

When Edward arrived to collect the children, Nelly stood before him, looking every bit a Vogue model, her vibrant red lipstick complementing her sapphire outfit.

"Well, I must say, Nelly, you look amazing. You don't look like you're about to do housework. Now let me guess," Edward scratched his chin thoughtfully, "you're going to the movies?" Nelly played the game and shook her head - *No*. "Mmm, this is a tough one because I know you'd never go to the races! So, I give up. Where are you going, Nelly, looking so beautiful?"

Nelly laughed out loud - a rare occurrence. "I thought I'd join you, Edward. Besides, I can help look after the children…."

"We're not *children*, Nelly, I mean Mum!" Grace glared at her mother.

Nelly took a moment to look at Grace and noticed she was almost at eye level. Grace had grown over an inch in the past six months, and she was already tall for her age. "Please, Grace, it's just a manner of speaking," Nelly said softly. "But I *am* sorry. You *are* growing up. Now, let's go and have a nice day. But remember, no gambling." She shook her finger like a school mistress, hiding her delight in venturing into the unknown.

*

The track was alive with the hum of the crowd discussing which horse to back, the relative merits of both trainers and jockeys, and which horse appeared the fittest in the parade ring. The exotic perfumes of the elegantly dressed women almost overpowered the heady aroma of leather and horses. Grace breathed it all in.

"This is like a dream come true; it makes my head spin," Grace murmured.

Edward touched her shoulder. "I'd like to introduce you to one of my friends, Grace. This is Mr. Blake; he owns a horse running in the last race."

"I'm pleased to meet you, Mr. Blake. Could we see your horse, please? I *love* horses," Grace said excitedly.

Errol Blake chuckled. "Of course, Grace, I was on my way. Follow me." As Errol took over the pushing of Walter's wheelchair, he bent over and whispered, "I'll use you to part the crowd, if you don't mind, Walter." Walter gave him a thumbs up.

"Thank you, Mr. Blake, you're very kind," said Nelly, admiring the tall, handsome man. She felt like a different woman: Her sense of relief at being temporarily free from her mother's scorn? Profound. Her delight at dressing up and being a part of such an exciting day? Overwhelming. Her initial sense of fear at ignoring her lifelong constraints? Dissolved. Nelly was, in fact, having fun.

Grace's heart thumped when they arrived at the horse stalls. She could reach out and touch the horse's silky coat, smell his scent, and feel her senses tingle from the warmth of his breath. Looking deep into his kind eyes, she was sure the memory of it all would remain indelible. Grace's passion for calling races had now catapulted her into another dream of riding and being with horses every day of her life.

"I'd love to ride him, Mr. Blake," Grace said longingly. He smiled and ruffled her hair just like Tom used to; it made her think how her dad would love being there with her and Walter. *On the right side of the fence, for once*, she thought.

31

"I'm sorry, Grace, he's a racehorse. Riding him would be far too dangerous. But my daughter would be about your age; she's fifteen. She has two ponies, and I'm sure she'd love for you to come and ride with her."

"Really?" Grace looked to Nelly, her heart doing back flips. "Would that be okay, Mum?"

"Well, that depends, Grace." Nelly turned to Errol." Where does your daughter stable her ponies, Mr. Blake?" Nelly asked, glowing. Grace knew that was a good sign.

"The ponies live at Ferntree Gully with us. You could perhaps catch a train, Mrs. Knight unless you have a car. It's less than an hour's drive from Caufield. My daughter rides every Sunday and almost every day in the school holidays."

It sounded plausible to Nelly. She turned to Grace. "We'll see, Grace. Firstly, Mr. Blake will have to ask his daughter. What is her name, Mr. Blake?"

"Emma, and I am sure it won't be a problem. Please, call me Errol."

"Thank you. I will." Nelly smiled and prayed her red lipstick hadn't smudged her teeth. "In that case, Grace, yes, you may take Mr. Blake up on his offer. But only if you keep your homework up to date and you receive an excellent report from school."

"Sounds fair to me, Grace," said Edward.

With the promise of fulfilling another dream, Grace relished the day, especially when seeing Nelly enjoying herself, flitting between one introduction to the next, Edward's guiding hand in the middle of her back.

Walter seemed only interested in studying the race book and duly marked the horses he thought would win, sometimes changing his choice after viewing the horses in the parade ring. Everyone introduced to Walter was courteous and attentive, making Nelly relax and appreciate the day even more. Grace was glad of this too, but she reckoned Walter's growing popularity had something to do with his skill at picking every winner. Their new acquaintances had been taking Walter's advice. She tallied up the amount Walter would have won - if he had started with a two-bob bet. A total of five pounds and ten shillings would have filled his pockets. This, of course, was unknown to Edward, who was too busy introducing Nelly to his friends, so there was little time for him to study the form and have a sneaky wager.

When they arrived home, Edward accepted Nelly's offer to come inside and for a light dinner. Later, in the lounge room, Grace discreetly showed him Walter's race book. "Look, Edward. Walter chose all the winners, " Grace whispered.

Edward hid his amazement behind the poker face he had developed from his legal experience. If he'd shown even the slightest sign of being impressed, asking Nelly if he could take Walter to the races again would have her smelling a rat. He'd keep this news to himself.

"Grace," Edward said, "how about you show me the problem you were having with your maths." He winked, and Grace smiled knowingly. Soon she returned with the winning calculations, hidden in her maths book. He raised his eyebrows and nodded appreciatively.

"Well, what about if I help you after church tomorrow, Grace? I'm a little tired at present; the old brain needs a rest after such a long and exciting day." He turned to Nelly. "Wouldn't you say so, Nelly?"

Nelly had a habit of sitting with her legs crossed, the upper one swinging up and down as if she were following a tune that only she could hear, her gaze on nothing in particular.

"Nelly!" Edward called.

"Oh, I am sorry - what were you saying, Edward." Nelly gave him a sweet smile.

"Never mind. I'd best be off and let you get a good night's sleep, ready for church tomorrow." Edward rose with caution due to his gammy knee; he took one step and emitted a groan. "I'll have to get this damn knee fixed one day."

"I'll see you to the door, Edward." Nelly sprang up like a lioness pouncing its prey, and before he could escape, planted a kiss on his cheek. "Thank you again for such a lovely day," she lowered her voice conspiratorially, "and remember not to say a word to my parents."

"Promise – not a word." Edward's words drifted into the night air.

CHAPTER 4

Grace smiled, watching the sunbeams dance their way through the kitchen window. They brought her a feeling of warmth and hope. And today was even more hopeful because Grace realized a dream had come true. She'd spent a glorious day o*n the right side of the fence*, and the memory would bring her happiness if ever she were sad.

Grace's reverie was suddenly disturbed. *What's that ruckus coming from Nelly's bedroom?* There were sounds of opening and shutting drawers and shoes thrown against the wall. Nelly was even Taking the Lord's Name in Vain. Oh, dear! It was late Sunday morning, and Nelly had obviously forgotten Church. It seemed she was too preoccupied with organizing what she'd wear to work on Monday – as well as the rest of the week by the sound of it.

Walter raised his eyes from the newspaper, glancing at the clock on the wall. "Aren't we going to ch…church, Gracie?" Walter asked.

Grace shrugged. "Doesn't look like it, Walter. It sounds like Mum's trying to sort out what she's going to wear for work tomorrow."

Nelly appeared wearing the beautiful silk dressing gown she had put aside for when she might have to go to hospital – something which had never eventuated. Grace and Walter couldn't contain their laughter.

"What's so funny, children? I know, I know - you're not children! Well, what's so funny?"

"Have you forgotten something, Mum?" Grace said with a cheeky grin.

"No, I think I have everything sorted for tomorrow. I've finally decided which outfits to wear to work each day. One has to look one's best, especially when one is a front-line representative for the company." Nelly's sense of self-importance swelled until Grace came in with a clanger.

"*Church*, Mum. *Church*! It's *Sunday*."

"Oh, damn! I mean, goodness me! Thank you, Grace. Are you

both ready?" Nelly was flustered. It was apparent they weren't, and she only had to look at their clothes, the ones she'd patched more times than she could remember.

"We didn't think we were going to Church, so me and Walter - "

"*Walter and I*, Grace," Nelly corrected.

"Yes. Well, *Walter and I* thought we'd go yabbying in the park today, so you have time to organize *everything* for work. It's going to be an extraordinary day, Mum. You don't want to bugg… I mean, you don't want to mess it up." Grace crossed her fingers under the table, hoping Nelly would agree.

"I don't know Grace. What will Grandpa and Grandma say when they don't see us at Church this morning?" Nelly looked worried.

"They'd probably say, 'I don't see Nelly and the children at Church this morning," Grace said, shrugging her shoulders, mouth downturned. Walter laughed. Nelly ignored him.

"I suppose you're right, Grace." She brightened perceptibly. "I *could* say I had a headache - and then ask God to forgive me?"

Grace couldn't believe her luck, but a feeling of unease tempered her buoyant mood. *What's gotten into Nelly, ever since… ever since Dad left, she's been so different. Sad to think she can only find happiness without him.* The thought chilled her.

The complications of marriage were beyond Grace and perhaps beyond Nelly, too. All Grace knew was that she missed her Dad terribly and sometimes cried herself to sleep, worrying about Tom's safety and if she would ever see him again. She wondered if Nelly did the same. But Grace had Walter to watch out for; Nelly had never been good at caring for anyone but herself. Yes, she'd cook and clean the house, and she'd dole out the discipline. But Nelly fell short of giving *the children* (as Nelly persisted in calling them) the affection they needed. *Maybe calling us children makes Nelly feel young, like if we never grow older, then she'll remain young.*

"No Church today! No Church today!" Grace sang as she wheeled Walter out of the house. She'd loaded him up with a yabby net and a bucket, and the bait and scissors sat on his lap. She was still thinking about the fact that her mother was uncharacteristically happy, while Tom was probably full of trepidation and on his way to fight in the Middle East. In his letters, he seemed proud of his achievements, especially on the firing range. Grace knew her dad had good hand-eye coordination;

it showed when Tom played golf, held a pool cue, or played tennis. You name it; Tom would get the ball in the hole or have it placed where he wanted. She supposed this talent would stand him in good stead when aiming and hitting his target - the enemy.

Grace took a left-hand turn into Edward's front yard. *He may not be up yet, but I'll take the chance.*

"Edward!" Grace called once, then again, with Walter joining her.

Edward appeared at the front door in his dressing-gown, glasses on the end of his nose and the Sunday paper clutched in one hand. "Where are you two going? No Church today? Nelly's not sick, is she?"

"Nup! We're going yabbying. Do you want to come?"

"I'll stay home and have the pot ready to boil for the load you catch. See you later." Edward waved the paper then closed the door.

The Summer morning promised a perfect day ahead, and Grace smiled as she pushed Walter's wheelchair towards their destination. Along the way, they enjoyed the different bird calls which Tom had identified for them over the years. Grace and Walter could now name most birds by their song, the ones who lived in the Caufield area, that was. The Dandenong Ranges had been Tom's preferred place to go bird watching, and before the War, he'd often taken Grace and Walter with him. Tom had gone alone when they were too young. He tried to explain to Nelly the enjoyment he derived from this hobby. "You're just using it as an excuse to get away from me!" she had argued, and in a way, he was. *Anything for a bit of peace*, he'd think.

Walter's attempt at imitating a bird call was interrupted by a familiar voice. Grace halted when she recognized the grey Mercedes Benz which had pulled up beside them. The window came down, and Grace could see Grandma's sour face, eyes squinting and jowls flapping as she yelled. "What on earth are you children doing! Go home this instance! Get out of those rags and into your best clothes and be at Church pronto, or I'll personally tan your hide with my leather strap! Look at you. You're a disgrace!"

"Yes, Grandma," Grace said, knowing not to argue with the most fearsome woman God had ever put breath into, as Tom would have described her, had he been there. The car drove off slowly, no doubt its occupants watching to see if Grace had turned the wheelchair around. She had, but only until the Mercedes turned the corner out of sight.

"We'd better go ho..home, Gracie, "Walter said, slumping in his seat.

"I suppose we'd better." Grace headed the wheelchair toward home, but seconds later, she spun the wheels around and took off at a run towards the park. "They're the enemy Walter, and we're the good guys! Let's get those yabbies for dinner!"

Walter laughed with pure joy; Grace knew she would carry the sound in her heart forever. To make him happy each day was her priority, and she could only imagine herself in his unenviable position. What must it be like to feel the frustration of being unable to achieve simple tasks without difficulty? Although Walter was getting better since she and Edward had begun to insist he does things for himself, there were still things he found a struggle.

The usual gang of non-God-fearing kids sat gathered around the dam. Grace liked them; they were not *hypocrites*. She'd just learned the meaning of this word, and the more she came to think about it, the word *hypocrite* described a lot of people Grace disliked or didn't trust.

"Hey Johnno, are the yabbies biting?" Grace called from the other side of the dam.

"They will if ya shut up, Grace."

Walter laughed. "Yeah, Gra...cie, you'd better."

"Don't be silly, Walter. Yabbies can't hear anything."

"You sound just like, M…Mum. I'm not silly. Yabbies feel the vib…ra...tion of your voice."

"Sorry, Walter, I know you're not silly - you're smart. Where did you learn that?"

"I read it in a fishing magazine."

Grace shook her head, "Walter, you'd read the bloody telephone book if there were nothing else."

After baiting the string and casting it into the water, Grace soon hauled in a catch with her homemade net. Johnno watched from the other side of the dam; he couldn't believe Grace was catching so many. He stood and stretched, pretending he needed a break. Johnno ambled around to Grace's side of the dam. His interest was aroused not only by Gracie's catch. He had always liked her. Being an only child, Johnno enjoyed the company. His father was headmaster at the local school, and his mother took in ironing, though she could have been a secretary; she was certainly intelligent enough. However, she chose to stay at home

37

and always be there for Johnno. His mother was not a martyr to her role, simply a caring, loving soul, and his father admired and loved his wife for it. Their affection toward each other was something Johnno thought occurred naturally with all married couples. Little did he know.

Grace intrigued Johnno; she was not like the other girls he knew. Most girls would scream if you put a yabby near them, but not Grace. She reveled in the catch. Grace was strong yet had a soft side - and she cared for and protected her disabled brother, Walter. Grace was *true- blue*, his mum had said. Johnno, at age fifteen, was two years older than Grace and thought she was pretty, for a kid. She'd inherited her mother's thick auburn hair, and her striking green eyes held the depth of an ocean. He'd known Grace for ages but had only just started seeing her in a different light. Something had changed within him, and instead of teasing and making fun of girls, he'd found himself attracted to their looks, intrigued by their scent. Despite this, most girls still annoyed him. Not Grace. She was special.

"You certainly have the right feel, Grace. We've been here an hour, and we haven't caught a bloody thing. Can I sit down?"

Grace patted the earth next to her. "Ah, yes, it's all in the tug, Johnno. You have to time it right and, of course, use the right bait." She noticed the serious expression on his face and laughed. "I'm only kidding. I don't know why I'm catching them. Maybe they just like this shady side of the dam?"

"I'll have a go then." Johnno threw his baited string in the water. Soon he was pulling in yabbies with the net Grace had made from Nelly's old stockings.

"There you go, Johnno," Grace said encouragingly. "And another thing - look for holes in the dam wall. It's a sign the yabbies are there, and they like chunks of meat best."

"We don't use meat. There's not enough to go around, so we use stale bread or a bit of cheese," Johnno said to Grace with his head turned sideways, a half-smile on his lips. *Yep, she's getting prettier*. His smile widened. "How come you have meat when there's rationing?"

"I have ways and means," Grace said with a wink.

"You're incredible, Grace. You mean you *stole* it?"

"Course not. Dad loves Camp Pie, but Mum says it's disgusting. He bought lots of it and hid the tins in the shed. It's the best bait there is," she said, nodding sagely.

Johnno studied Grace again until she asked what he was looking at,

"You're growing up, Grace. Do you have a boyfriend?"

"Are you joking? Why would I want a boyfriend?" She blushed, embarrassed. Walter laughed, and Grace whacked him on the arm. "I like boys as *friends*, but I'm not ready for a *boyfriend* - yet. Besides, I have Walter to keep me company." Grace smiled and gave Walter another punch on the arm.

"Stop hitting me, Gra…cie!" Walter said, rubbing his arm.

"Sorry, Walter," Grace said, mussing his hair, "but you'd stay with me if I needed you, wouldn't you?" She turned to Johnno. "Walter's mowing lawns now. He's got a job mowing Edward's next door!"

"Good on you, mate. Though I reckon you could do better than that, Walter."

"I agree," said Walter, nodding his head.

Grace felt suddenly ashamed. She'd derided Walter's intelligence, albeit unintentionally.

The morning ended with their bucket full of yabbies. Grace insisted Johnno have some. He refused politely.

"Go on," she pressed. "I know your dad loves yabbies, and I like to keep in sweet with him. After all, your dad is our Headmaster."

Johnno laughed, and Grace noticed how deep his voice had become. He was a good friend, and Grace realized he would have to put up with a bit of ribbing when he returned to his mates. She knew Johnno would take it with good humour; he was what Tom called *empowered*, meaning he was his own person. She liked Johnno for that.

"See you, Johnno. We'd better go home and face the enemy. God knows what Grandma's said to Mum after we didn't show up at Church."

"You'll handle it, Grace, don't worry." He walked a few steps away, then over his shoulder, called. "If things get too rough Grace, you and Walter can always come over to my house. Mum thinks you're both bonza."

"Really?" Grace asked, a little surprised.

"Yes. She does, Grace."

As they drew closer to home, Grace drew in a deep breath then let out a sigh of resignation when she saw Grandpa's car in the driveway. "We're in for it now, Walter. Keep calm and carry on!" Grace leaned forward and asked, "Did you know those words are on red banners all around London, Walter?"

"Yeah, I do. I read the newspapers, Grace!"

"I know you do. You read everything. And you are smart, Walter, but sometimes you're a smart *arse*. Though I reckon you can pick winners better than anyone. So, pick this one, mate. Who's going to win this fight?"

"B…b…buggered if I know. Let's go inside and see."

Grandma stormed from the house before Grace could push the wheelchair up the ramp, followed by Grandpa - a lamb to her lion. Grandma huffed indignantly as she pushed past.

"You children will go straight to Hell if you don't mend your ways!" Grandma said, hate oozing from every pore. After her initial thunder and lightning onslaught, Grace couldn't believe she had let them off with a warning, albeit a dire one. Usually, she was faithful to her word, and the leather strap would be used without compassion - if Tom weren't around to stop her first.

They entered the house and heard gentle voices coming from the kitchen. Grace was surprised to see Edward consoling Nelly, holding her in his arms and rubbing her back while she whimpered.

"Mum, what's wrong?" Grace asked, adding quietly, "Silly question, really."

"Oh, Grace! Grandma has just cursed us all. She said we would burn in Hell. She said - "

"Don't go over it, Nelly. You know she talks a lot of hogwash. Your mother is devoid of love and common decency. Don't cry, love. I'll help you when you need it," Edward said, holding Nelly out at arm's length.

Gracie's ears pricked. *Love? Edward called her love, and she didn't mind? And he even rubbished Grandma. Holy shit! And Nelly didn't defend her?*

"You're a good bloke, Ed…ward. When can we go to the races again?" Walter asked with a smile and a dribble which he immediately wiped up.

Edward laughed. "Trust you to put the right slant on things, Walter." Edward nodded. "Let's say next Saturday; there's a meeting at Flemington." He turned to Nelly - still teary. "What do you reckon, Nelly? If you're ever going to show your parents you're in control of your own life. Then this is it! Let's go to Flemington!"

Nelly sniffed, dried her eyes with her apron, and said defiantly, "I don't see why not, Edward. It seems we have been disowned by my parents, anyway. So, what the heck!" She moved closer to give Edward a cuddle, which he clearly welcomed.

Grace fought the urge to step in and physically separate them. *There's a little too much affection going on here.*

"Nelly, I mean, Mum, look at the yabbies Walter and I caught today. Do you reckon there's enough for a good feed?"
Edward peered at the squirming catch and declared, "Let's boil the water, Nelly. There's plenty enough for dinner, especially with bread and butter."

With a sigh, Nelly admitted she had run out of butter. "I don't think I'll ever get used to rationing. I used it all to make pastry for an apple pie." That announcement soothed their disappointment.

CHAPTER 5

"How do I look, chil… I mean, Grace, Walter?"

"You look wonderful, Mum! You'll be the best dressed in the office, I reckon," Gracie said. Her sincerity was not lost on Nelly.

Edward concurred with Grace, even though he wasn't looking at Nelly. He was helping Walter spread jam on his toast - a change from his usual Vegemite. Edward didn't need to help him, but it justified the 'caring for Walter' agreement.

"Well, I'm all set then. Don't be late for school, Grace." Nelly threw Edward a charming smile. "And thank you again, Edward. I don't know what I'd do without you." She hurried across the room and kissed Edward on the cheek.

Grace turned her cheek to Nelly, but no kiss came her way. She rolled her eyes and shrugged. Walter laughed, wondering where she got her devil-may-care attitude and her dry sense of humour. Her resolve had always seemed to be well beyond her years. From very early on, Grace had hardly ever cried; she'd simply screw her face up, determined not to let anyone or anything beat her. Walter felt blessed she was his sister, as well as being his best advocate. Grace had an enormous heart and a capacity to tackle anyone in any situation. He leaned forward and kissed her on the cheek.

"Thanks Walter. At least *someone* loves me," Grace said with a wink.

Nelly settled quickly into the routine of office life. Her initial nerves disappeared as she was made feel welcome and helped to learn the role of receptionist, which was not as difficult as she thought it might be. Nelly was gracious to clients and mastered the switchboard within the first hour, though she wished the damned thing wouldn't light up like a Christmas tree all the time. "One at a time, *please*," she'd mutter through gritted teeth.

The business had moved premises since Tom had worked with

the company. Nelly's desk was on the fifth floor of a modern building, only recently built and fitted with the latest and most tasteful furnishings. It was so fashionable that Nelly felt like she was on a movie set, and Peter O'Toole might walk through the door and kiss her hand at any moment.

Edward and Walter launched their study program at home, though not before they'd peeled potatoes for dinner. As it was their first day working as a team, Edward had decided that a celebration was called for in the shape of a chicken and vegetable casserole, which required sacrificing his youngest chook. "Sorry, darling, I'll make it quick," he'd said, as his razor-sharp ax came down with sudden force.

Walter's lessons, Edward had obtained from the Education Department'Home-Schooling Program; developed for children on farms and stations in remote areas of Australia. Edward was surprised at how easily Walter coped with the program's demands, quickly realizing that Walter was a brilliant young man. At fifteen and a half, he was well in advance of the lessons set for what Edward had assumed would be Walter's ability level.

"Walter, you're a bloody genius!" Edward later proclaimed after Walter had come dangerously close to beating Edward in a chess game. Walter laughed. "Dad's taught me w…well, don't you r…reckon?"

"Absolutely, Walter. I think you're wasting your time sitting at home doing nothing. I think you should be at high school. I'm sure you'd do extremely well, and then you could follow a career. What do you say Walter?"

"I'd r…really like that, Edward. Although I do r…read a lot. Non-fiction, of course. Definitely not Mum's *Mills and Boons*!"

They shared a laugh.

Okay, then. I'm going to try hard to make it happen. It would help if you were with young people your age, plus your intelligence should be acknowledged. Just because you're in a wheelchair most of the time and have some trouble controlling your limbs, it doesn't mean you can't learn and achieve things. I'm proud of you, Walter," Edward said, giving Walter a solid pat on the back.

During the weeks that followed, Edward met with many local school principals, both private and public. He gave convincing arguments that disability should be weighed against ability. After all, Walter would attend school for academic learning, not to play sport, and he'd soon

43

show he was as capable as the next young man his age. He should be allowed to determine his own future. There were plenty of professions where Walter could excel - the law, for one. And as Edward had been an experienced lawyer before retirement, he would be the one to guide Walter in that direction.

All arguments, both for and against, were discussed at length in the chosen schools. It became clear that Walter was the victim of the general ignorance about his condition. It always seemed to come down to the fact that Walter would need help with all his personal needs. This wasn't strictly true, as Walter had been practicing and was, to all intents and purposes, pretty much self-sufficient. *The main argument was that his difference would stand out in the classroom and distract his fellow students*, and Edward could not disagree, except to say it was about time to change things. He asked them if they thought no soldiers would be permanently injured or disabled by the war returning home to Australia. These brave soldiers, some of whom would have to live the rest of their lives in a wheelchair or be missing limbs, would need re-training to find work and be a part of the workforce and society. These statements were met uncomfortably and with sympathetic murmurs and eyes lowered in either embarrassment or respect, but it didn't change their decision; they would not be enrolling Walter.

Edward was incensed by this injustice. He knew it a waste of time taking Walter to a sheltered workshop where he'd only learn to weave baskets or make pencil cases. Edward was sure he could teach Walter what he needed to know until it was time to sit the exam to enter university and study for a law degree. Edward had to go to the universities and make sure they would accept Walter, provided he passed the test. That would be his next step.

Meanwhile, the odd day at the races wouldn't do them any harm, especially with Walter's talent for picking winners. However, as Caulfield was out, they would have to travel to Flemington, as the Army had officially taken over the grounds.

Grace was content with her world, although it was not perfect. With her father at the War and his letters being less frequent, her heart ached, especially at night after she'd said her prayers for his safety. Tom was a gunner in the Middle East Desert Campaign. He must be busy, Grace reckoned, or nowhere near a post office. Eventually, she learned from the newspaper that the Army had mail runners who serviced

44

soldiers everywhere. It was a dangerous business to be in, as they were sitting ducks for snipers. Grace tried to imagine galloping a horse flat out, ducking bullets just to collect and deliver letters. She proposed these soldiers were the ones deserving a medal!

Johnno had taken to waiting for Grace after school. She was in eighth class now, and Johnno was at a boys' college, a block away from Grace's school. She didn't mind Johnno keeping her company on her walk home, especially since she'd been the target of bullying from a new girl.

"One day, I'll knock her block off!" Grace said to Johnno, who laughed at her ferocity. "But I don't need trouble, I'm on Nelly's Good Behaviour Bond, and I desperately want to ride Emma's pony next Sunday. I've been invited." Seeing Grace's sad expression, Johnno just wanted to hold Grace in his arms and kiss her. But he'd have to wait.

"So, you're really that keen on riding horses, Grace?" Johnno asked, sneaking a look at her profile. He loved her aquiline nose and the way her long dark eyelashes curled upwards. And her rosebud lips; how he wanted to feel them on his own.

Grace's mood lifted. "You bet. I can't wait. I've only been led around on a pony before. But I'd *love* to learn how to ride properly. I wish we lived at Ferntree Gully or somewhere where I could keep a horse."

"What about asking my Uncle Charlie – he's the Clerk of the Course at Caulfield - Charlie Norman. He's Mum's second cousin. I reckon he'd be able to teach you to ride." Johnno felt uneasy when he saw Grace's shocked reaction. "Well, I'm sorry, Grace. I didn't know you were *that* keen on riding. I just thought you loved calling races?"

Grace's surprise had her tongue-tied for a moment. "You mean… you *knew* I loved *all* things to do with horses, Johnno, and you never told me about your uncle? Or is he a cousin?"

"He's my cousin, but I call him Uncle because he's Mum's age. I could introduce you to him, Grace. I'll ask Mum tonight."

Overwhelmed by Johnno's offer, Grace suddenly realized that doors into the horse world were now opening for her. First, her mum now enjoyed attending the races instead of abusing her family for merely watching them from *the other side of the fence*. Nelly had also listened with interest when Grace called a race and had seemed most impressed. Then, meeting Mr. Blake and his daughter, Emma, and now, Johnno's uncle. She was finding it hard to contain her excitement.

"Oh, Johnno, that would be wonderful! Do you think he'd mind teaching me how to ride? I'd love to call a race for him and see if he thinks I'm any good. What do you reckon?" Grace's eyes shone with the possibilities before her.

"I reckon we take one thing at a time, Grace. Don't get too eager. Charlie may not have time. He works, too. He's not just Clerk of the Course. He's a builder."

Momentarily, the wind was taken out of Grace's sails. Silently, she prayed it would work out with Charlie; it would mean the beginning of another dream coming true. She couldn't wait to get home and tell Edward and Walter.

Grace's news came in such a rush that Edward had to sit her down. "Now, take your time, Grace. We're not going anywhere."

"Okay. First," Grace said after she'd taken a deep breath, "do you think you could drive me to Ferntree Gully this Sunday, Edward?" Edward opened his mouth to speak. "No. Don't answer that. Not until I tell you the big news! Johnno's uncle is Clerk of the Course at Caufield. His name's Charlie Norman. Johnno said he might teach me how to ride. So, as well as me going to Ferntree Gully to ride Emma's pony, I'll have lessons with Charlie! Isn't that wonderful news?" Her face turned as red as a Christmas bauble. "I'm getting a leg up, as they say in the horse world." Grace deepened her voice for effect.

Edward imagined it all happening for Grace. She was as determined as a charging bull at times. He sighed, then took her hands in his. "Grace, this all sounds wonderful, but you know petrol is rationed. I'll have to see if we have enough to get us to and from The Gully. And I do know Charlie, but he's a busy man. If you offered to muck out his horse stalls and maybe feed and water his horses after school. He might just find time to give you lessons, Grace. There's a big park nearby where I'm sure you can ride. That's where I reckon he'd teach you if he has time." Edward gave the hint of a smile. "Don't go getting your hopes up, Grace. But I'll have a talk to Charlie for you," he said, ruffling her hair.

Grace wished he wouldn't do that but smiled and said, "Johnno said his mum would talk to Charlie, but I suppose it wouldn't hurt to have two people on my side. Thanks, Edward."

*

Luckily, there was enough petrol in the tank. Edward drove Grace to Mr.

Blake's home, and they found him most welcoming when entering his impressive bluestone manor. The front entrance was as big as Nelly's sitting room, it sported marble tiles, and a grand chandelier hung center stage. French Provincial furniture placed strategically provided total elegance. Grace gazed around in awe until Emma came running to meet them.

"Hello! I'm Emma. You must be Grace, and I know *you*, Uncle Edward. Hello, Uncle." She jumped up to plant a kiss on his cheek. Grace turned to Edward,

"I didn't know you were Emma's uncle," Grace said, surprised.

Edward smiled warmly. "It's just a figure of speech, Grace. Since he was a young lawyer, I've known Mr. Blake, and Emma wasn't even born. I like to think I helped Errol learn the tricks of the trade, so to speak." He gave Grace a wink.

Errol smiled, nodding agreement as he showed them through to the oversized kitchen, where double glass doors opened out to a vine-covered terrace, and from there, they could see green paddocks, dotted with various gum and wattle trees, all enclosed by tongue in groove fences. Shaded under the vine leaves, they sat drinking tea and homemade lemonade, served with the fanciest little cakes Grace had ever seen. *Too fancy to eat*. "Instead of eating one, may I take it home to show Walter?" They laughed.

"Of course! You can take as many as you like home, Grace, but please eat some first. They are Cook's specialty." Emma held out the plate to Grace. "Cook said if Dad ever fired her, she'd open a shop and only sell tiny cupcakes." Emma gave a delightful giggle.

Grace immediately liked Emma. She was so full of life and laughter, particularly for someone who'd lost her mother only six months before, as Edward had told her on their drive there. Grace wondered what her secret to happiness was. If Grace even thought about her father dying, she would… she didn't want to think about it. *Too terrible*.

"Are you ready for a ride, Grace?" Emma jumped up, scanning Grace's attire. "No, you can't ride in those trousers or those shoes. I'll lend you some. As a matter of fact, I have a pair of jodhpurs and boots you can have. You're thinner but the same height as me," Emma said, chin in hand, "even though you're two years younger. Amazing. What shoe size are you, Grace?" Emma laughed. "You could be a jockey! No, on second thought, I think you're too tall."

47

"Please don't put any more ideas into Grace's head, Emma," Edward said with all sincerity.

Emma's friendliness and warmth towards Grace continued when she guided her to the stables within a massive barn. They were every bit as impressive as the house. After showing Grace how to saddle up and place the bridle in the pony's mouth, Emma helped Grace mount Bobby's old pony. Grace would never have guessed he was twenty; he was fat, and his coat gleamed.

"Bobby's really gentle, Grace. He taught me how to ride. We'll just walk and trot today. He can't take too much work, and anyway, you're not ready to go fast. Dad says, we have to crawl before we walk." Emma's charming smile showed a small piece of cake trapped in her braces.

"You've got…ah…you've got…." Grace pointed at her mouth.

Emma ran her tongue over her teeth. "Thanks, Grace. Most people are too frightened to tell me. I like you; you'd make a good friend. You know good friends will always stab you in the front, not the back!" Emma ran her tongue over her braces a few more times. "Has it gone, Grace?" Emma bared her teeth like a horse, and they laughed like hyenas. Beginning slowly, they rode through the bush along a well-worn trail until Grace felt connected to Bobby. Then Emma led the way going faster, trotting, jumping over fallen tree trunks, and ducking low branches. Grace managed to stay on board, even when Bobby shied away from a rabbit bolting across their path. Emma was impressed at Grace's lack of fear, her quickness to learn, and her knowledge of the local bird life. After spending two hours chatting, they realized how alike they were, agreeing on everything - and both loved horses with a passion.

Edward smiled as he drove home, listening to Grace's excited description of her afternoon; she barely stopped for breath. Grace couldn't believe how friendly Mr. Blake and Emma were and told Edward so with vivid animation, and it amused him.

"I'm so happy for you, Grace," He gave a sideways glance. "I knew you'd fit in. It was such a shame when Errol lost his wife. She died of cancer. Far too young, only thirty-six." Edward shook his head in sorrow.

"Yes, I know. Although I don't know how Emma could be so well adjusted and happy after losing her mum." Grace frowned.

"Mr. Blake is the kindest, most considerate man I know,"

Edward said. "Except in court, then he becomes a tiger. He's now the most successful criminal barrister in the State of Victoria. His family comes from old money; it's set him up financially. Emma's his life now, but I think she's a little lonely. Not many kids live nearby, and he's not one for a lot of noise in the house. Well, not at the moment - he's still in mourning."

*

Within a short time, Grace began working for Charlie Norman. Both Edward and Johnno's mum had talked to Charlie about giving Grace riding lessons in exchange for her mucking out his horse boxes. Charlie's horse set-up adjoined his home and was not far from the park.

Gracie's job was to pick up the horse manure from the small paddock, scrub the water buckets, re-fill them, and muck out and add straw to his two stables. She'd also bag the manure and put it out front with a sign - *Flowers grow faster with horse poo! Sixpence a bag!* She'd have all this done and be waiting for Charlie to give her a lesson on his return from work. This routine began after she'd spent three Sundays in a row with Emma. During this time, she insisted Grace saddle up Bobby then Emma would give Grace instruction on basic riding skills.

Charlie had given her a spare key. It was to unlock the shed that held the tools for the work and his saddles and bridles.

After a quick inspection at the end of three weeks, Charlie said, "You've done well, Grace! And to see Charger and Freddie, brushed, saddled, and ready to go is very impressive. You're a good worker. I'll give you that, Grace. You've learned quickly in such a short time - the place is a credit to you. Now, let's see how well you're riding."

Grace led Charger toward the park. The old grey, whose coat was almost white now, had taken a real liking to Grace. Maybe her giving him an apple every day had something to do with it. They reached the park, and soon Grace was on board and rising to the trot like a pro.

"I reckon you're ready to canter, Grace," Charlie called to her. "Sit down in the saddle - plant your behind- make it part of the horse. Now push him on with your seat and legs. He'll get the message. That's right - keep pushing. He can be a lazy old bludger! That's it! You're lookin' good, Grace. Hands down and heels, too. *Now* you've got it! Well done!"

In the past few weeks, Grace, it seemed, had transformed into what Nelly called "a complete horse nut." All Grace could think about was riding horses. However, she still loved calling races. It seemed horses were in the marrow of her bones. After working for Charlie for three months, Grace even dared to call a phantom race. The 1941 Caulfield Cup was coming up in October, held at Flemington, and Grace had been following Velocity, the horse she thought would win. This year, the race fell on her fourteenth birthday.

"Go on Grace, call it like you imagine it was happening, and we'll see if you're right next Saturday," Charlie said, sitting on an up-turned feed bin in the shade of the stables. He was intrigued by Grace. *She's got more confidence than any kid has a right to,* he thought.

Using two glasses held up to her eyes for binoculars, Grace started, "And they're away and racing in the Caulfield Cup…"

Charlie could see the race unfolding, as Grace called it. As the field turned into the home straight, Charlie's adrenalin level soared. It felt so real, and he was desperate to know who would make it to the post first. Grace's voice rose as they approached the finish." And Velocity with a run sent from Heaven is storming up the rail…fifty yards to go and he's neck and neck with Gunner…head-to-head… nose to nose… eyeball to eyeball…and on the post…it's a bob of the head… and it's Velocity, yes Velocity! He's pulled off one of the biggest betting plunges ever! Oh, no! The bookies have made a run for it. Somebody stop them!"

Charlie doubled up - laughing, coughing, and spluttering. "Oh, my God, Grace! That was one of the best race calls I've heard. How do you keep it up? Bloody hell, you're a star! I must introduce you to Ken Howard. He'd be most impressed, I'm sure."

"Really? Do you know him, Charlie?"

"Of course, I know Ken - who doesn't?" Charlie gave her a nod. "I'll see what I can arrange."

Grace smiled as if she had won the Cup herself.

CHAPTER 6

Saturday the 21st of October 1941 was Caufield Cup Day, and to Grace's delight, she was woken by Nelly and Walter. They handed her a present. She shook it. It rattled. Chocolates, maybe? A game?

"Open it Gra...cie!" Walter urged, protesting at the delay.

To tease him, she opened the box slowly. A pair of binoculars with her name engraved in gold sat nestled in the mauve tissue paper.

Speechless, Grace looked from Walter to her mother and dissolved into tears, her shoulders shaking with emotion, moved more by the meaning of the gift than the gift itself. Her mother had finally realized and accepted her dream of becoming a race caller. It was the best present Grace could have wished for.

Nelly looked sadly at her daughter, thinking that Grace's dream would never become a reality in the male-dominated racing world, where women were simply there to add glamour and elegance to the Sport of Kings. She hugged Grace and said, "Happy Birthday, Grace."

However, thanks to Edward, Nelly was more than happy to make a personal contribution to the glamour and elegance of racing. She now looked forward to their race days. Her parents, it seemed, had completely disowned her and the children. She hadn't heard a peep from them since what they called *Yabby Sunday*. Nelly couldn't have cared less; she was finally free of their hateful, judgmental personalities. Well, her mother's, at least. Dad wasn't so bad. Nelly, and the friends she had made at work, enjoyed meeting up with Errol Blake at the races, and now his lovely daughter, Emma, had taken an interest in joining him, seeing as Grace also went.

Edward had become her Guardian Angel; Nelly felt she wouldn't cope without him. Why hadn't she ever realized what a charming man he was when Tom was at home? But then, there was a lot that had changed since Tom had left. A tremor went through Nelly's heart - it shook her feelings back to order. She was not missing Tom like she should, even

51

though she still loved him. Nelly would never tell the children this. She felt guilty enough.

A record crowd of over seventy thousand attended the 1941 Caufield Cup at Flemington, and Nelly felt privileged that Edward had organized for her to become an Associate Member. "It's much more civilized in the Members' Enclosure," Nelly said haughtily. Grace hated it when she spoke like this.

Nelly had said that the girls were old enough to wear smart hats and dress up, as young ladies should, and everyone duly commented on how beautiful they looked. Secretly, Grace would rather be in trousers and climbing the broadcast tower to sit with Ken Howard. She was sure to meet him one day soon because Mr Blake knew him, as did Charlie Norman. They'd both promised. And since Ken had moved to Melbourne after accepting an offer from 3KY Radio Station, the meeting would be more accessible.

Grace delighted in showing her new binoculars to Edward's friends, assuring them, "I'm going to be a race caller one day, and that's why Mum gave them to me." Her confidence waned a little as most laughed at hearing this, but Grace's determination remained. She stood alone and quietly called the next race. Her new binoculars, the perfect size, had an excellent field of view. Grace was so intent on her call she hadn't noticed Emma quietly come up behind her.

"I can't believe you just did that, Grace. You amaze me. How do you do it? How do you remember all the colours and the names of the horses?" Emma whispered.

"I've done it pretty much since I could talk, Emma. My Dad taught me. We'd study the fields on Friday night and on Saturday we stand down a laneway behind an old fence adjoining the Caulfield Racetrack. I've called horse races for years - it's what I want to do." Grace looked defiantly at Emma, expecting her to laugh, but she didn't.

"If you want something badly enough, Grace, you'll make it happen. Never give up. My mum said that before she ..." Emma lowered her head and Grace held Emma's arm searching for her eyes.

"I feel sad for you, Emma. You know Dad's away fighting in the Middle East. I pray all the time that he'll come back to us, and I don't know what I'd do if I lost him."

"Yes, you would, Grace." Emma's assurance made her stand straighter. "My Mum said we all have our *own* life to live. Our spirits will always be entwined with those we love, but our minds and bodies are *ours* to do the absolute best we can. Mum said I would let her down if I were to be sad the rest of my life. She wanted me to be happy, be compassionate, and help others. But most of all, she wanted me to live my life to the fullest. I'm trying to follow her wishes. It's the least I can do." Emma gave Grace a warm smile and kissed her cheek. "Now, let's be happy. Let's go and take a look at Dad's horse, Coin Tosser. He's in the last race, so he should be here by now."

Grace thought about Emma's words; they made sense. Grace felt her dad's absence deeply, but now it made her more determined to live her own life and look out for Walter - no matter what happened.

Hand in hand, the girls threaded their way through the crowd to the horse stalls, just in time to see Coin Tosser arrive and be tied up in his stall by his strapper, Peter.

"He looks wonderful, Peter," Emma said before lowering her eyes, a shy smile upon her lips.

Grace noticed and whispered, "Do you like Peter, Emma?"

Emma giggled, "yes."

Grace took a closer look at the spiffy young Peter, who wore a pinstripe suit, crisp white shirt, and green tie. His riding boots were so highly polished she could almost see her reflection. His fair hair looked to be slicked back with Brylcream. He was handsome to the point of being a little feminine, she thought. She flashed him a smile.

"Do you think he has a chance of winning, Peter?" Grace asked openly while Emma remained coy.

"Yes, I do Grace. I think it's his day. That *is* your name? *Grace*?"

Emma flushed bright red. "Oh, I am sorry, I didn't introduce you. Grace, this is Peter Falkner, and Peter, I'd like you to meet Grace Nobel." Emma beamed.

"Nice to meet you Grace. I've heard about you."

"Really?"

"Yes, I've heard you can call races as good as anyone."

"Really?"

Peter laughed. "Is that all you can say? Really?"

"No," said Grace, "but I'd like to know who told you, Peter."

"The racing fraternity has its own grape vine. Anything special or different gets talked about."

"But who told you?" Grace persisted.

53

"Can't remember," Peter said as he untied the horse. "I have to go and wash Tosser now; I'll see you, girls, later. In the winner's circle." He gave them a wink and led the horse out of the stall.

Emma flung hand to heart, heaving a dramatic sigh. "Don't you think he's handsome, Grace?"

"Who, the horse?" Grace asked. Seeing the scowl on Emma's face, she quickly added, "Oh, you mean *Peter*. Yes, he is - he's almost pretty. How old is he Emma?"

"He's nineteen. He's going to be a lawyer, like Dad. He loves the races, so he's strapping to earn money to put himself through university."

"That's good. Peter seems nice. But I wouldn't get too serious. Don't you think you're a bit young to be in love?"

Emma sighed again. "That's what everyone says. But I say, when you meet Mr Right, you just know. Your heart tells you. I can wait, though." Emma's blue eyes sparkled with the magical thoughts of romance.

"Well, I'm glad I'm not interested in boys - yet. Who knows, maybe I'll never be? I like boys as friends, and I have a good friend, Johnno. He's alright. And of course, Walter, he's my best friend, but he's my brother."

"You're lucky to have a brother, Grace. I wish I had a brother or a sister. I get lonely. Dad works long hours, and I've only got Cookie to keep me company. Dad says he should send me to boarding school, but I don't want to go." Emma shrugged. "Maybe I'd find more friends there, but anyway," Emma linked arms with Grace. "I have you now, Grace." Emma searched Grace's eyes. "You will always be my friend, won't you?"

"Of course I will, Emma. You let me ride your pony, and we love the races." Grace peered at Emma's teeth. "And I tell you when you have food stuck in your braces." They laughed. "We'll always be friends!" They shook hands and made their way back to the Members' Enclosure.

The crowd was becoming restless, with everyone hustling to find the best vantage point to view the Caufield Cup. Earlier, Nelly had asked Edward to push Walter's wheelchair closer to the fence near the finish line while, a little concerned, she searched for Grace. Relieved, she spotted Grace struggling with Emma, pushing their way through the crowd. "Mum! Mum, we're here!" Grace waved.

"Thank heavens! I was beginning to worry about you, Grace.

You never know what sort of people lurk in a big crowd. Somebody could abduct you!"

"They'd be bloody stupid - I mean they'd be silly if they did, Mum. You're always telling me what a troublesome child I am. I reckon they'd soon give me back."

Emma burst out laughing, but Nelly simply grabbed Grace's hand and pulled her towards the space Edward had commandeered near the fence.

Errol Blake turned and smiled. "There you are ladies. How did Tosser look, Emma?"

"He looked a treat, Dad. Peter's confident. He thinks he'll win today."

"Excellent! Let's hope so. They're moving up to the start, so push in here, ladies, and hang onto the fence."

For the first time ever, the horses lined up within the wooden barriers, and, as they jumped as one, a mighty roar rose from the seventy thousand spectators. Soon the best gallopers in the land found their preferred positions. Velocity jumped first but was quickly headed and gradually settled back fifth on the rails. He was the only horse Grace watched. With all her heart, she silently urged him. *Stay there, boy, keep your strength for the end, they'll weaken, and you'll get there! Relax. Wait for the straight. Please, God, let there be a run. Let him win!* Grace was transfixed, her heart pounding in time with the thundering hooves.

The Caulfield Cup, run over a mile and a half, had Grace calling it silently until the final four furlongs when she found her voice. Unrestrained, she called every horse in the correct order, with some quick banter in between, much to the surrounding spectators' approval. With her new binoculars making her job easy, Grace was unaware that all within earshot were amazed by the race call from this young girl. Instead of cheering their favourite horse, they watched in silence as the field flashed by the post.

"Velocity! Yes! Velocity has *won* the 1941 Caulfield Cup!" Grace held her binoculars in the air as a triumphant salute.

The crowd immediately surrounding Grace applauded, some patted her on the back, and some shook her hand in congratulations. Grace, surprised by the well-wishers, hadn't realized anyone was listening. *But how could they not - she had been screaming!*

Finally, Errol Blake rescued her and kissed her on the cheek.

"Well done, Grace. Edward told me how well you call races. And now to hear it for myself - I'm stunned. I can only hope when you're old enough, the powers that be will allow you to call professionally. You're a very clever young lady!"

"Thank you, Mr Blake. I can only hope so," Grace said humbly. The day ended with Coin Tosser winning, albeit after a protest, which took ages for the stewards to determine. The happy group, including many of Errol Blake's friends, celebrated at the Windsor Hotel, where Errol hosted them to dinner in the Grand Dining Room.

Grace was almost trembling with the accumulated excitement of the day. If she was honest, she felt a little inadequate to find herself eating in such a fancy place. Grace looked around, enchanted by glimmers of glassware and silver cutlery in the warm light of the chandeliers, and the crispness of the table linen, finding it nearly overwhelming. *But not Nelly,* Grace thought; *she's swanning around, full of airs and graces, pardon the pun.*

Nelly's mind was reeling with the romance of the rich and famous that she so loved reading about, and tonight, it was like her fantasy come true. Well, it would be - if only the charming Errol Blake would ask her to dance.

Errol will fold me into his arms. His strength and love will guide me effortlessly around the dance floor. He will lower his head, gently pressing his lips against my slender neck, and whisper 'Je t'aime', making me blush and almost swoon against his broad chest. Oh, how beautiful it will be.

She gave a contented sigh before noticing Grace's pained expression. Nelly narrowed her eyes, sending Grace a telepathic message.

Yes, I know what you're thinking, Grace. And yes, I am happy to be here, receiving attention from a handsome and powerful gentleman like Errol. You think I don't care about Tom. Well, I do. I love him, and I always have. But there's no romance anymore – not that there ever was. It's a duty that binds him to me – not love. And it's not enough.

Nelly glared at Grace, who could almost guess what her mother was thinking. Grace decided not to upset herself as, after all, this was the best time she had ever experienced, especially since Mr Blake's other guests were being so kind to Walter.

One charming lady at their table told them she was a member of a charity raising funds to help the new Spastic Centre, which helped cater to the needs of people with cerebral palsy and their families. Edward took the opportunity to explain to the group the trouble he was having enrolling Walter into a mainstream school. The conversation became too political for Grace, and she was glad when the band struck up, and the couples chose to dance.

Nelly was also thankful for the interruption, delighting in dancing with Edward, then Errol. Nothing went unnoticed by Grace. Her mother's delight stoked Grace's anger. Grace needed to shift her focus. She glanced at Walter, who sat tapping his feet in time to the music. *Maybe another feather in his cap?*

"Would you care to dance, Walter?" He smiled and proceeded to lift himself out of his seat. Slowly, they walked to the edge of the dance floor, where Grace held him tight.

"Now concentrate, Walter. Just sway with the music. You don't have to do any fancy steps. That's right, just relax and feel the music."

Grace closed her eyes, not wanting her confidence to be undone by the gawps of couples gliding past them. Together they swayed and occasionally attempted a few steps. When the music stopped, she realized the entire crowd was applauding *them*. Emma walked to their sides, clapping enthusiastically.

"May I have the next dance, Walter?" Emma asked, her emotion clearly evident. They danced together for the rest of the evening.

Edward extended his hand to Grace, inviting her to dance. She suddenly felt quite grown up.

*

Grace found it hard to sleep that night. Her thoughts scattered like confetti on a windy day. Tom had not written her for her birthday. Actually, she hadn't received a letter for over two months, and it worried her, almost to the point of tears. She also thought about how her mother was behaving like some *Mills and Boon femme fatale* towards any man who would show interest in her. It was embarrassing and sad, especially since Tom was stationed in the Middle East. He was out there trying to survive a stinking hot desert and fight for his country and, God only knew, his own life. And what was Nelly doing? Having the time of her life.

Please, God, don't let me be like my mother. I can't understand her. How can she love my father when she is so happy in the company of other men? Please, God, keep Tom safe and show Nelly that she is misbehaving. Amen.

CHAPTER 7

Over the next two years, life progressed along the same path for Grace; school, study, and phantom race calls. Walter had taken on helping Grace by drawing the jockeys on their relevant horses, and he'd then colour them in so Grace could imagine how the race would pan out. It was an excellent method of training her memory, though Walter wouldn't win any prizes for colouring in. Although he was making a name for himself in the local neighbourhood. Nelly took little notice of Walter's legal studies, a real shame because he was making fantastic progress, and word had spread on how Walter, with Edward's help and support, was going to beat the education system!

Walter was maturing into a confident young man - he'd even told his Grandma where to go on the day she and Grandpa had paid an unexpected and *unwelcome* visit. Grandma had long suspected something sinister was going on between Edward and Walter.

"Why else would an older man give so much time to a helpless young boy? And, as you know, Edward and his wife never had children, so maybe he didn't have a proper relationship with; what was her name? Sylvia, yes, Sylvia. A lot of men are like that. They never own up to being homosexual; they simply live a disgusting lie!" Grandma had declared to Grandpa, bringing home the point with her eyes bulging.

Maybe she has a thyroid problem, Grandpa had thought, *she should have it seen to.*

"And today, we will catch them at it! We will then send Walter to a home for afflicted children - where he should have been - *from the start!*"

Walter had been deep in his studies with Edward when they arrived. Grandma had barely begun her speech before Walter had stopped her mid-blast with a withering assessment of her mean-spirited nature, followed by a very clear suggestion as to what she could do with her baseless accusations!

Nelly was on her return from work. Her emotions were caught off-guard by her parents' uninvited, surprise visit. The total absurdity of her mother's accusations had Nelly crying until her eyes became so swollen she found it hard to see. Edward, as usual, consoled her. He had definitely become a calming influence, for which Grace was thankful.

"I find my mother's degenerate mind simply too impossible to deal with *anymore*, Edward." Nelly wept; the words muffled by his tear-stained shoulder into which she pressed.

It was some consolation that Walter had succeeded in delivering a vulgar but intelligent rebuff to his grandparents. Edward repeated to Nelly, word for word, what Walter had said. Nelly had listened, astonished by Walter's strength of character and genuinely proud of her son, which showed with her warm hug of approval. Nelly immediately picked up the telephone and, in a defiant tone neither her Mother nor anyone else had ever heard before, declared resolutely, 'Never *ever* set foot in my home again!" Good for Nelly!

*

It was November 1943, and Grace sat listening to the radio, which confirmed what the newspapers had claimed, that the Allied Forces stood an excellent chance in restoring world peace. It was in stark contrast to her own opinion of how the war was going, although she, too, hoped the war would end soon. Grace read aloud, sitting at the kitchen table. Walter sat opposite.

"*Australia has withstood the bombing of Darwin, Broome, and the far Northwest coastline of Australia* - without too much damage, they say, Walter. It's *bullshit*!" Nelly was out shopping; otherwise, Grace wouldn't get away with swearing. "They just don't want to alarm us – the helpless citizens of Australia! *Boo hoo*! And what about the invasion of Sydney Harbour by those Japanese mini-submarines? They've understated that too! Like it was nothing, really!" She looked up at Walter, shaking her pretty head and went back to reading. "*Confidence is therefore maintained, and any future attack on Australia, the Government says, will also be thwarted.* Yeah, well, I'm not so sure. What do you reckon, Walter?"

"I'm with you, Gracie. But wh...what will we do if the Japs come here?"

"We'll defend our home to the death, Walter! Let's start collecting big stones for our sling shots!" Grace laughed. "Don't worry Walter, I think they're right. We will win this bloody war! I only hope it ends soon. Though I wouldn't be this confident if the Yanks hadn't joined the fight after what happened to them at Pearl Harbour."

Walter nodded then went back to studying the Form Guide.

Tom's letters had been infrequent. But recently, he'd been injured and sent to Cairo Hospital and was able to find more time to write.

...nothing serious, don't worry, just a scrape. I'm lucky I turned around to see my mate who'd just copped a bullet. If I'd been standing front on, I'd be dead with a hole in my chest. The bullet took out a chunk of muscle on my right arm. It doesn't matter; I've got plenty to spare. They say I'm too good a shot to be sent home just yet. We're known out here as 'The Desert Rats' - I think that title explains pretty much how things are.

Love to all.
Tom xxx.

His bravado and humour was intended to quell their worry, but the truth was, he was leading a tormented existence.

Grace excelled at high school, though she still held onto her burning passion for being a race caller. She loved her job with Charlie Norman but desperately wished for the war to end and her dad to return home. Tom's ardent belief in her talent for race calling kept Grace from folding under the unrelenting criticism she experienced whenever her ambition was mentioned. It came from ignorant traditionalists who wanted to see nothing change, especially for women: *I'm sure there are many more suitable jobs for girls*, they would say condescendingly. It also came from well-intentioned people, not wanting to see her heart broken by something they believed was unachievable. *'Not in our lifetime, dear- don't get your hopes up,'* they would offer with a sad smile.

"Patronizing old buggers," Grace would mutter under her breath when confronted by these types.

However, Grace also had her share of staunch admirers, especially Johnno. She appreciated his friendship and valued his support, but her dreams were full of a solitary excitement – she saw herself alone, not married. Grace believed that one day she'd be calling the best races in the land. Especially after she'd met one of her idols in the racing industry, this meeting had propelled her dream forward – considerably!

Yes, the entire race day she'd spent with Ken Howard had been excellent, never to be forgotten. At first, Grace sat speechless, her throat so dry and raspy it would have stripped paint off a wall. She knew she'd have to overcome her nerves if she were to make an impression on her idol. Grace sat focused all day listening to Ken's flawless race calls. At the end of the day, Ken turned to her with a smile, "so Grace, would you like to do a phantom call? Maybe the last race shouldn't be too hard as there were only seven runners, and it was a long-distance race?" Consuming three glasses of water and drawing several deep breaths, she then sized up her blessed life against the lives of soldiers fighting the war and living in squalid conditions. These thoughts had given Grace the composure needed to relax and call the chosen race with her unique flourishes - and she had excelled.

During her call, Ken's eyes grew wide, and his mouth gaped in disbelief. When it was over, he regarded her with sincere admiration, saying, "Well, I'll be damned. You definitely *can* call a race. You're a very talented young lady, Grace."

Grace's invitation from Ken had come via *his* friend, Errol Blake. Ken had been most charming and seemed genuinely impressed because he'd told Grace. *"If you remain dedicated and focused, Grace, I may be able to help you fulfill your dream. Always remember, nothing is impossible."*

From then on, listening to Ken Howard call races, replete with his embellishments and dry humour, added another layer to Grace's delivery. Not that she copied Ken, she owned a similar style. With her natural wit and ease of speech, Grace soon became Ken's invisible protégée and learned all the information she could, storing it like a squirrel would nuts. There was no doubt that this was *Grace's* chosen profession - but would the profession choose *her*?

A boyfriend was not even remotely on her agenda, and the thought of becoming a mere housewife made her shudder. She supposed Johnno was a *sort-of* boyfriend. Grace held his hand at the pictures, but only because she saw other girls doing it. She didn't want to be *too* different. Yes, she liked Johnno – a lot. Apart from Walter and Edward, he was her best friend.

However, one memorable day, the universe seemed to tilt its axis when Grace and Johnno were alone in the park, hidden beneath the fresh fomenting leaves of a weeping willow. The day was hot and sultry, and

Johnno's excuse was, 'It's much cooler under here, Grace.'

They lay on their backs, feeling the coolness of the earth and fanned by a gentle breeze. Johnno dreamily fixated on the light shifting through the dense canopy. It gave him a moment of resolve, and he took Grace's hand.

"I'm eighteen, Grace, so I'm going to join the Army." He felt Grace's sudden grip, and Johnno sighed recognition. "Mum, of course, doesn't want me to, and Dad says it's not necessary. He says there are enough brave, dead young men to fill the quota. I just feel it's my destiny - my duty, Grace. So, I'm leaving."

He turned to see Grace's shocked, injured look, relaying what she truly felt. It had taken Johnno's declaration of leaving for Grace to realize what she actually felt for him. It had suddenly awakened in her a real depth of affection, not a girl's giggling infatuation. It made Grace's heart race and heat suffused her body. The fear of losing him hammered her soul. She leaned her trembling body against Johnno's chest and breathed in the clean smell of his shirt, reminding her of how his mother worshipped him. *How would she cope if he were killed? How would I cope?* Grace looked deep into his soft brown eyes and her love for him spilled over into a passionate kiss and a sensation Grace had never before experienced. It ignited an intense fire and her body ached. She wanted, needed him in a way she had never thought she would. His tender lips full of love and desire held her captive. She was slipping away, never wanting this moment to end until she realized she was losing herself - and her childhood. She placed her hands on his chest, pushed him away, and sat up. The fear of the consequences in giving herself to Johnno right then had overwhelmed Grace's senses. It frightened her.

Grace's lips tingled. Part of her revelled in the new sensation, while another part fought to recall her childhood delight at finding the first Spring daisy to start a chain. She tried to resist her transition into this new world, but she knew it was as natural and as inevitable as the daisy's appearance. There was a season for everything. She needed to explain, in the best way she could, how she felt.

"Johnno, I can't tell you - or show you in any other way - how I truly feel about you. I won't try to talk you out of joining the Army. But I want you to know if anything happens to you," she paused, drawing up her knees, and rested her head on her folded arms, muffling her words, "it would break my heart." Grace rose quickly and ran towards home.

Johnno smiled his emotions in turmoil. Never once had he thought of pressuring Grace to go any further than holding hands in the pictures. He was prepared to wait for her, sometimes doubting she felt any affection for him at all. His feelings for her were a heady mix of respect, admiration, and physical attraction – and yes, desire. And now he knew she had similar feelings, *that kiss!* he felt privileged that he'd been the one to stir those feelings in Grace. For a brief moment, this welcome news made him consider changing his mind. *Should I stay with Grace and assure our future together? No. I have to go and fight – and help win this bloody war. Grace would surely see me as weak if I stayed just to be with her.* Johnno wasn't weak; it was one thing he was certain of about himself. He had tremendous admiration for Grace's dad Tom enlisting while secretly feeling a little ashamed of his own father. But then his father had health issues - or so his mother said.

Johnno stood, slowly stretching his lean form before he headed home, satisfied with his decision and happily distracted by the remembered feeling of Grace's kiss; it was a memory he knew he would cherish. One day, he was sure, they would have a future together to create more wonderful memories. That alone was worth fighting for. He would survive and he would keep Grace safe in his arms - forever. He somehow knew he could never in his lifetime find love with anyone but Grace.

After running and crying all the way home, Grace arrived breathless. She hated herself. She hated Johnno and the free-fall she felt when they'd kissed. Her heart and body had betrayed her. Grace didn't want to be like Nelly, who desperately needed men to admire her and love her in that physical way. Grace couldn't comprehend what was happening to her - her body was a traitor! She was held hostage by her hormones! What was she going to do?

*

Since Yabby Sunday, it had been a rare occurrence for Nelly, Grace, and Walter to attend Church. But to Nelly's surprise, on this particular Sunday morning, Grace asked if she could take Walter to Church, that was if he wanted to go. Grace felt she needed a little guidance from above to help her deal with her conflicted feelings. And Walter could always do with another prayer going his way.

"Are you coming, Nelly?" She asked her mother, who had finally accepted Grace's form of address.

"No, Grace. I have to catch up on the housework. Besides, I don't want to bump into your grandparents. I'm still not over their terrible behaviour. I may never be," Nelly said, her blood rising at the memory of her mother's interference.

"Fair enough, but they don't frighten me, and if Grandma gives us any trouble, Walter can practise his new lawyer skills. He's learned a few tricks from Edward that will put the wind up them." Grace smiled at Walter, who gave a thumbs up.

Nelly may have been surprised by Grace *wanting* to go to church, but Grace was even more surprised when she saw her grandmother approach them – her eyes lowered, her hands clasped nervously in front of her. She was the very picture of humility.

"Hello, Grace," Grandma said softly, almost tenderly. She looked down at Walter, who immediately stood, towering over this short, solid woman. She stepped back slightly before raising her face to Walter with a wan smile. "Walter. How are you?"

"Good," was all he said.

Grace, for one brief moment, was dumbstruck. "Are you… are you trying to be *nice* - Granny?"

"Of *course*, I'm being nice, Grace! But I should just remind you about how…" she stopped when Grandpa gave her a gentle nudge. Grandma cast a sideways look at her husband, and her voice softened. "I'm delighted to see you both at Church. I was going to telephone and ask your mother if we could come and visit later this morning."

She lowered her head, and for a moment, Grace thought she could see Grandma's eyes watering. It couldn't be tears? Surely not?
"I need to tell you all something very important." Grandma's tone was serious.

Grandpa nodded and said, "Yes, it's essential, Grace." He tilted his head and smiled up at Walter, who had remained standing.

"Hmmm," Grace was skeptical but acceded to the request. "I reckon it would be all right, as long as you don't give us any more lectures, Granny. Mum has a lot to deal with, with Dad away fighting in the War."

"I promise I won't, Grace. And if you could *please* go home straight after church and tell your mother, we will be dropping in a bit later this morning. And, please," Grandma hesitated and looked to her husband, who smiled encouragingly. "Tell her I am asking for her to forgive us – I mean, *me*. It was a terrible thing I accused Edward of, and

I've written him a letter of apology." She dabbed at her eyes.

Grace looked at Grandpa, noticing a subtle change in how he stood beside his wife, close by her side rather than half a step behind her. And he seemed taller and stronger looking, somehow. His shoulders lifted and dropped as Grandpa gave a deep, satisfied sigh, his mission accomplished. "Come, Gertie," he said, and Grace and Walter watched in astonishment as Grandma, as meek as a lamb, was led away.

"This is going to be interesting," Grace whispered to Walter as they walked down the aisle at sat down on one of the cold hard pews. Grace shifted uncomfortably – the seating was another reason Grace didn't enjoy going to Church, but today she'd put up with it if, in return, she could get some guidance and sort her feelings out. *Come on, God, I need some advice*, Grace prayed silently. *What am I going to do?*

*

Nelly paced the lounge room floor after hearing the news of the impending visit. "What on earth does she want? It must be some sort of trick! Buttering us up so she can get up on her high horse again and tell *me* what to do. If she thinks she is going to tell me how to raise my children - well, she's got another think coming!"

"We're not children. We're…" Grace said automatically, trying to drive her point home.

"I know, Grace, I *know*. And you *have* been wonderful since I've had to work. You're growing up to be a responsible young lady. You too, Walter - a young man, that is."

Nelly stopped pacing, and at the couch where Grace and Walter sat, she placed a kiss on each of their respective heads. "Walter! What on earth is on your hair? It tastes awful!" Nelly scrubbed at her lips with her handkerchief.

"I like to use Brylcream," Walter said mildly, smoothing down his hair.

Grace laughed. " But what does the advertisement say, Walter? *A little dab'll do ya!*" No doubt Nelly knew which pillow slip belonged to Walter when she did the weekly wash.

The doorbell Edward had recently fixed rang a happy jingle. Nelly looked puzzled. "Surely that can't be them. They always just barge in!"

"I'm telling you, Nelly, they've changed their tune entirely. Well, not Grandpa. He's always been Grandma's reluctant accomplice,

I reckon. I feel sorry for him. I'll get the door." Grace rose from her chair and automatically straightened her skirt, flicked her hair behind her shoulders, and opened the door to greet them. "Granny! I can't say it's a surprise, can I? Please, come in." Grace moved aside, a wry smile curling her lips.

Nelly stood stoically in front of the fireplace, Walter, her sentinel, alongside her. For reasons unknown, Walter's constant trickle of saliva had ceased – almost. He looked handsome and completely composed. Grandpa noticed and he smiled broadly as he shook Walter's hand.

"Before we discuss anything, Walter, I must say how proud of you I…I mean, *we* are, of your being accepted into university to study Law. I'm sure you will pass and do us all proud." Grandpa turned to Grandma. "Isn't that so, dear?"

"Yes," was all she could muster, her smile fixed.

Nelly thought she could smell a rat, but she managed to be gracious and asked them to sit while she was on the kettle.

"I assume you would like tea and cake?" Nelly said a fraction chilly before she moved towards the kitchen, leaving Grace and Walter to sort out the small talk before discussing the real reason for their change of heart and attitude.

*

It had been a week after Grandma had accused Edward of sexual impropriety with Walter that Grandpa's conscience finally got the better of him. He had been deeply troubled by his wife's accusations, not because for one second he believed them to be true; they had known Edward for years, and there had never been, even the merest hint of impropriety, either in his personal or professional life. Grandpa's concern was focused on his wife. She had always been devout, some would say a *fanatical* Christian, but her intentions had always been good, mostly. Grandma had been a product of a rigorous family, and he had made allowances for her throughout their marriage, even though he had at the time, thought her to be far too hard on their daughter. For the sake of a peaceful life, Grandpa had taken a back seat when it came to Nelly, letting his wife use the threat of eternal damnation to make their daughter walk the straight and narrow.

It had been a terrible disappointment to them both when Nelly *had* to marry Tom. Not because Tom wasn't a good man, but because Gertie had seen it as her failure, and she had become increasingly full of bitterness and self-loathing. It had become worse when Walter was born, as Grandma had seen his affliction as the manifestation of Nelly's sin. However, he knew if he was ever going to make a stand, that the time had come.

He had told his wife, in no uncertain terms, that enough was enough. "Gertie, you have taken things *too far*," he had said, "and it is time for you to put things right. I am not going to lose my daughter and my grandchildren because of your misplaced belief in the sins of others. *Let he who is without sin cast the first stone*."

Grandma's eyes widened in disbelief. Her husband had never taken that tone with her before. She was furious. "Now listen here –"

"No! *You* listen. And I am only going to say this once." Grandpa pointed a dominant finger at her. "You are going to apologize – to Nelly, to Edward, to Grace, and Walter. You have done your best to make that family's life a misery, and to *their* credit, you have failed. If anything, it has made them stronger. No, don't interrupt," he added, holding up his palm towards Gertie as she opened her mouth. " Listen carefully, my dear. Either you do as I say, or you can leave. That is my ultimatum. I have had enough, and you need to make a decision. Now."

It had been the longest speech Grandpa had ever made and the only one where he had expressed exactly what he felt, rather than replying *Yes, dear*, whenever his wife suggested a course of action.

He had gone into the kitchen, made a cup of tea, and waited. Twenty minutes passed before his wife came in, her head bowed and her eyes red. Grandpa looked at her sternly. He was sad that it had come to this, but his resolve was not shaken. "Well?"

Gertie took a deep, shuddering breath. "I'm sorry, George. I don't want to leave," she said softly. "I know I've been too hard - on all of them. I don't know what turned me into such a horrible person." She began to weep silently, the tears dripping unheeded down her cheeks.

Grandpa thought back to his pretty young bride, so afraid that anything enjoyable was some sort of sin, and how that guilt had made her want to stop herself from enjoying anything in her life. He stood and walked over to her, enfolding her in his arms and stroking her hair. "It's never too late to change, love. Let go of all that hellfire nonsense and come back to your family."

*

Nelly remained highly suspicious of what lay behind this change of heart. She acknowledged her mother's apology and her promise never to interfere in Nelly's life, or the children's, ever again!

"I'm so pleased you've stepped down from your high horse, Mother. As they say, it is never too late." Nelly smiled and gave her an awkward but warm embrace, surprised to feel her mother's initial stiffness dissolve.

"So, Mother. How is your charity work going?" Nelly asked, now at arm's length, looking eye to eye. At first, their conversation was stilted, but several glasses of sherry before the Sunday roast was consumed eased things along. The day ended most amicably. Grace felt relieved; it was not in her nature to be at loggerheads with people, especially family. She at once remembered Johnno was leaving the next day for Army training. That night, Grace's sleep was disturbed by nightmare visions of battlefields, with Johnno fighting alongside Tom. Shoulder to shoulder, they dodged bullets that came so close, Grace woke up screaming, "Get out of there! Get out!" Hyperventilating, she turned on the light to make sure she was in her warm bedroom. No guns here, no death - just a safe place to be. It made her think about the many children in the war-affected countries who, she knew, would be cold, hungry, and in fear for their lives. She suddenly wanted to do something to help. *If Granny can help, so can I. She can't be all that bad. I reckon something must've happened to her to make her so mean.* Grace was on the right track but never learned the truth.

The bright sunshine, which Grace loved so much, was absent this morning. Only a dull light filtered through her window. It turned everything a shade of grey, and she felt the same.

"I'm not going to school, Nelly," Grace said. "I have to say goodbye to Johnno. He's leaving today, and it's important because…. because he may not come back. So many young men we know have died." Tears came as Grace tried to come to terms with the horrid truth.

Nelly could do nothing else but hold Grace in her arms. "Shush, Grace, Johnno will be fine." Her offering solace gave Nelly a quiet moment to accept the reality of the War. She felt far removed from it at times; it was easy to live in another world here. They were sheltered, with the fighting and related carnage so far away. Their only suffering, other than rationing, was Tom's absence and the anticipation of his return. She thought about Mrs Fleming, who, only two days ago, had received a pink telegram from the Government to say her son was killed in action.

Mrs Brown also received one yesterday. It was too sad, too terrible to contemplate. Nelly prayed no telegram would come to her.

CHAPTER 8

Johnno held Grace at arm's length, searching her eyes for what he so desperately wished to see. Love. Yes, it was there. Reflected in *his eyes*; regret, regret at having to leave her and face the reality that he may never see her again.

Since she had last seen Johnno, Grace had changed; she had grown up. She'd weighed up the magical experience when they'd first kissed beneath the same willow tree where they now stood. It added more confusion about what was happening to her body. *Do I really want a man to kiss me – to love me?* She hadn't even thought about this until she faced the possibility of losing Johnno. Something inside had suddenly clicked, like an electric switch that turned Grace from a girl into a woman. The initial shock of it frightened the child in her. Now, in Johnno's arms, the woman in her welcomed the change.

"You know I love you, Grace. I've always loved you. I don't think you know how special you are. You're selfless, strong, and beautiful." His smiling lips met hers in a moment of such tenderness, and Grace wanted his kiss to last forever. Reluctantly, she drew apart.

"You forgot Johnno. I'm *funny*, too. You're always telling me how funny I am." They laughed.

"Of course, how could I forget, Grace? Now, promise me you'll write and tell me only the funny things that happen - or a joke, you're good at telling jokes. I love the way you act out the characters. Maybe you should be on the stage?"

"Yep, the first one out of town!" Grace quipped.

Johnno's mouth curved into a smile that matched his dancing eyes. He brushed a loose strand of hair from Grace's face and held her tight, swaying back and forth. "I have to go Grace before I find it impossible to leave you."

Grace's eyes filled with tears, and she struggled to hold them back. "Yep, you'd better. But I'll be right here when you come home,

Johnno. I promise." She stood on tiptoe to kiss his cheek, turned abruptly, and ran from under *their* willow tree.

"Remember, Grace. You said you'd be right here when I get back!" Johnno called, smiling and trying hard to hide his heartbreak. Grace stopped mid-stride and, turning, called back, "I will. I'm just going home to get a tent and some food!"

"Hilarious, Grace," he said softly, his smile fading as he watched her leave.

*

Grace, at sixteen, was old enough to join The Australian Women's Land Army and attempted to do so with all the eagerness of a lion cub at play.

"Not now, Grace. Your schooling is more important. I won't allow it!" said Nelly. "There are enough young women who have left school and need employment and are the preferred age. You're such a bright student. You could be anything you want. Stay at school one more year, and then we'll discuss it. All right?" Nelly hoped Grace would see common sense.

Reluctantly, Grace agreed. It *did* make sense to wait until the end of the year when she gained her Victoria n Certificate of Education. At least while Grace attended school, her mind was occupied and not drifting off to the perils of war. She knew in her heart that Australia, along with the Allies, would soon win, but at what cost? It worried her continuously.

Walter was nearly nineteen, and much to everyone's delight had passed the Law exam set by the University of Melbourne. Edward was the proudest of all. He needed a bit of a steadier to calm him down enough to hold his pen steady when writing the news to Tom. The Chivas Regal ran smoothly down his throat, and he waited for its effect before pressing pen to paper. The letter included all the family news. Apart from their pride in Walter, he wrote of how Grace was excelling at school, and even though she wanted to leave and join The Women's Land Army, she was reluctant to do so without Nelly's permission. On a different note, Edward explained that Nelly's mother had recently had a change of heart. Why? They didn't know, except that Grandpa had stood by with a self-satisfied smile while Grandma had almost begged for forgiveness.

...after the domineering way she preached the fear of God into you all, relentlessly, for years! And given orders in what to think and

71

what to do. I ask you, Tom, how come it's only now that's she realized how it ostracised her from her family? I tell you, Tom, you need not worry about Nelly and the kids. They are now free from her tyranny. All is well, except Grace is heartbroken after Johnno left to join the Army. We pray for both his and your safe return. Don't be a hero, Tom. Come home to us.

Edward sniffed away a tear, folded the letter, placed it in an envelope, and fixed a stamp in the top right-hand corner, ready to post. His conscience was clear, and he'd done all he could to keep everyone happy, and things were ticking along for Tom's family. Well, Edward felt like it was his own family, too, albeit a de facto one.

*

Tom read Edward's letter while convalescing, yet again, in the Cairo hospital. This time was a result of suffering a scorpion bite. He couldn't complain, the food was edible, and the nurses were lovely – especially one.

"I still can't believe, Sergeant," Nurse Lucy said, "that you have dodged bullets left, right, and centre - but then you get bitten by a damn scorpion!" She continued to soak the inflamed flesh on the back of his calf. "So, what do you have to say for yourself, Sergeant? I'd say it was carelessness. Do you agree?" Her smile dazzled him.

"Damn lucky, I'd say Nurse. Though the Arab who brought me here said, it was one of the *least* deadly. I thought all scorpions were the same and you were dead meat if they bit you."

"Well, you have quite a bit of *red* meat here Sergeant. Though it's beginning to heal, finally. You'll live to fight again." She rose, and with dish and cloth in hand, gave him a wink and glided away.

"Jesus, I wish she wouldn't do that," Tom muttered. "Giving a bloke a wink in Australia meant something more than just being cheeky. Maybe in America, it was different, and Lucy was indeed a candidate for Miss America. Her alabaster skin was the perfect canvas for her pink cheeks and enhanced her naturally full lips, which Tom imagined would be luscious to kiss. But more than this, Lucy was grounded and funny. She told it like it was.

Am I falling in love with her? Maybe I should stop right now. Lucy would be ten years my junior. Why would she even look at a bloke like me if I weren't her patient? And I'm married with kids!

72

Tom needed to get back into action; it was becoming more dangerous in hospital than at the Front. He could handle a gun and knew every trick in approaching and keeping the enemy at bay. But this beautiful, blonde timebomb? Was it all in his mind, or had he noticed Lucy looking at him in that certain way when she didn't think he could see her? Sure, she was professional, with a few funny quips thrown in when she was nursing him. But there was *definitely* an attraction between them - he'd seen that inviting look plenty of times before. In the end, he was too old to be acting like a love-struck schoolboy. *Pull y'self together, y'silly bugger.'*

*

"Nelly!" Grace had to shout to break Nelly's reverie as she sat staring at her wedding photo. It seemed a hundred years ago when she had walked down the aisle, and if she was honest, she had been surprised to see Tom waiting. Nelly knew he was duty-bound to *marry* her – but not to *love* her. She looked up, tears filming her eyes. "Yes, Grace, what is it?"

Grace noticed. "It's okay, Mum. Don't be sad. Dad will come home. I know he will." She walked over and placed a hand on Nelly's shoulder and smiled into her eyes, seeing in them the reflection of her own.

With a sigh of acceptance, determined to hide from Grace her true feelings, Nelly rose and positioned the photo back on the mantelpiece. "Yes, I know he will, Grace. Now, what is it?"

"Mr Blake phoned and asked if we would like to go to Ferntree Gully tomorrow. It's Emma's birthday, and they're having a few friends over for a barbeque lunch. Edward's invited too."

Nelly, a little sad, nodded obligingly. "Yes, that would be lovely. And I am sure Edward should have enough petrol because I insisted he take the money I offered to help pay for his monthly ration. I'm sure he won't mind driving us there. It's much nicer than sitting in that dirty old train. Go and talk to Edward, Grace, and if he has enough petrol, then we'll go." She noticed Grace's reluctance, "Go on, Grace. Go and ask Edward."

Grace's hesitancy was due to the thought that only a few months ago, Nelly would have *crawled* to Ferntree Gully to see Errol Blake, who, Grace knew, was Nelly's very own heartthrob. What had altered that? Nelly seemed to be changing like the wind these days.

*

73

Perfect Autumn weather accompanied Emma's birthday, and Errol's manicured gardens were the perfect setting for the guests to enjoy the festivities.

"Would you like another glass of champagne, Nelly?" Errol asked solicitously, bottle tilted at the ready.

"Goodness me, Errol! You'll have me tipsy!" She grinned with no agenda other than simple happiness. "Just one more. Thank you."

Nelly smiled indulgently at hearing Grace and Emma's laughter. "They get on like sisters, don't they, Errol?"

"Yes, I couldn't be happier. Emma's, at last, has found a good friend. A soulmate, as they say." He turned to face Nelly. "Now, tell me about Walter. He seems to have improved out of sight since Edward's been tutoring him. Not only with his aim of becoming a lawyer but also with his social skills. It's amazing, utterly amazing what Edward has done for Walter. Not to say that your husband, Tom, would not have done the same if he were here in these important years of Walter's life. Turning a boy into a man is not easy, but in Walter's case, even harder, I would think."

Nelly sipped her champagne and nodded in agreement. *Walter has changed, thanks to everyone who believed in him. I've changed, too - thank heavens. I realize now how wrong I was – I was stifling Walter's progress. And Grace, well, she's still the same. She's the only one in our family who has always spoken her mind and instinctively knows what's right and what's wrong.*

"Yes, we're fortunate to have Edward. He's been our rock. I don't know what I would have done or how I would have coped with Tom in the Army and Walter needing extra care." Nelly giggled and nodded her head in Walter's direction. "Though, I don't think he needs extra care now. Look at him with that lovely young lady - he's charming her, I'm sure. Thank goodness his dribble seems to have gone." She tilted her head. "I wonder why that is, Errol?"

"Maturity, perhaps. Sometimes, hormones play a major role in correcting defects." Errol cleared his throat and gave Nelly a worrying look. "About that *young lady*, Gillian. She looks younger than her years, and she is, in fact, a lawyer. She works for me." Nelly noticed him blush when he gazed at Gillian. Errol then turned to Nelly. "I have become very fond of Gillian." He took a huge slug of champagne before continuing. "It's even to the point where I am considering asking her to marry me."

74

He saw Nelly's stunned expression. "I'm sorry, I didn't mean to shock you, Nelly. I simply blurted that out. You see, I'm just so happy that I had to share the news with someone. I hope you take it as a compliment that I spoke to you first." He placed his hand gently on Nelly's shoulder. The gesture immediately arrested her surprise.

"Yes, I do, Errol. I'm sorry for appearing shocked. It's just so sudden. Grace hadn't mentioned it…I mean, why would she? It's only that she is so close to Emma, and I thought perhaps Emma would have confided in her." Nelly looked inquiringly into Errol's eyes. "I assume Emma *does* know how serious you are with Gillian?"

"No, not really. I don't display my affection for Gillian in front of Emma. She thinks we're close because we work together. I feel guilty, not telling her." A troubled look briefly crossed Errol's features. He continued, "But in my defense, I've only just realized how much Gillian means to me. It started when she tendered her resignation a month ago. Her father was retiring from his law firm and wanted Gillian to take over. She'd never really seen eye-to-eye with her father before. She said their problem stemmed from him wishing she'd been born a boy." Errol noticed Nelly's frown. " But when he announced he wanted her to take over the practice, she jumped at the chance. It was also a chance to reconcile with her father. He had told Gillian that either she took over the reins, or the business his grandfather started would be closed down." Errol sipped his drink.

"I could see all the responsibility and the massive workload it all would involve separating us. So, I asked Gillian what kind of future she wanted. Was marriage at all on her agenda?" He smiled at the recollection. "She looked straight at me - with a bit of a mischievous glint in her eye, I might add - and asked, *Is this a proposal Mr Blake?* I laughed, of course." He turned his gaze towards Gillian, who seemed entertained and engaged by Walter's conversation. "Then I became serious and said, *Yes, I suppose it is. I certainly don't want to lose you, Gillian.* She said, *Well, then. Let me think about it. Can I take some time off today? We could have dinner tonight and discuss the future.* I agreed, and for the first time, I kissed her. And I knew then that I loved her." Errol smiled, no doubt reliving the moment.

All of Nelly's fantasies about making love to Errol and him telling her how much he loved her and that he could not live without her melted away as quickly as fresh snow under a scorching sun. It had all been a dream. *Don't be silly, Nelly*, she chastised herself. *Be happy for him - he's such a lovely man and deserves happiness with another woman. He has suffered so much sadness, and it needs to be replaced with love - the only healer.*

Nelly's eyes filled with tears, and she held him close for a brief moment.

"Thank you for feeling you could confide in me, Errol. I like to think I'm your friend, and I wish you every happiness. You deserve it." Nelly sniffed. And for once, her being overdressed for a barbeque and wearing gloves helped to wipe away her tears.

"Thank you, Nelly. We *all* deserve some happiness." He looked steadily into her misty eyes, "I pray you will regain yours when Tom returns." And with that, Errol went to join Walter and Gillian, leaving Nelly to sip her champagne – alone.

Will I be happy when Tom comes home? How could I possibly know? He may come home changed by the war, as so many have, either mentally or physically. So many scenarios, too many to think of right now. Nelly sighed and, stoically accepting her new circumstances, straightened her stance, swigged the last of her champagne, and wandered over to where Edward stood talking to another of Errol's lawyer friends. She smiled charmingly and tried to enjoy the rest of the day.

*

School holidays arrived, and Grace was delighted to have been invited to stay with Emma at their home. Emma had explained over the phone that there would only be themselves and Cookie, as her father had to go on a business trip with Gillian.

"But just between you and me, Grace, I think he really likes Gillian. So, it won't be *all* business, I'm sure!"

She doesn't appear upset by it at all, Grace thought. *How would I feel if it were my dad? Oh well, I'm too young to be worried about all the 'what ifs.'* And Grace also had more important, more immediate things on her mind. "I can't wait to go riding every day, Emma, and the Healesville Races, wow! That will be amazing, especially when hardly any races have been held at Healesville since the Depression. But now, they're trying to lift their game."

"Oh, Grace, you know so much about racing - you're funny. See you on the weekend." Emma hung up the phone.

*

Music from the radio drifted through the house, and Nelly, standing at the sink, dreamily sang along, *"For all we know... we may never meet again...Before you go...Make this moment sweet again..."*

"Nelly!" It seemed to Grace that she was still having to wake her mother from one daydream or another. Some things never change. "Have you seen those fawn jodhpurs Emma gave me? I can't find them *anywhere!*"

"Oh, Grace! You startled me. Yes, they needed mending; they're in the sewing basket. I'll do it in a minute."

"But I'm leaving on the bus in twenty minutes."

"It's all right, Grace. I'll have them mended by then. And I'm still not sure about you going on the bus by yourself." Nelly wiped her sudsy hands on the tea towel. "You must *promise* to be careful and not talk to strangers!"

Walter laughed, "I hope someone warns the str...strangers not to talk to Gracie!"

Grace ruffled his hair. "That's right, Walter, I'm not to be messed with!"

"Oh, stop that, you two! You are to behave like a lady *at all times*, Grace."

Grace gave Walter a wink, and in a posh voice, Grace said, "Yes, Mother, I shall."

"I still feel bad about you not being here on Walter's birthday, Grace. You have never been apart on either of your birthdays." Nelly was about to sniffle but strengthened her resolve.

"I know, Mum, but I'm hoping to give Walter his best birthday present ever. I'm going to talk to the broadcaster at the Healesville Races and he just might let me call a race. Especially if I tell him it's for Walter's birthday!" She kissed Walter on the cheek. "Happy Birthday, champ."

*

On the bus, sitting in the window seat, Grace gazed at the changing scenery. The further they travelled from Caulfield, the more sparsely populated and greener the country appeared. Horses and sheep now dotted the paddocks, with the occasional herd of black and white dairy cows. Grace thought back to when she was much younger and the country trips the family would sometimes take. *I remember when I was about four years old, I think, and I asked Dad, 'How many bottles of milk does a cow lay a day, Dad?' and Nelly had laughed out loud. It's one of my happiest memories. The sound of Mum's laughter felt so good, knowing she was happy, if only for a moment. Most times, she seemed sadly disconnected to us all. Good memories are like old friends. They give so much comfort. And now, I suppose it's time to make my own happy memories.*

Of course, I want to call races, but I hope my life will include Johnno, somehow. I dream about him every day, and I know he would never stand in my way of becoming a race caller – he's said so. But what if we did get married and I had children straight away? Then having a proper career may be impossible... Stop it, Grace, she scolded herself. *It's a problem you don't need to worry about, not for a long, long time.* All Grace wanted to do right now was ride horses and practise race calling. Maybe Mr Blake could help make that happen, given he was President of the Healesville Race Club?

The bus finally pulled over, and after thanking the bus driver, Grace jumped down onto the last step. Forgetting how heavy her suitcase was, she nearly fell into Emma's arms. They giggled, hugged each other, then proceeded to walk the mile home to the farm.

Emma shot Grace a serious look. "You know I feel as close to you as any sister could, Grace. We are in tune with each other. So, I have to ask for your advice because you're so wise." Emma stopped and, turning to face Grace, looked deep into her eyes. In them, she saw awareness as deep as the sea. *Maybe Grace is an old soul?* Emma thought. "It's just that I wonder what my life would be like if Dad married Gillian? Do you think I would have to play the second fiddle in his life? Do you understand, Grace?" Grace nodded. "At first, I was happy for Dad to have found someone. But more and more, he's left me alone, so he and Gillian could go away on what he calls *business matters*." Emma looked forlorn. "And though she's nice, Gillian is not the type to be spending time talking and doing things with me." Emma picked unhappily at a loose thread on her jumper. "I'm beginning to feel a bit jealous of her, to tell you the truth. I feel excluded, and I'm upset that Dad hasn't noticed." Emma's eye shone with unshed tears. "Oh, Grace, I feel so miserable at times, like I have to weigh up my feelings against Dad's happiness - and I know he *is* happy when he's with Gillian."

Grace put her suitcase down and hugged Emma. "Why don't you just tell him how you feel, Emma? I'm sure he'd listen and understand. I think he's so obsessed with Gillian; he hasn't realized the effect it's had on you. He *loves* you, Emma. Just *talk* to him." Grace gave Emma a reassuring smile.

"I know you're right, Grace. It's just if he says, *Don't be silly, Emma.* I'll feel like I will be all alone, especially with Mum gone. We have no other relatives; I only have Cookie." She gave Grace a warm smile. "And you, of course."

"That's right Em, you'll *always* have me, and I know nothing can ever make up for you losing your mum. I truly feel for you and I want you to know I'll always be there for you, no matter what. I promise. Come on. My arm's about to fall off lugging this thing!" They both laughed and started walking.

They reached the massive oak door, and before they could twist the knob, Cookie swung it back with a smile warm enough to break ice. "Welcome back, Grace! I have a birthday surprise for you."

Grace's heart raced. "It's not *my* birthday. It's Walter's. But is the surprise about me standing with the race caller at the Healesville Races?"

Cookie laughed, "Oh, you and your race calling, Grace. Do you really think they'll let a *girl* call races?" She tut-tutted as she guided Grace through to the back patio. From there, they could see a chestnut horse in the adjoining paddock. Grace turned to Cookie.

"So?"

"*So*, she says!" Cookie chuckled, rolling her eyes. "He's been given to you by our neighbour, Mr Stenning. He says he's *very* quiet and a good stock horse. Mr Stenning doesn't ride anymore, so; *you* can have him, Grace." She saw Grace's expression of disbelief. "Well, go on, go say hello to your new horse. I think his name's Carrot. Yes, that's it, Carrot the horse." She laughed again.

Grace was wildly excited about actually owning a horse, but Cookie's dismissal of her chosen career had stung like a bee, even though she knew she'd have to get used to similar comments. She was not about to forget Cookie's rebuff, but she would forgive her. *Cookie hasn't heard me call a race yet. And that'll change her mind, for sure.*

"What do you think, Grace?" Emma chirped, trying to lighten the hurt she knew Cookie had inflicted on Grace. "Shall we go and say hello to Carrot, *your horse?*"

Grace shook herself. "Yes, of course. But can we go and thank Mr Stenning straight after? It's very kind of him." She turned and did her best to muster a grateful smile. "Thank you for arranging it, Cookie."

"Not a problem – not a problem at all, Grace. I've been watching you, and I suspected you were up to riding something with a bit more spirit than old Bob. Besides, I think he should be retired now, don't you, Emma?" Cookie didn't look at Emma as she spoke; she was still studying Grace's subdued expression. Hardly what she'd expected from the girl after such a pleasant surprise, *oh well*, she thought, *can't please 'em all.* "Now, I'd better get dinner started. You girls won't be long, will you?"

"Not too long," Emma called as they walked out. Once out of the house, she added, "I'm sorry, Grace. Cookie shouldn't have said that about race calling, I mean. And I'm sorry I didn't stick up for you." Grace kept her focus on Carrot. "You're okay, aren't you, Grace? I mean, it *will* be hard to follow your dream. It doesn't matter *how* good you are. Women just don't seem to fit into some professions."

Grace didn't trust herself to answer. Her pride was wounded, and deep in her heart, she feared Emma's words might be the truth. Grace took a deep, steady breath and made a promise to herself. She looked squarely at her friend. "Emma, I'm going to be the best race caller Australia, and maybe the world has ever heard! And I don't want to talk about it *anymore!*"

"I'm sorry Grace. I didn't mean to be a Doubting Thomas. I simply don't want you to be hurt if it doesn't happen, that's all. But I know if *anyone* can make it happen, *you* will. And I promise to support you in any way I can why I'll even talk to the Racecourse Manager at Healesville to see if you can join the broadcaster. Cyril's his name, and he's a real character. I know he wouldn't mind a bit. How's that, Grace?"

Mollified by her friend's generous offer, Grace turned and hugged her. "It seems we both have problems, Em. We'll work them out together, okay?"

Grace entered the paddock and introduced herself to Carrot, gently stroking his neck and telling him he was the most handsome horse she'd ever seen – even though he wasn't. However, Carrot now belonged to her, and she would love him unconditionally. With this thought, Grace calmed herself, realising just how fortunate she was. She and Emma climbed over the fence to thank Mr Stenning, who was so thrilled to have them visit and offered them a shandy featuring his homemade beer. The girls were more than happy to accept and settle themselves in the chairs on his veranda, where they discussed the familiar woes of the war.

"So far, my son, Phil, is safe," Mr Stenning said. "And I reckon the war will be over soon. He was only seventeen when he took off, not even old enough to have a beer in the pub." He shook his head with the memory. "It's a bloody crime, the Government sending our kids to war so young. Still, he's a damn good shot, so I reckon he'll shoot his fair share of those Jap blighters!" He nodded at the picture he'd painted for himself.

"My Dad, Tom, he's a Desert Rat at Tobruk. He's a real good shot, too. Where's your son stationed, Mr Stenning?" Grace asked.

"He's in New Guinea, on the Kokoda in the bloody jungle. Terrible hard it is. But I'm sure he'll make it home," he said with determination.

"Yeah, we hope so, too. I'm sure, with the Yanks helping, they'll get those Japs to retreat," Grace said, trying to sound more optimistic than she felt.

"Phil turns twenty-one on the tenth of June next year. Wouldn't it be great if he came home to celebrate?" Mr Stenning said with a broad smile.

Grace raised her glass. "Let's drink to that, shall we?"

The girls had downed three shandies each before swaying home, late for dinner and receiving the sharp end of Cookie's tongue. Trying hard not to giggle, they apologised, avoiding blaming Mr Stenning for both their delay and their carefree attitude. It would be their secret.

"I hope he doesn't lose his son, especially after his wife died not so long ago," said Grace much later. "We could try and cheer him up by taking him to the races on Saturday."

"That's a nice thought, Grace. I mean, he'd love to go to the races, I'm sure." Emma gave a coy smile. "Peter's also coming. I've been seeing him a bit lately. I like him, and I'm eighteen, so I'm old enough to have a steady boyfriend if I want to. Why some girls are even *married* at my age." Her decisive nod confirmed Emma's approval of this statement. "But we're not going steady yet," she added, sighing dramatically, "because Peter says he is *too busy with his law studies*. And he's also still working at the training stables where Dad's horses are." Emma held Grace's hand and looked her in the eye. "You do like him, don't you, Grace?"

"It doesn't matter if *I* like him or not, but yes - Peter seems nice." Grace didn't want to tell Emma that Nelly had seen Peter with a pretty young woman on his arm in the city. Nelly had tried to say hello, but when he saw her coming, he had turned and walked the other way.

81

"Is Peter strapping a horse at the races, or is he coming with us for the outing?" Grace asked.

"He's actually in charge of the horse. Peter's Foreman for the day. But he said the horse is in the first race, so the rest of the day he can spend with me – I mean *us*."

The following morning the girls saddled up and rode nearly all day. Carrot turned out to be '*a real bottler*', as Grace told Mr Stenning.

"I'm so happy he's got a lovely young lady to love him, Grace. Though I suppose Emma will help care for him, seeing as you live in Caulfield most of the time?"

"Yes, but I might see if I could bring him back home and stable him with Charlie Norman's horses, near the racetrack. Then I could ride Carrot every day! I'd bring him back here on school holidays, of course."

"Sounds like a plan. I hope it works out for you, Grace!"

"Thank you, Mr Stenning," Grace smiled. "Carrot is the best gift I've ever had."

*

A glorious day greeted the racegoers; the sunshine was warm, and a slight northerly breeze made it perfect for Emma to wear her new floral dress. She smiled knowingly at Grace, who had donned a pair of slacks and a bright blouse, ready to climb up to the Judges' Box. Emma had been successful in her plea for Grace to join Cyril.

"Wish me luck!" Grace said as she walked briskly towards the ladder, her binoculars slung around her neck.

"You're not calling races *yet*, Grace!" Emma called. "You're just there to learn." Emma laughed, especially when Grace gave a backward wave – a sign that Emma knew, *go away!* Grace pretended it was her first official race call, even if she only called it to herself. She steeled herself and climbed the ladder to meet, perhaps, her future mentor.

"Hello, young lady." The friendly greeting came from a small man whose head appeared far too big for his body. Grace towered over him as they shook hands. "I'm Cyril, and you're Grace, right? So, you want to call races, do you? Have you had any practice?" he asked, his eyebrows raised sceptically.

"Yes, I have. Quite a bit, actually." Grace tried hard not to sound defensive. "I used to stand with my Dad and my brother behind an old wooden fence that adjoined Caulfield Racetrack. We live just down the road. We'd study the horses and the colours every Friday night, and then

I'd take it in turns with Dad to call the races."

"You never went into the racecourse? You stayed on the outside, is that right?"

"Yes, but it changed recently; we go to the races often now. It's a long story. Mum wouldn't let us go before. But now Dad's away fighting in the war, Mum's changed her mind. Well, " Grace smiled, "I think Edward changed it for her. He's a family friend and lives next door, and he's helping us while Dad's away."

Cyril nodded his understanding or was it his assumption, and Grace gave a nervous grin. "Okay. Did you take a look at last night's *Argus*? Do you know the names of the horses and the colours of the jockeys' silks, Grace?"

She nodded. "Yes, I did. I studied the form, and I've followed all the races. I know every horse who's racing today, and I remember the owners' colours." Grace beamed. "I've even met Ken Howard once, and he listened to my call, and he said I had a real talent for it."

Cyril smiled. "Did he just?"

"Yes, he did."

Cyril was secretly impressed. "Well, then. In that case, we'd better give you a go. What do you reckon?"

Grace's nerves exploded; her stomach churned, and her hands trembled.

"You...you really mean it?" she asked breathlessly.

Cyril placed his hand upon her shoulder. "I'll tell you what, Grace. You stand behind me, and try to remember my call, then as soon as I'm off-air, you call the race back to me. If - and I mean *if* you get it near right, every time, I'll think of some excuse so that you can call the last. Then you can do your best. Do you think that's fair, Grace?" He looked up into her green eyes and smiled when he saw the depth of her emotion. "Now, now - don't go getting all *girly* on me. Keep your nerve, Grace." He looked down at his highly polished shoes and said in a low, serious voice, "I've heard you're a bloody good caller." He paused and continued, much louder, "So! Don't let yourself down. Okay?" He gave Grace's shoulder a slight shove. "Now stand at my back, use those nice binoculars and concentrate, because the horses are coming into the enclosure."

*

Emma hadn't taken her eyes off Peter. She'd watched him lead his horse around, hose him down, walk him again, tie him up and brush him - all the while thinking, Peter would never pay *me* that much attention. Emma wasn't entirely sure whether Peter liked her or if he were just being nice because she was the daughter of not only the owner of many horses in Peter's care but also a successful lawyer *and* the one he wished to work for, as he'd told her.

Emma promised herself. *I'll just come right out and ask him if he likes me because I'm not going to waste my time on him if he doesn't.*

Emma's heart soared when Peter approached and gave her a peck on the cheek. "Hello, Emma. I'll be with you as soon as *Avalanche* races. You go and mingle. I'm sure you know lots of locals. I'll find you, don't worry."

A bit condescending, Emma thought, *but then I probably asked for it after following him around like a lost puppy.*

"I will, and I hope he wins, Peter. He looks *reasonably* good," she said a touch sarcastically. Her pride regained, Emma walked away thinking, *Don't you worry, Peter. I fully intend to get 'lost. You're going to have to look very hard to find me!* Although, in reality, there was not much chance of *that* happening at a small country race meeting, even though the crowd *was* building fast.

Emma took advantage of the time on her own, chatting to neighbours and friends from school. Everyone seemed to be there, perhaps to take their mind off the war, if only for an afternoon. Time passed quickly with her social interactions, and soon Avalanche was lined up, ready to race. Emma laid an each-way bet with the bookies, then stood close to the fence, opposite the winning post.

The race began, and Avalanche settled nicely, travelling easy on the fence, where his jockey chose to stay and ride for luck, hoping the field would spread out and offer him a clear run. But none came; he was trapped behind tiring horses and ran an unlucky third.

Disappointed with the outcome, Emma walked to the mounting yard to see Peter fuming at the jockey. She couldn't quite hear what he was saying, but his body language and the shocked expression on the jockey's face relayed the message. Her disappointment doubled; she would never have believed Peter could act in such an unsporting manner. When something like that happened to one of her father's horses when he was there, he'd simply shrug philosophically, thank the jockey for his work and say, 'That's racing.'

*

Grace had succeeded in calming her nerves by breathing deeply – a technique Tom had taught her. She'd focused so hard on the previous races that she'd given herself a headache. However, so far, Grace had managed to repeat Cyril's call for every race or, at least, her *impression*. She had seasoned her commentary with her unique vocabulary and used a deeper voice than usual. Cyril laughed, enchanted by her comic turn of phrase. '*If that straggler doesn't get going, we'll send him a packed lunch! Uh-oh, he heard me; he's rounding the field.*'

"Okay, Grace. You're on. Don't tell a soul that I faked being ill, or I'll lose my job, and God knows what they'll do to you!" Standing on tiptoes, Cyril gave her a peck on the cheek. "Jeez, are you tall enough, Grace?" he asked with a shake of the head. "Mind you; I do have ducks' disease."

"What's ducks' disease, Cyril?" Grace was genuinely puzzled.

"Think about it, Grace…my bum's too close to the ground!"

Their laughter quelled her mounting nerves.

Cyril started giving his observations of the horses in the last race parading in the mounting yard, interspersing his descriptions with several coughs, each followed by '*Excuse me*. When the horses lined up to start, Cyril made exaggerated gagging sounds and continued until the horses were just about ready to jump. With one last croaky, '*You'll… have… to excuse me,*' he turned the microphone in Grace's direction. So convincing was his performance, Grace silently mouthed, '*Are you all right?*' Cyril gave her a thumbs up and smiled, leaving Grace in charge. She took over seamlessly.

She braced herself and found the courage to call the last race precisely as it played out, and even as several horses battled it out on the line, Grace called the winner by a nose. The crowd had been cheering for their chosen horse to win and seemed almost oblivious to the call. However, shocked silence descended when the race was over before people started muttering, '*Who was that?… It sounded like a girl…Nah, it couldn't be. Girls can't call races.*'

Emma stood behind a particular group of non-believers. "Excuse me! I'll have you know girls *can* call races! And that was *my* best friend, *Grace Nobel*. Aren't you *impressed*?" They looked at her dismissively.

Emma walked off in a huff, then, despite wearing a dress, scaled the ladder leading up to the Commentator's Box. She gathered Grace in her arms. "Grace, you were amazing, and you sounded so professional like you'd called races all your life!"

Grace extricated herself from Emma's embrace and looked deadpan into her eyes. "I have, Emma."

"Oh, I *know*! Of *course*, you have! I just meant, well, you sounded so professional. It was - "

Before another word was spoken, the thumping sound of heavy boots ascending the ladder shook the flimsy box. The three of them stood fixed to the spot, looking like condemned prisoners.

The enormous frame of the Racing Club Secretary - cum Course Manager; cum Holder of Any Official Position to do with Healesville Racetrack - filled the doorway. Meaty hands upon his generous hips, he demanded, "You do know that what you just did is illegal, Cyril?"

"You mean, nearly choking on my own vomit just before the last race was underway, George?" Cyril, barely containing his laughter, tried to look offended. He knew George's bark was far worse than his bite.

"No, you idiot!" George roared. "That *girl*!" He pointed toward Grace. "She's not allowed to call races. It's *illegal*! We could be struck off for this!"

"Oh, that's a bit rich, George. What did you expect me to do when I was nearly choking to death? Leave the horses to race *without* a call?"

George looked around and gave an exaggerated sniff. "Where's the vomit, Cyril? I can't *see* any, and I can't *smell* it." George squinted and crossed his beefy arms. "But I *do* smell a *rat*!"

Grace and Emma stood shoulder to shoulder. Emma gave Grace a wink, assumed a superior look, and addressed George. "Mr Green, I *assume* you know the exact details of the *law* allegedly broken? Would you please explain which section of the law states that a girl cannot call a horse race? Especially under such *life-threatening* circumstances?"

There was no answer, just a dumbfounded expression on George Green's florid face. "Hmm. Just as I thought, Mr Green," Emma said haughtily. "I think your *accusation* should be explained to the Race Club Committee, of which my father is the President, as *you* well know. I suggest you let the *Committee* decide the appropriate measures to deal with this. Thank you, *Sir*."

Emma took Grace by the arm. "Excuse us, gentlemen, we must be leaving. Come, Grace." Still in shock, Grace meekly allowed Emma to steer her to the doorway and guide her down the ladder.

Back on solid ground, Grace regained her senses, and they ran, trying to stifle their laughter that was threatening to explode. Emma had utterly forgotten about Peter in the excitement of the situation and her delight at handling it. *Oh, well, bad luck!* She thought. *I'm not going to go searching for him now,* which was just as well, as Peter had found a pretty, sympathetic strapper to take his mind off his woes.

CHAPTER 9

After his release from the hospital, Tom took every opportunity to meet Nurse Lucy for a beer or a coffee. A strong friendship had resulted from their shared interests and sense of humour. Nothing looked like developing further because they each respected, the other was married. Tom mainly spoke of his children and little of Nelly. However, Lucy often told Tom how much she loved her husband, Sam, an officer in the U.S. Navy. They had no children as yet, but after the war, they intended to have two. "A boy and a girl," Lucy told Tom, then giggled at her assumption. "As if we could simply order the sex of our children." She drifted into melancholy. "Though a pigeon pair *would* be perfect. *If* we survive this war."

"You *will*, and so will Sam. Don't be sad, Lucy." Tom held her hand across the table. "Nelly and I were lucky enough to have one of each - you don't need to have any more kids, then. That is unless you want them."

Lucy smiled and squeezed his hand.

Later that month, Tom had another leave pass and waited for Lucy in a bar, which Aussie soldiers had taken over. After waiting an hour, he decided to walk back to the hospital, a little concerned that Lucy had not met him as planned. Tom's mind was preoccupied with Lucy, as well as his thoughts of home. Lucy had told Tom that her father was a race caller back in America - information he knew would excite Grace. What a treat it would be if one day they could travel there to meet him? And catch up with Lucy, of course. He wondered what would it be like to *live* in America? Would it be possible to follow his dream of becoming a race caller in the U.S. of A.?

Tom knocked on Lucy's bedroom door, and her roommate, Jenny, answered with a worried look. In the background, he could hear sobbing.

"What's wrong, Jenny?" Tom asked, trying to get a glimpse of

Lucy, who lay prostrate on her bed, the pillow pressed against her pretty face, muffling her heart-wrenching sobs.

Jenny stepped outside the room, placed her hand on Tom's arm, and shut the door behind her. She kept her voice low. "Lucy's just had a telegram, Tom. Her husband, Sam, has been killed. A Jap torpedo got their ship in the Pacific. I'm sorry, Tom. I know you and Lucy are good friends, but I'd better handle this. I'm sure she will talk to you later - maybe tomorrow if you're around." She closed her eyes, tears trickling down her cheeks. Taking a deep breath, she wiped her face and gave Tom a wan smile. "I'd better go." She rubbed Tom's arm affectionately before stepping back into the room, closing the door quietly.

Tom, sensing Lucy's pain, wanted nothing more than to stay and hold her, to comfort her, and to tell her he would always be there. *Oh Christ, what am I thinking?* He was a married man, and Lucy was simply a good mate, albeit a woman - and what a woman. *She's nothing more than a friend. And I'm too old for her.* But he knew there was more, much more to *his* feelings.

Tom strolled, kicking stones along the road, turning his thoughts to home. Sudden death had a way of making him confront his mortality. *The kids -what would they do without me?* He felt guilty, as his feelings for Lucy had dulled the ache of being away from Walter and Grace. He couldn't consider Nelly because as hard as he'd tried, Tom had never been able to love her, not the way he should have, not the way *Nelly* wanted. Why the hell *was* that? In the beginning, Nelly had provided for all his needs with genuine pleasure. She had loved him with every fibre of her being. And what had he done? He had merely tolerated her. He had tried to be a good husband, to say nice things to her, but his heart had never been it, or in anything, he did for her. Maybe that was it. Gradually, when she wasn't loved back, Nelly had become bitter. Her mother hadn't helped, filling Nelly's head with God-fearing rubbish, telling her that Walter's disability was a punishment because he was conceived out of wedlock. It still angered Tom. Walter was more like a gift from God. He was intelligent, charming, and had a bloody good sense of humour, *and* he never complained. Walter was the best son a bloke could have. And Gracie, he knew she thought the same. Grace was a gem - a diamond, hard to crack, but with a heart of gold. *I don't think I could ever leave those two, not even if Lucy asked me to.*

Tom's reverie ended outside the noisy bar. He entered, smiling when he heard the Aussie slang, witnessed the rough camaraderie, the slaps on the back, and the odd smack over the earhole. *Ah, a slice of home.* He wandered through the crowd towards the veil of cigarette smoke engulfing his mates. Soon his worries were washed away by a few pints of lager.

The following day, a little seedy, he ventured to the nurses' quarters to see Lucy. She sat forlornly in the communal living room, being consoled by her friends. He paused at the doorway, wondering if he should impose.

Lucy looked up. "Oh, Tom, I'm sorry, I couldn't speak to anyone yesterday. Please, come and sit down." Lucy patted the space beside her on the couch. The others shifted away and busied themselves making tea.

Jenny, standing in a shaft of sunlight next to the sink, spoke from across the room. "Would you like a cuppa, Tom?"

"Yes, thanks. Black, no sugar."

Lucy's eyes were swollen and red from crying. She held Tom's hand tightly. "*Please* stay safe, Tom. I don't think I could bear to lose you, too. She lowered her eyes, and a faint blush coloured her pale cheeks. "What I mean is, you are *such* a good friend, Tom. I feel I can tell you anything. Thank you for that. I treasure our friendship."

Tom was perplexed. *What was she trying to say? That even though her husband is dead, there could never be anything else between us but friendship?*

"Of course, Lucy. We'll always be friends. If there's ever anything I can do for you, you know you only have to ask. I'm so sorry for your loss."

A moment of silence and Lucy placed Tom's hand back on his lap. She gazed into his eyes, seeing in them the love she knew he held for her. "I'm going home, Tom," Lucy said, despite what she saw. "I can't let Sam's parents cope with this alone. He was their only son. They had a daughter, but she died of pneumonia at sixteen. It was incredibly hard for them, and now..."

"I understand completely, Lucy. I thought you might go home. You must. I'll be sorry to see you go. I'll miss you."

Tom stood to leave, but Lucy tugged his sleeve. "No, please stay, Tom. Besides, Jenny is bringing your tea." Lucy's sad smile convinced him, and Tom sat down, a fraction closer. The space between them charged. They sipped their tea in silence until Lucy asked, "Would you

90

take a walk outside with me?"

"Of course. I know a sheltered spot where we can talk." The two left, and the remaining nurses exchanged speculative looks.

Some distance from the nurse's quarters, a white-painted pergola gave support to a crimson bougainvillea. The lush foliage provided them with both shade and privacy. Tom brushed the wooden bench seat free of dust and indicated for Lucy to sit. Hoping to break the uneasy silence, Tom asked conversationally, "Did you know, Lucy, Australian First World War soldiers erected this pergola?"

"No, I didn't."

"Well, it was. The Soldiers built it when they were recovering, and they made it to thank the nurses who'd cared for them."

"Wow, that *is* something, Tom. I'm glad you brought me here. I never knew that." She focused on the dancing shadows thrown by the paper-thin Bougainvillea leaves. "It's beautiful. I've always admired it and wondered who built it. Now I know. It should be our special place to sit and talk." She sighed with resignation. "What am I saying? I'm going home, and this will probably be our last chance to talk."

Tom, hesitant at first, gave in to temptation. Stretching his arm slowly around her shoulders, he gently held her. Lucy came alive in his embrace; she felt loved and safe. She leaned her head on his shoulder.

"I don't know what's going to happen, Tom. Am I going to spend the rest of my life consoling my parents-in-law and, with that, give up my chance of finding happiness? I'm duty-bound. That's my nature. But I'm young, and I wanted to have children, be happily married to the man I loved. It's all gone now. My life has changed in an instant. I'm not alone in this tragedy, I know. There are so many young wives, mothers, and fathers who have lost their loved ones. I shouldn't feel like this. I'm being selfish." She lifted her head and turned to face him. " But what should I do, Tom? Tell me, please." Lucy moved into his arms, their eyes locked before their lips met in a soft lingering expression of all they meant to each other.

A voice made them pull apart abruptly. "Lucy, there you are!" It was Jenny. "Phone call for you. I think it's your Dad, from America."

Lucy blushed, and Tom straightened himself before he stood and helped Lucy to her feet. "I have to go, Lucy. I'll write to you." He turned and walked away, leaving Lucy to unscramble her emotions. She lowered her gaze and followed Jenny to the telephone.

91

"Hi, Daddy," Lucy said brightly before dissolving into such a flood of tears.

"Darlin'... oh, don't cry, Darlin'. Hear me out. I know you're comin' home especially, so you can help Jack and Frieda. But Mom and I can do that. We want you to do whatever makes you happy, Honeybun. It's not your fault what happened. Goddamn, this bloody war! Don't cry, Honeybun. You're doin' a great job. Your Grandpappy would be proud of you for mending all those brave soldiers over there. Why if it weren't for him bein' injured in the First World War and bein' helped by one particular nurse in the Cairo Hospital - well, you and I wouldn't be here."

Lucy gained control of her tears as she recalled the reason she had volunteered. She sniffed and said, "I know, Dad."

"That's better, Honeybun. All I'm sayin' is follow your heart. Please don't feel like it's your duty because it ain't. Your Momma says that, too. You're young. You can find happiness again. I know that might seem a little heartless at the moment, especially since we're all gonna miss Sam, ver' much. He was a great young fella, but you know as well as I do, he wouldn't want you to waste your life cryin' over him. Give him the respect he deserves. After all, he fought for your freedom, Honeybun. I know it will take time for you to come to terms with your loss, but you're like your Grandpappy, tough and resilient. That's all your Momma and I wanted you to know, Darlin'. The decision is yours. Come home if you want, but don't do it for anyone else but yourself. Or stay there and help the war effort. We love you, Honeybun. Stay safe and try to be happy."

"I love you too, Daddy. Tell Mom I love her, and I won't do anything in a hurry. I'll take some time and think about what's best for me at this stage. Bye, Daddy." Lucy hung up the phone.

It wasn't the time to tell her father she had a special friend she could lean on. She knew Tom would be able to comfort her, more to the point, hadn't he shown her with his kiss? With this thought, a wave of relief washed over her. If she ran, she could catch up with Tom and tell him what her father had just said. Yes, she would run as fast as she could, and that was *damn* fast; she'd won many track events at college. However, Lucy's effort was in vain. Tom had vanished. She stopped to catch her breath, shading her eyes to scan the campgrounds.

Maybe it's a sign. Perhaps I should just let Tom go and see what happens. But he might be killed, too, and then where would I be? Best not to get my hopes up in this bloody war. I have to get over the loss of Sam on my own. Oh God, I loved him so much! How can I have almost the same feelings for another man? I have to be strong. I can't rely on anyone else to help me come to terms with this. Best not to overthink. I just need to get on with my job - keep my mind busy and let my heart rest.

Lucy wandered back to the hospital, emotionally drained and physically exhausted. She had been given the day off and knew she needed to try to catch up on the sleep which had eluded her since she'd received the terrible news about Sam.

CHAPTER 10

Eventually, both Grace and Walter received separate letters from Tom, written while in the hospital.

I've been talking to my American Nurse, Lucy, and I must repeat the age-old saying, 'the world is a small place.' Well, not that I knew Nurse Lucy before a damn scorpion bit me, but her dad's been a race caller down in the South for the past fifteen years. Lucy said we are all welcome to come and stay with them when all this business is over. She's sure her dad would give you a go on American radio, Grace. Wouldn't that be something? Anyway, Lucy heard yesterday that her husband, Sam, a U.S. Naval Officer, was killed in a torpedo attack. I feel incredibly sad for her. She's such a great girl. She's nursing here because her Granddaddy fought in the Middle East. He was injured in the First World War, and his nurse became his wife. I know it prompted Lucy to become a nurse and volunteer.

Anyway, how are you managing over there? Not having too much trouble with Nelly, I mean, Mum? I hope she's enjoying her job and not spending all her money on new dresses. I know how she likes to dress up for a minor occasions.

I've written a separate letter to Walter. I thought it best. Now he's not a kid anymore. Edward tells me how he stood up to your Grandma. It appears Walter put her right in her place. I always felt sorry for Grandpa - I hope this is a sign that he's woken up. Never too late, they say.

I'm not permitted to write about where I am or what's next for me. All I can say is, do your best, whatever it is. But that's not necessary – it's what you always do. I'm so enormously proud of you, Grace.

All my love,
Dad xoxoxo.

Walter was thrilled to receive his letter from Tom, written man to man. Tom even asked if he had a girlfriend, and Walter desperately wished he did. Emma was his *pinup girl*, an expression Walter knew was used by the armed forces when they hung up a photo of their favourite girl. Walter hadn't gone quite that far, but only because he didn't have a picture of Emma.

Walter wrote back to Tom with much less difficulty than before he'd commenced his studies with Edward. He wouldn't show Grace his letter. It was *men's business*. He only hoped Tom could decipher his unruly handwriting. Even the question about him having a girlfriend boosted Walter's ego. The fact that he'd recently topped his university law class also gave him cause to feel satisfied with his lot. He was on his way to independence, and the feeling was empowering.

Later, a pensive Grace encountered a beaming Walter in the living room, and he immediately noticed she was subdued. "What's wrong Gracie? I thought you'd be *happy* to hear from Dad. You w...were w...worried because we hadn't heard from him for ages."

"I'm okay, Walter. Did Dad mention a Nurse Lucy to you in your letter?" She slumped into the armchair.

"No, Grace. Dad never mentioned any nurse. But he did ask me if I had a girlfriend." Walter chuckled and, embarrassed, added, "As if! I mean, who'd want me?"

His question brought Grace out of her funk. She sat up, suddenly animated. "How can you *say* that, Walter! Any girl would be *proud* to have you as her boyfriend!"

"You mean any *nice* girl, Grace. Usually, they make fun of me. But I'm not worried. It is what it is. And I'm lucky to have a sister like you. You've always looked out for me. But I tell you, Grace, I'm a m...man now, so I'll fight my own b...battles. Christ, if I can put our ferocious bulldog Grandma in her p ...place, I reckon I could t...tackle anyone. Maybe not physically." He paused and smiled. "Maybe I should carry a sword or a gun. Then I'd be safe. What do you think, Grace?" He laughed.

"Oh, shit! Don't do *that*, Walter. A cricket bat would do. You wouldn't get into trouble with a cricket bat! With the police, I mean." Grace stood and walked briskly from the room.

"Hey! Wh...where are you going, Gracie?" Walter called.

"You'll see!" She returned carrying a hand mirror and pushed it up close to Walter's face.

"Take a good look in the mirror Walter. What do you see?"

"I see me."

"Yes, of course. But describe your features."

"Oh, okay. My hair is streaky b…blonde, my complexion is slightly b…brown, 'cause I love the sun." He smiled. "My teeth are white. Thanks for helping me clean them, though I can manage it myself, now," he said proudly. "My nose isn't too b..big. Actually, it's a good nose. It's straight at least. But I've got a b…big mouth!"

"No, you haven't, Walter. You have *kissable* lips," Grace told him, smiling.

"Yeah, when I don't dribble."

"You *don't* dribble anymore, but *if* you do you wipe it straight away."

"Do you think I have k…kind blue eyes, Grace?" he asked shyly, "because that's what Emma said."

"Oh, did she now? Give me another look, Walter." He lifted his eyes to meet hers. "Yes, definitely your best feature. Your ears stick out a little." Grace pushed his ears flat against his head. "Nothing a bit of glue won't fix. I might just do that when you're sleeping."

They were still laughing when Nelly entered. "What are you two up to?" she said light-heartedly.

"I'm convincing Walter that he is quite handsome and how any *nice* girl would find him attractive." Grace hoped her mother would back her up.

"Well, I don't…" Nelly thought about what she was going to say and abruptly changed her mind. "… I don't see why any girl *wouldn't* find you handsome, Walter. Because the fact is, you *are!*"

"Thank you, ladies," said Walter, while making an elaborate bow, feeling satisfied with himself. "Your compliments are accepted. Thank you. And now, may I offer you both a cup of tea and show you that not only am I *handsome*, but I am also capable of doing, well, p… pretty much *everything*!"

Nelly was stunned. She turned to Grace, asking, "When did all this happen, Grace?"

"When you weren't paying attention, Nelly," Grace said with an accusatory tone.

Nelly had the good grace to look a little shamefaced and gave an apologetic smile. Walter walked to the kitchen and, before too long, returned, balancing a tray laden with all the essentials, and carefully proceeded to place it on the coffee table. Nelly and Grace watched; their breath held in anticipation of a disaster. Walter lowered the shaking tray; it made a noisy but safe landing, all things remained upright and intact. Three breaths were released in unison.

"Would you like me to pour, ladies?" Walter looked up, smiling his relief.

That may be pushing things a little, Nelly thought. "No, thank you, Walter. You've done a wonderful job, and I'm still the head of the household. I'll pour."

Grace, happily contemplating Walter's self-sufficient future, started when she heard a knock on the door. "I'll get it," she announced. She strode to the door and opened it to find a smiling Edward. "Come in, Edward. Walter has just made afternoon tea."

"Thank you, Grace. Don't mind if I do." He turned to Walter, "Well, Walter, this is a nice surprise! I thought you may have needed another practice, but I can see you have accomplished yet another exercise. Good on you, man!" Not only had Edward been tutoring Walter with his legal studies, but he had also been teaching him some life skills.

"Yes, you have taught me w…well, Edward. Thank you."

Turning to Grace, Edward said, "However, the reason I'm here is to tell you, Grace, about the Healesville Race Committee's decision." He took a deep breath, then exhaled slowly. "They said you were unqualified to call the last race. Well, we all knew that, anyway. But now, the *Victorian Race Club Committee* has also given their say on the matter. They weren't happy."

As Grace's unofficial male guardian, Edward had stepped up to speak on her behalf. The outcome had been a double-edged sword; her talent drew a raft of genuine compliments, but both committees gave stern warnings against any further infringements of regulations.

Unfortunately for Cyril, he had borne the brunt of their wrath and stood down for ten race meetings. '*Deceiving the public*,' they said, '*by bringing into play an unapproved, amateur race caller.*'

Although he didn't say anything in defence of either himself or Grace to either of the committees, Cyril *did* speak to the sports journalists. "It was worth it! This young lady, Grace Nobel, will be one of the best race callers Australia has *ever* heard. You mark my words!"

Grace's heart plunged when Edward read out the verdict. She

was banned from attending race meetings anywhere in Victoria for six months. This was implemented by the VRC, not the Healesville Race Club. They had been more lenient, perhaps because of Errol Blake being president. After her ban had expired, she would have to apply in writing to be allowed back on course in the future. Grace would never be permitted to call another race unless under contract with the VRC.

Edward placed the letter on the coffee table and looked squarely at Grace. "If you want, I will fight this for you, Grace."

Grace shook her head. "No, Edward. As Cyril said, it was worth it. I can wait six months."

Edward was secretly relieved by Grace's philosophical acceptance of her punishment. He didn't want to fight a case when there was no certainty of winning.

Grace continued drily, "After all, Mum banned me from racetracks for thirteen years. What's another six months?" They all saw the humour in that remark.

Even Nelly laughed. "I have an excuse for doing that," she protested, "My mother brainwashed me!"

"Ahh, but you have not seen the errors of your ways, my child," Grace said in a deep, sinister voice. "Racing holds the lure of easy money - it is the greatest temptation of all! You will soon suffer the fire and torment of hell!"

"Oh, don't be silly, Grace," Nelly said dismissively. "There's nothing wrong with a little flutter to accompany the thrill of watching those magnificent horses race." Nelly looked pointedly at Grace. "Besides, I was talking to a Catholic priest at Flemington last Saturday, and he goes to every meeting held there. If he wins, then the money goes in the Poor Box on Sunday. Isn't that nice?" Nelly said with an innocent smile. Grace rolled her eyes.

The phone, which sat permanently beside Nelly on her lamp table, shrilled suddenly and cut short any further discussion. She picked it up. "Hello? Who is speaking please?"

'It's Emma, Mrs Nobel. I was wondering if Grace was home?'

"Yes, she is, Emma. But first, how are you and your father?"

The conversation went on until Grace mimed for Nelly to hand over the receiver.

On hearing the sound of Emma's name, Walter's heart instantly filled with warmth. He fantasized about the day he could dance with her again. She'd held him close that night at the Windsor. *Maybe it was only to help me stand,* Walter had thought at the time, but once she realized he could dance, she stopped and, at arm's length, gazed into his eyes. *"You have lovely, kind blue eyes, Walter,"* Emma had said before she held him close again. How could he *ever* forget that moment?

Nelly stood up, offering Grace her armchair, then headed toward the kitchen carrying the tray. Edward followed. "Thank you, Edward, but I don't need your help. I'll wash up and Grace will dry them later."

"It's no trouble, and I need to talk to you alone anyway."

"Oh. We don't have a problem, do we, Edward?"

"No, not us. It's just…well, it's Walter." Edward looked decidedly uncomfortable and eyes averted, mumbled quickly, "He asked me about…how do men... I mean, how does a man, ah, you know… make love…to a woman."

"Oh, my goodness!" Nelly was taken aback. "He's not ready for those shenanigans, is he? And besides, I'm not sure he could…" Nelly stopped washing, the teacup poised in mid-air. "Do *you* think he could… you know..." Nelly briskly resumed the washing up.

"Yes, I know. And yes, Walter could. There's nothing wrong with him, Nelly. He's a physically healthy young man, and he's twenty years old - soon to be twenty-one. His hormones are racing. All I want to ask is, is it all right for me to have a man-to-man talk with him? I told Walter I'd ask you first before we talked about the subject again."

Nelly sighed deeply, "I suppose I have to admit it. Walter is growing up. He amazes me how much he's learning, not only academically but physically, too. I never thought it possible. I always thought he would get worse, not better."

"If you don't mind me saying so, Nelly, you made him believe he was pretty much useless. If someone keeps telling you, you're this or that, sooner or later you become whatever it is they say you are."

"Yes, that's true, and I feel terrible, Edward. I know I keep blaming *my* mother for *my* shortcomings. She told me terrible things all my life until I was almost too frightened to live." Nelly's eyes filled with tears. Edward put his tea towel on the sink and held her close.

"Don't cry, Nelly. Look how far *you've* come and how *Walter* has progressed, too. Thank God for Grace, she relies on her gut instinct, and she has the inner strength to stand up for herself."

"Grace gets that from Tom," Nelly murmured into Edward's

chest.

Grace entered the kitchen. *Right, this is a bit too close for comfort!*

"Every time I see you two, you're hugging. I want this to stop right now! Do you hear me?" Grace wagged an admonishing finger at them, her tone light but the glint in her eye meaning business.

Edward laughed, but Nelly took two steps back. "Your mum is going through a lot, Grace. I was just consoling her, that's all," Edward shrugged.

"Well, console her from the other side of the room, Edward!"

"Yes, Grace," he said meekly, his tongue firmly in his cheek.

"Right," Grace said with authority. "Emma asked if Walter and I could stay with her next weekend. Mr Blake is going away with Gillian - *again*. And Cookie wants the weekend off." Grace lightened her tone, "Please, Mum. It would be fun just the three of us. And Saturday night, we're going to cook a three-course dinner for Cyril, seeing how wonderful he's been to me. It's the least I can do."

Nelly turned to Edward. "What do you think, Edward?"

"It's not up to me, Nelly. Though I'm sure, they're all old enough and responsible enough to do the right thing. And, as Grace said, they would have a bit of fun. Wouldn't mind being a fly on the wall."

"Alright, Grace." Nelly smiled. "It should be fun. But be careful when you're cooking. You don't want to burn down Mr Blake's beautiful home."

"Thanks, Nelly. Though I don't think there's much chance of that, after all, it is solid bluestone!"

In the lounge room, the phone rang again. This time Walter picked it up.

"Hello, Nobel residence. Walter sp…speaking."

Grace, Nelly, and Edward stood in the doorway from the kitchen listening with expressions of curiosity. Walter was nodding his head and grinning like the Cheshire Cat.

"Yes, I'd like that. I understand. No, pay until I pr…prove myself. Yes, of course. G…goodbye for now."

"Well, *tell us*, Walter. Who was that? What was it all about?" Nelly demanded anxiously.

"That was the Editor of *The Argus* n..n..newspaper," Walter's excitement got the better of his pronunciation. "H…he w…wants me

100

to write a t…tipping column for the r…races. I don't know h…how he knows about m…me?"

Edward smiled knowingly. "I told Keith. I thought a bit of extra money would help see you through university."

"Jesus, I hope I don't get too n…nervous. It was just a bit of fun before. But to pick winners and be p…paid for it, and h…having to wr… write about it, too? I d…don't know, Edward."

"You'll be fine, Walter. No pressure. As Keith said, it's just a trial to start with, but you'd better call him Mr Dunstan."

"I will. I mean, I did on the ph…phone. He said I could start this S…Saturday. I have to have the tips to him by early F…Friday afternoon."

"Does that mean you won't be able to go to Emma's with me, Walter?" Grace asked, disappointed.

"I d…don't see why not. You g…girls can help me. And all I have to do is phone through my spiel and tips to Mr Dunstan's secretary. Easy!" Walter's face simply beamed.

CHAPTER 11

"Edward, I must agree with Mum. You are, indeed, Our Saviour. It's much easier being driven than going by train and bus. Are you coming in for a cup of tea?" Grace said as she knocked on Emma's front door.

"Absolutely. I wouldn't miss seeing Emma. I won't stay long, though. I know you three have a lot of studying to do. Especially if you want Walter to pick a winner – or two."

"Sorry I took so long to answer the door," Emma said, "I was up to my arm-pits in flour. I thought I'd try Cookies scone recipe. I'm about to put them in the oven. Come in." Emma's eyes were fixed on Walter as she spoke. *Mmm, he's so handsome! No one would even think he had Cerebral Palsy, at least, not until he moved.*

Their overnight bags they flung in the expansive hallway before following like puppy dogs promised a treat.

Grace grabbed the dishcloth and began wiping surfaces with gusto, while Walter surprised Emma by offering to make the tea. Emma raised an eyebrow.

"It's okay, Emma. I've been here before, and I think I know wh…where everything is." He smiled, praying that his infrequent dribble wouldn't make an unscheduled appearance. Good - he was safe.

"Why thank you Walter, and you too, Grace. It seems we're a good team. Maybe we should open a Tearoom. Though I think we might need Cookie's help," she added as she watched her flat scones browning in the oven.

They shared Walter's perfectly brewed pot of Bushells tea, along with Emma's slightly crunchy scones. However, topped with homemade strawberry jam and whipped cream, the botched attempt went down well.

Edward stood after finishing his second scone. "Now, I must be going. Don't do anything I wouldn't do if let off the leash!" Edward said with a wink. "Thanks, Emma, I must say your rock cakes…I mean, your scones were delicious. I'll pick you up Sunday afternoon." Edward said, inclining his head towards Walter and Grace.

"We'll be here. Thanks again for the l...lift, Edward." Walter stood, focused, and shook Edward's hand. Perfect, not even a tremor, Emma noticed.

They cleared the kitchen table to spread out the race fields. Walter, with pen in hand, sat and studied the first race. The girls stood behind, looking over his shoulders. Their discussion became quite animated at times but always ended in laughter. Walter enjoyed the banter but finally had to protest.

"Okay, ladies, I have your opinions safely on board. Now, I'm the one who has to call the sh...shots so, if you don't mind, I need s... some peace to pull this all t...together. Remember, I have to write a short spiel on each horse and explain why I p...picked it to win, and it will take some time."

"Do you want me to take shorthand, Walter? I'm rather good now that I'm in Secretarial College." Emma gave him a coy smile.

"I think that's a great idea," Grace said decidedly. "Besides, I'd like to ride Carrot." She left to get changed into her riding gear.

"In that case, I would love you to stay and take shorthand, Emma. As long as you can tr...translate it for Mr Dunstan's secretary?"

Later, with help from Emma, Walter phoned through his tips to the Sports Section of the Newspaper. He hung up the phone and sent a silent prayer. *Please, Lord, help me by bringing those horses home in at least a place.*

Emma kissed him on the head. "Good luck, Walter. I'd better get dinner ready; I hope you like bangers and mash." She turned with a cheeky grin. "The sausages will be underdone, and the mash will be crunchy!"

"I hope not. Maybe I'd b...better help you, Emma."

*

Saturday night came all too quickly after a day of the girls riding in the morning and Walter doing some study. In the afternoon, all three slaved in the kitchen while listening to the races. That evening, Cyril sat head of the table, impressed with their team effort. They'd put a very edible three-course dinner together, especially for him, their guest of honour. He was touched by their friendship and completely bowled over by the fact that Walter had tipped six out of eight winners, and the other two horses ran places.

"You're a bloody genius, Walter. I'm amazed. Usually, those newspaper tipsters couldn't pick their noses!"

They all laughed, especially Emma, who'd proudly placed her arm around Walter.

"Yes, he is a genius! My dad said Walter will be a top solicitor one day."

"How does your dad know th…that, Emma?" Walter turned his curious expression to Emma.

"Don't you worry, Walter; Dad has his eye on you. Apparently, you came top of your university class in a difficult legal exam."

"I didn't think it was *that* hard," Walter said modestly. "Wait until they give us something impossible, then see how I go."

"I'm sure you will do just as well, Walter," Emma said, kissing his cheek.

Grace, more than intrigued, studied the emotional to-ing and fro-ing match between the two, and Cyril couldn't help but notice Emma's affection toward Walter. He felt a little concerned. He knew Emma was interested in boys, and he'd seen her flirting at the Healesville races. *I'm sure she has her eye on that young strapper who works for her father… What's his name? Peter somebody. Anyway, she'd better not play around with Walter's feelings. A bloody cruel joke if she does. But, it's none of my business, I suppose.*

Cyril considered the dinner a success and took his leave after his offer to help clean up was resoundingly rejected.

"You're our *guest*, Cyril! Of course, you're not helping! Just drive home safely," Emma instructed him as she saw him to the door and returned to the kitchen where Grace and Walter had already made a start on the dishes.

Walter took himself off to bed, luxuriating in the beautifully appointed guest room. "Fit for a king," Walter said to himself as he snuggled under the feather quilt. Within minutes, he'd drifted off into pleasant dreams about Emma.

Meanwhile, Grace and Emma sat on their beds in their shared bedroom, knees up under chins.

Grace looked squarely at her friend and, without preamble, said, "I have to ask you, Emma, you seem to be…how can I put it? Showing affection toward Walter. What is that? Do you like him? I mean, as a boyfriend. I thought you were in love with Peter?"

"Wow, Grace, so many questions." Emma bought time, rearranging the pillows behind her back. "Firstly, I'm *not* in love with Peter. He was just a passing attraction. Besides, he doesn't show me enough attention. I like a man to at least like me back, if you know what I mean. And *yes*, I do like Walter very much. He's intelligent, handsome and I know he likes me. I don't care if he has Cerebral Palsy. He's normal as far as I'm concerned. Does that answer your question?" Emma gave Grace a challenging look.

"Yes, I suppose so," Grace said, somewhat mollified by Emma's forthright response. "I just wouldn't want to see Walter get hurt. So please, *don't* take it any further unless you're serious, Emma."

"Okay, Grace. Of course, I won't. I'm just very affectionate; I need someone to love. And as long as they love me back, I'm happy." Emma began playing with her toes. "Do *you* think Walter likes me, Grace?"

"Yes, he does, Emma. *A lot*," Grace said without hesitation. "So that's why I say be careful with his feelings. Please."

"Oh, that makes me so happy. I won't ever let Walter down. Not ever!"

"I hope so, Em. Now let's get some sleep. I want to go riding again in the morning." Grace switched off her bedside light, her head hit the pillow, and within moments, her lights went out, too.

Emma lay awake, thinking about what her life would be like married to Walter. *Would people be cruel to him and me? Would I be strong enough to stand the criticism or the pity? Would I be a good wife? Am I too young to be thinking about such things? Should I travel the world like Dad wants me to, that is, when the war is over. Oh well, too many questions I can't answer tonight. I'll just see where life leads me. But Grace is right. I never want to hurt Walter. I think I love him.*

Grace woke when hearing the rain on the roof. She rolled over to face the window. Her vision blurred as she watched the rain bucketing down. "Bugger! We won't be riding today, Em." She turned to see Emma snuggled under her quilt. "Are you awake, Em?"

A muffled, "Yes, sort of," came from the depths, followed by a knock on the door before it opened slightly.

"I've made pancake b…batter; it's ready to pour ladies if you're r…ready," Walter said, with a broad smile. Life couldn't be better.

Emma's grin widened as she crawled out of bed and went over

105

to give Walter a quick kiss on the lips. "Thank you, Walter. I'm starving. Come on, Grace, let's stay in our pyjamas until it stops raining, or if it doesn't, we could eat pancakes with different toppings all day!"

Walter's laugh filled with joy and a little pride. *At last, I'm not a nuisance; I'm independent and helpful. But best of all, I know Emma likes me. One day, I'll work up the courage to ask her out.*

Sadly, it didn't stop raining, but they were happy enough to spend the day enjoying each other's company, playing cards, and Monopoly, and taking it in turns to make pots of tea until Edward came to drive them home.

*

Grace sat quietly in the back while Walter chatted incessantly about his studies. It gave Grace an excuse to go over what she was feeling about Emma. *Is she simply flirting with Walter? Would he be heartbroken when Emma has had enough of him? Has she genuinely finished with her infatuation with Pete?. Why do I feel this way? Surely, it's not jealousy! Or am I worried someone else could be more important in his life than I am? I only want happiness for him, but somehow I feel Emma and Walter's relationship could end badly.* Grace looked out the car window at the dismal weather, feeling a little glum herself.

Filled with guilt, Nelly sat in her armchair reading Tom's letters to Grace and Walter. *I know I shouldn't, but I need to know how he's written to them. Does he open his heart?* Her letters contained mundane things, *'Just trying to stay alive'* was all Tom wrote her. He hoped Nelly was still enjoying her job, he was sorry she needed to work, but maybe it would be good to meet new people and so forth. Tom had not written one word about wanting to come home, see her again, hold her in his arms and tell her he was a different man now and how it had taken him a long time to realize how much he loved her. No, not one word of love.

"But what are you staying alive for, Tom?" Nelly asked bitterly, out loud.

Reading Grace's letter, Nelly shuddered at Tom's excitement when he mentioned his new friend, Lucy. Reading between the lines, Nelly was angry when *Tom sounded pleased that Lucy's husband was killed in battle. That's terrible, don't think like that, Nelly. Lucy must be a lot younger than Tom. What's he thinking, getting involved with a young nurse? Okay, maybe he's not romantically involved. Not yet.*

Nelly jumped on hearing car doors open and shut. Quickly she shoved the letters under the cushion and hurried to open the door.

"Hello, did you have a good time?" Nelly said brightly, her nerves on edge, hoping she'd find a moment to place the letters back where she'd found them.

"Absolutely," said Walter before kissing Nelly's cheek.

"That's wonderful, Walter. I'm so pleased. And how about you! Picking six winners out of eight! You're the talk of the town. Well, at least with our neighbours. They've been knocking on the door wanting to congratulate you, especially Mrs Carol! She had a small wager on each of your tips, and the dividends paid her gas bill!"

Grace pecked Nelly's cheek before hurrying to her bedroom. Edward raised an eyebrow, lifting his shoulders.

"I'll go and talk to her," said Nelly.

"Okay, I'm off home." Edward waved. "I'll see you tomorrow, Walter. Bright and early, we have a load of revision to do, mate."

"Yep, I'll be there, Edward," Walter said, his face reflecting his concern about Grace's behaviour.

Grace sat cross-legged on her bed, gazing out the window, watching the red and green King Parrots flitter around the back yard, flying from a Lilly- Pilli hedge to a Cootamundra Wattle. Nelly was unaware that Tom had deliberately selected these particular trees to attract such a beautiful array of winged visitors. Seeing them now made Grace miss him fiercely. She remembered clearly how a familiar King Parrot perched on Tom's shoulder one day and ate nuts from his hand. The memory put a smile on Grace's face.

Why couldn't everything just stay the same? Even Mum's relentless ordering us about, or her drifting off into one of her romance books. Dad shaking his head at Nelly's theatrics and suggesting he take us kids for a walk. 'We'll go and see if we can find a King Fisher, Nelly.' It was Dad's way of escaping the drama. Grace longed for the uncomplicated life she had well and truly left behind.

Grace, burdened by the heavyweight of adulthood, pondered on how many problems there were to solve. So much had changed over the last four years, and with it came worry. *I shouldn't say worry. Dad hates that word. 'Concern's a better word,' he'd say. Well, I got plenty of 'concerns' right now,* Grace thought morosely.

Nelly tapped on Grace's door. "May I come in, Grace?"

"Yes, Mum."

"What's wrong, Grace? You're quite - unlike you, especially after spending time with Emma. Is it Johnno? Are you worried about him?" Nelly rubbed Grace's back, and she stiffened, a little surprised at her Mum's show of affection.

"No, I've just received a letter from Johnno, he's good. It's…it's, well, it's Emma and Walter…"

"Oh no, they haven't…" Nelly's hand flew to cover her mouth.

"No, of course not. It's Emma. She was flirting with Walter all weekend, and I just don't want her to hurt him." Grace rubbed her face and threw her hair behind her shoulders. "Should I be worried?"

"I think at this stage, Grace, Walter is brave enough to get hurt and learn from it. I know what you mean though, his feelings are more vulnerable than most young men. I'd talk to him and point out that Emma has a flirtatious nature if I were you. He should tread lightly at first and see how sincere she is and then put Emma to the test."

"What do you mean, Nelly?"

"I mean, Walter should ask Emma out on a date. See how she reacts if people stare at them or if someone makes an unkind remark. Could Emma cope, or would she fold under others' judgment of their relationship?" Grace threw Nelly a wry smile.

"You've been reading too many romance novels, Nelly," Grace giggled. " Though I think you may have the answer. But we mustn't help Walter if Emma accepts his invitation, okay? He will have to meet her or pick her up. In a taxi, maybe. Now that could take some time because he'll need money, so he'll have to wait to get paid for his tipping column."

"Devious, aren't we Grace?" Nelly smiled conspiratorially.

"I love you, Mum, and I'm proud of you," said Grace, holding Nelly close. "Especially how you have risen to the challenge. Not only with Dad being away but also standing up to Grandma." Grace stood apart and searched her mother's eyes. "Funny, isn't it, how life changes and we all change with it. It's this bloody War! Though I suppose it has to bring some good; it's certainly made us all stronger."

Grace kissed Nelly on the cheek and thought about Tom's *Nurse Lucy*. She prayed her instincts were wrong. "You know what I feel like, I feel like grilled cheese on toast and tomato soup for supper. Do we have any cheese, Nelly?"

"Now, that's another strange thing, Grace. I was about to eat the last piece of cheese for lunch, then changed my mind. So, it's all yours. And I love you, too."

Together, they walked into the kitchen where Walter sat reading the Sunday paper, especially the accolades he'd received for his tipping performance.

"Did you read this, Mum? I'm almost f…famous!"

"Don't let it go to your head, Walter. You may not be successful every week," Nelly chided.

"I know. I'm only joking!"

Nelly and Grace chatted while preparing their simple supper, then sat at the kitchen table, from where Walter hadn't moved.

"Grace told me Emma took shorthand for you, Walter. How did she go? Was she efficient?"

"Too right she was, Mum. Emma loves Secretarial College and pl…plans to be a legal secretary for her dad. She said she didn't have enough p…passion or the d..dedication to go through a Law Degree. Law does interest her, though, but not to the p…point where she wants to stand up in c…court, defending a murderer. I suppose that's fair enough. Personally, I can't wait. Though I'd rather sit d…down and d…defend them. Lazy, aren't I?"

Nelly laughed. "I am proud of you, Walter. I never dreamt you would or could become a lawyer." She looked at Grace for encouragement. Grace nodded. "Um, Walter. Do you like Emma? I mean, would you like to take her out to the movies, perhaps?"

Walter near choked on his soup, and Grace smacked him on the back. He turned, "Grace, have you been saying s…something to Mum?"

"Not really. Just that you two seemed to get along so well, I suppose Mum thinks it's time you had a girlfriend. And Emma likes you, Walter, so why don't you ask her out on a date?"

"I will, but I need money. I'll have to wait and see how much I get paid." Walter's cheeks turned the colour of the tomato soup. Nelly noticed and smiled.

"Good thinking, Walter," Grace sputtered, her mouth full of melted cheese and toast.

CHAPTER 12

Two months of Saturday race meetings flew by, and such was Walter's prowess at picking winners that he'd become a minor celebrity. It was Friday afternoon, and Walter sat alone at the kitchen table; his concentration focussed on tomorrow's fields of racing thoroughbreds.

"Walter!" Grace called suddenly.

"Oh! Jesus, Gracie! You sc…scared the shit out of me!"

"I sincerely hope not. And if so, you will have to clean up the mess." Grace's cheesy grin made Walter laugh.

"What do you want, *dear* Gracie?"

"I have just been looking at what's on at the flicks. Do you have enough money to ask Emma out on a date yet? It's been over three months." Walter rolled his eyes, and Grace threw her arms out in desperation. "Don't be a dill, Walter. You don't have to take her to the bloody Ritz!"

He took little notice of her jibe, asking instead, "What's on?" *If I don't like the sound of the movie, I can postpone the inevitable question. 'Emma, would you like to go to the movies with a cripple?'*

"The movie is *Going My Way*. At least it's not about war. It's a musical, and I've heard it's terrific. It's got Bing Crosby in it. Why don't you ask Emma?"

Walter read the Movie reviews when Grace shoved under his nose.

"Okay, I'll phone Emma, see if she's free on Su…Sunday. I'd rather go to a matinee." Walter mentally rehearsed what he would say and, smiling to himself, decided to leave out the bit about him being a cripple. *It's not like she doesn't know that already.*

Emma, just about to go for a ride, walked past the phone and picked it up as it rang.

"Oh, hello, Walter. No, I'm free Sunday. Yes, that would be wonderful. Is Grace coming too?"

"No, just you and me, Em. Is that okay?"

"Yes, of course. Will Edward drive you? I could meet you in the city. Dad said Sunday is the safest time to travel by train as it's full of families out for the day. Though if I ask him nicely, he might drive me there."

"I'm having driving le…lessons, Em, so I'll be able to b..buy my own car and pick you up. I've been saving my money."

Emma, momentarily speechless, soon relayed her surprise.

"Really, Walter? How amazing! I mean, good on you! I can hardly wait." *Well, I never imagined that.* "Where would you like to meet, and what time? Okay, I'll see you then. Bye." Emma gently placed the receiver back in its cradle. She smiled as she left the house, thinking about Sunday. Suddenly she stopped dead in her tracks. *What on earth am I going to wear?*

The discussion between Nelly, Grace, and Edward about how Walter would meet Emma on Sunday at the Regent Theatre became heated. And it confused Walter to the point of him throwing his hands in the air.

"Okay, if you can't or don't want to drive me, Edward, I will take a bus. It's not a p…roblem. I know Joe. He's driven the same route into Me…Melbourne since I was a little kid. He's a good bloke. He'll help me up and down the steps, if I n…need it."

Edward tried to defend himself, 'that's not wha…..

"You can't possibly go without your wheelchair, Walter," interrupted Nelly. "You'll get tired walking all that distance. And if anyone bumps you, you'll fall over and won't be able to get up!"

Grace shook her head. *There's the old Negative Nelly again. Looking for all the ways it can go wrong.*

"Oh, Nelly, *please.* Walter will be *fine*," Grace said shortly. *She hasn't remembered our go-it-alone deal.* "He has a walking stick, and if he gets tired, there's plenty of seating throughout the city where he can sit for a while. And he's good at getting up off the ground now." Grace smiled at Edward. "Edward's been encouraging Walter to do push-ups. He's getting stronger every day."

Edward gave the nod. "That's right, Nelly. We - meaning Grace and I - think it a good idea for Walter to go it alone." *I didn't, but Grace insisted.*

Nelly shrugged and crossed her arms. "I hope you're right.

111

That's all I can say."

Walter approached Nelly in his unsteady way and wrapped his arms around her. "I love you, Mum, but y…you *have* to let me go, and I need to stand on my own two w…wobbly feet." He looked her in the eye and saw a tear begin to trickle. "Okay, Mum?" He said softly.

Nelly hugged him back. "Yes, all right."

*

Joe, the bus driver, smiled in admiration as he watched Walter climb the steps, pay his money, and take a seat – alone - unaided.

Grateful to Joe for stopping the bus ten yards from the Regent, Walter shook his hand. "Thanks, Joe."

"Good luck, Walter. Have a nice time, mate."

Full of anticipation, Walter made his way as best he could toward the entrance of the cinema, where to his delight, Emma stood waiting. She wore a dazzling, deep pink dress, with matching shoes and handbag: white gloves and her white fitted jacket contrasted with the pink perfectly.

Emma threw her arms around Walter, to the point of almost knocking him over. She giggled. "Oh, Walter, I'm so happy to see you." Said while looking him up and down with approval. "I like your outfit. Now, that sounds silly. What do you call a man's clothes?" She laughed, with Walter along with her.

"Just say I look good, Emma. That will do."

"Okay. You look good, Walter."

"And you look st…stunning, Em."

Walter thought the dark theatre provided the perfect place for his first date. *People can stare if they want to, and I can't see them*, he thought as the usherette showed them to their seats. Emma held Walter's hand and leaned close to him as the dim lights went out.

Going My Way was an excellent choice to lift the spirits in this time of death and destruction, highlighted in *The News of the World*. The newsreel at first placed a dampener on things, but optimistic predictions of an Allied victory at the end, left the patrons feeling hopeful.

Interval arrived, and the lights came up. *Thank heavens I don't need to go to the toilet*, Walter thought. However, Emma did.

"I must powder my nose, Walter. Shall I bring some drinks back?"

"You won't h...have to, Emma." He nodded towards the

112

refreshment trolly. "You go. I'll b...buy the drinks. D...don't be long, though."

Emma smiled and squeezed past Walter, who was sitting in the aisle seat. Two youths had arrived and sat in the row in front just as the theatre darkened. They now turned to watch Emma walk up the aisle after they'd heard Walter stutter, and they laughed hysterically. Walter could have kicked himself. *Why did I have to stutter now? Nerves, that's what it is.*

The taller of the two boys, with greasy hair and bad teeth, turned around in his seat to take a good look. "What's wrong, mate? Back from the war with st...st...stuttering shellshock?" The idiot said,

His equally unappealing friend laughed coarsely. "As if! 'Ave a look at 'im! The Army don't take spastics." They doubled up laughing again.

Walter steeled himself; he'd suffered similar verbal attacks before and was grateful it hadn't occurred in front of Emma. He ignored them, but they persisted, hurling insults until the young boy trundling the refreshment trolley arrived. After Walter's purchase, Emma returned. She'd caught wind of the exchange coming back down the aisle. The two idiot youths gaped, her beauty completely overwhelming them. She smiled sweetly at them as she took her seat, then exacted her vengeance by turning to kiss Walter on the lips.

"Thank you, Walter. I just love popcorn, don't you?"

Lost for words, the oafs turned back to the screen which had illuminated for the main feature. They didn't say another word.

When the movie finished and the lights came up, Walter placed his hand on Emma's arm. "Just wait until everyone l...leaves, Em. Is that okay with you?"

"No. Let's go now, Walter. I know what you mean, and I'm not ashamed to be seen with you struggling a bit to walk. You're a better man than anyone here! Especially those vulgar boys in front of us!" She said, loudly enough for all to hear.

The two idiots choked and sniggered, and one whispered, "He must have a big dick." Though not quietly enough to escape Emma's keen hearing. Immediately, the youth felt the hard blow of a pink handbag smacking his ear.

"Shit!" He said, holding his aching ear. "What the fuck are you playing at, bitch?" He stood up and leaned threateningly over the back of his seat. With that, Walter threw a punch knocking him over and into the aisle, where he landed like a rag doll. Walter then gave idiot number two a back-hander that rendered him almost deaf.

Whistles blew, and uniformed police ran into the theatre, grabbing Walter by the arm and escorting him outside to the wild applause of the patrons who had witnessed the incident. Emma was beaming with unconcealed pride.

After giving their statements at the Russell St. Police Station, the two were released into the care of Edward, who had been called by the Police Sergeant, who knew and respected Edward.

"Yes, I know exactly what happened, Edward. Walter and Emma were understandably provoked by the verbal abuse they'd received. However, as you know, physical violence is an offence. I will let them off with a warning this time. But if any further disturbances occur, I'm afraid they could be charged. And *you* will represent them in court, no doubt." The Sergeant, with a wry smile, shook Edward's hand.

"Understood, Sergeant. You won't be seeing them again. I can assure you," Edward said gratefully.

Nelly became more and more distraught after Edward phoned, thinking her son was in jail. He wasn't. Walter was only being questioned, but of course, Nelly was *still Nelly* - the Drama Queen. However, later, when a joyous and animated Emma told the whole story, Nelly saw the humorous side to their actions. She was also enormously proud of her son.

Errol Blake later arrived to collect his daughter. On hearing what had happened, he tried to hold back his laughter, which ultimately escaped. He congratulated Walter on defending Emma's honour. "I shouldn't laugh; it could have turned nasty." Errol's expression was solemn as he faced Emma. "Imagine if those degenerates had a knife or another weapon - you could have been injured or even killed. Don't think I'm condoning your behaviour, Emma."

"Oh, Dad, I *had* to hit that idiot. Did you hear what he said about Walter? He said… I won't repeat it. But he said *awful* things!"

"I know what they said, Emma. I've read all the statements. Let's put it behind us, shall we?"

The entire episode had Grace satisfied that Emma had proven her love for Walter, and her loyalty, too. She released a deep contented sigh before gathering Walter and Emma in her arms. "I love you two so much."

The following morning, Grace slept in; maybe it was the late-night they'd shared, hearing *the Walter and Emma drama* over and over, which had led to other similar stories being related into the small hours. Grace felt churlish and groggy.

"Grace! You'll be late for school," called Nelly.

"I know, Nelly, but I think I'll take a sickie today. I'm exhausted."

"All right, Grace, but make sure you study later. I'm off to work. Somebody has to put food on the table!" Said with as much theatre as Nelly could muster first thing.

Grace curled up under her woollen blanket and drifted off to sleep. Her dreams, filled with Johnno, especially his battle to stay alive and return safely to her. He'd been away for so long. Surely the War would end soon? She could even hear his voice, "Grace, wake up, Grace. I'm home." Gracie moaned. If only her dreams were true. Another call, louder. "Grace." She turned slowly from the pillow to feel his soft lips caressing hers. Suddenly, her eyes flung open, and she sat bolt upright to see what she had thought to be an illusion. Johnno smiled. Grace shook her head and rubbed her eyes.

"Is it really you, Johnno?"

"Yes, it's me Grace." He stood up, and she noticed him leaning on a walking stick. "Oh, my God. What happened, John?" Grace rose quickly.

"Nothing much, just a bullet through my leg. It took a hunk of muscle and a piece of bone. After that, I was unfit to do battle, so they sent me back to work on the Home Front. The Army's put me in charge of training our Home Guards."

"I've prayed day and night you'd come home safe, Johnno." Grace smiled into his eyes. "And my prayers have been answered."

"Yes, but you said you'd be waiting under our Weeping Willow Grace." He brushed the tousled hair from her eyes.

"Shut up and kiss me!" she demanded.

Johnno's passionate kiss had Grace suspended in time, melting her like a snowflake in the sun as their limbs entwined.

Walter laughed as he walked past Grace's room. "You could have shut the bloody door, Johnno. I didn't want a fr…front row ticket!"

CHAPTER 13

It was the eighth of May 1945, and Nelly stood in the lounge listening intently to the news on the radio. She collapsed into her armchair, overcome with relief and happiness. Grace, in the kitchen, heard the radio blaring from the lounge room. Something about the war ending: she hurried in to see her mother smiling, tears of relief running down her cheeks. Nelly mopped her eyes. "It's over, Grace. The war has ended."

Grace yelled. "Walter! The war's over!"

They hugged each other and danced around the lounge room. The front door flung open, and Edward joined in their rejoicing.

Celebrations all over Australia had begun. Not one able-bodied person stayed inside. The streets of Melbourne and outer suburbs were jammed with crowds bestowing joy and affection upon strangers. The eighth of May 1945 would be a day to remember throughout history as the day good had triumphed over Hitler.

However, a small band of Australian soldiers, airmen, and seamen in the Pacific still fought bravely alongside the Americans to defeat the Japanese.

*

Tom hurried back to Cairo and into the arms of Lucy as soon as it was possible. Their love had grown beyond their expectations, and Tom was still struggling with what he should do, especially now the war had finally come to an end.

Should I go home and explain to Nelly and the children what has happened? But I don't want to let Lucy out of my sight. Should I go with her to America and explain to her parents how deep my love is?

He'd done nothing but think about it, chew on it, argue with himself. After a difficult two months of anguish, Tom was sure what he must do to find happiness.

I'll give up my life in Australia, including sacrificing the respect of my children. Though I hope they'll understand and still love me, no matter what. But will they be old enough to know how I feel? I simply can't let Lucy go; she's the only woman I've ever genuinely loved. I can't. I won't return to a loveless marriage. I deserve more than that, and so does Nelly.

*

Nelly leaned back in her armchair, staring at the wedding photo which had kept her company on many occasions throughout the long years of the war. The picture rekindled memories and provoked questions. How would Tom be when he returned? Was he mentally fatigued by the years of relentless battle? Silly – of course, he would be. And, *of course*, he'd be changed; they all had. The war had transformed everyone.

But more importantly, will Tom see the change in me? Nelly asked herself. *Will he like me now? He might even begin to love the new me. I haven't altered, really, but my attitudes certainly have. Yes, I've rejected all those awful ways of thinking that were drummed into me by my domineering Mother, although she has changed – a little. At least I've freed myself from her power, and we rarely even speak. I'm my own person now, and I've begun to like myself. I only hope Tom will, too.*

She sighed deeply and rose to place the photograph back on the mantelpiece. "I promise you, Tom, no matter in what condition you return, I will love and care for you." Nelly kissed Tom's face and braced herself, ready for the next battle.

Grace lay in bed, wondering if Nelly had read the letter Tom had sent her. It had been moved slightly from where she'd carefully placed it, underneath her petticoats in the top drawer of her dresser. She didn't know whether she should be annoyed with Nelly or feel sorry for her. *Should I mention Lucy to Nelly?*

At that moment, Nelly walked into her room. "What are you reading, Grace? Is it the last letter Dad sent you?"

"Yes, Mum, it is. I don't like to ask, and, truly, I'm not angry if you have...but *have* you read it?" Empathy shone through Grace's eyes, inviting Nelly to tell the truth.

Nelly sat down on the end of the bed. "I'm sorry, Grace, I have. I just needed to know how different the letters your father wrote to you were compared to the ones he sent me." Nelly took a deep breath and composed herself. "I think you realize, Grace, that your father and I were not on good terms before he went to war. But everything changes in wartime, including people. I have, and I assume your father has, too.

117

However, his letters to me remained the same. Platonic. Do you know what that means, Grace?"

Grace nodded. She felt terrible, seeing the sadness on her mother's face.

Nelly said in a small voice, "Not *once* did he send his love to me, not like the love he declared to you and Walter." Her composure broke. She knew Tom had found someone to love, and the silent promise she'd just made to his photograph was pointless. The flood of tears she had been struggling to contain escaped. Grace immediately moved close and held Nelly tight, rocking her back and forth.

"Oh, Mum. I'm *so* sorry. If Dad only knew how strong you've become and how compassionate and fair you are with Walter. I'm so proud of you."

Nelly pulled away and looked her daughter in the eye. "Be honest with me, Grace. What did you make of that *Nurse Lucy*? Do you think he's having a love affair with her?"

"I don't know, Mum. I hope not." The truth was too painful to contemplate. "But I tell you one thing if he doesn't come home if he goes to America with that…that *woman* – I swear that I will *never* speak to him again!"

"Please don't stop loving your father, Grace. It's not his fault if he doesn't love me. I know he only married me because of my being pregnant with Walter." Nelly realised her blunder. She'd never admitted this fact to Grace or Walter.

"What! I didn't know that. Oh, you poor thing, Mum. I always blamed *you* because Dad didn't love you or treat you right. I thought it was because of the way you behaved. You know, with your God-fearing ways and the way you always read those romance books. You were off in another world, shutting us all out at times. Though sometimes Dad *was* okay to you, *wasn't he*?" Grace lowered her head in thought, then suddenly, she looked pleadingly into Nelly's eyes. "He *was* nice to you on your birthday." Grace knew that was feeble. "I'm old enough now, so you can talk to me about anything, Mum."

Nelly needed no prompting. She opened up and told Grace her full and unadorned story. Grace then held her mother tight, her way of giving comfort, she hoped. It was, as Grace had always thought - her mother was a broken soul who needed mending. It was only now Grace realized what would heal her mother, unconditional love. *Don't we all need that?* Grace thought.

"I'm going to write to Dad, Mum. I will tell him to bloody well get his act together and come home where he belongs. And while I'm at it, I'll tell him how wonderful you are and always have been. It was just that you were under the influence of your mother, and you have now virtually disowned her. And I'll tell him how Edward has taught Walter so much, how he believes in Walter's intelligence, and how he's educating him. And Dad had better love you like you deserve to be loved. He's the one to blame for your unhappiness. How could he be so cruel as to have kept you at arm's length, never treating you like his proper wife? I can see it now. It's all clear to me. And you know what? I've seen *Edward* show you far more affection than Dad *ever* did. Dad knew you were hurting but didn't do anything about it. That's all it is, Mum. You were hurting, and you didn't know where to turn or who to turn to. He shouldn't have married you if he didn't love you!"

Nelly smiled lovingly at the daughter she'd begun to appreciate over the last few years. "That's a bit harsh, Grace," Nelly said with a wry smile. "Your father saved me from a terrible fate. Imagine if I had been forced to put Walter up for adoption? That's what my mother promised would happen. Walter would have become a ward of the State – he would have been seen as damaged goods and never have had the love we have all given him. I'd never have seen him again. And, of course, if Tom hadn't married me, you would have never been born, Grace." Nelly smiled and kissed Grace on the cheek. "And what a lost opportunity to the world *that* would have been!. Imagine, there would never be a female race caller in Australia. And imagine having to live with my parents. Well, Mum, at least. I'd have eventually been committed to a mental asylum."

Grace gave the nod. "Yeah, you're right. Life's bloody hard, isn't it, Nelly?"

Nelly giggled and ruffled Grace's hair just like Tom used to.

"You *are* a funny girl, Grace. Honestly, I don't know where you came from; maybe I picked up the wrong baby in the hospital?" They embraced again, this time almost as equals, and showed their deep love and understanding of the other.

After talking with Grace, Nelly felt she could come to terms with losing Tom if she must. She sat back in her armchair, looking up at her wedding photo. *You've left me for another woman, Tom. Deep down, I've always feared this would happen one day.* She stared into space, not interested in opening the pages of her book.

Trust Walter to stir her from her reverie and brighten her mood. He sat down on the couch, grinning from ear to ear.

"Mum, do you re…realize I will be twenty-one in f…four days?"

Nelly smiled despite her heartbreak, "Of course I do, Walter. I've been discussing with Edward what we should do to celebrate. Though I think the decision should lie with you. So, what would you like to do, Walter?"

"I know money is short, Mum, so I don't want a b…big birthday bash. But if you can afford it, I'm thirty pounds shy of b…buying my first car."

Nelly burst into laughter, both at the vision of Walter driving a car, which she'd never thought possible and at the sum of money he'd mentioned. She could have thrown him a *huge* birthday party with thirty pounds.

"What's so funny, Mum?" Walter asked, hoping she wasn't laughing at his driving ambitions. "You know Edward has been giving me driving lessons, and he reckons I'm ready to go for my licence!"

Nelly gulped back her laughter. "I know, and I'm proud of you. I'm laughing, Walter, because, for thirty pounds, I could give you a *magnificent* birthday party!"

"Oh, I see. Yes, of course, silly comparison. Well, what do you th…think, Mum? Is it a possibility?"

Nelly agreed. It was markedly so, which made Walter tear up and hug her hard.

"Walter, you're squashing me!" Nelly filled with pride for her son, the son she could have destroyed if it hadn't been for her waking up to herself. "I love you, Walter."

"And I l…love you too, Mum."

*

With Tom's passion spent, and his desire satiated, he held Lucy to him; their naked bodies blended from the intensity of their lovemaking.

Although the last thing on Lucy's mind was to end their embrace, Lucy huskily breathed her words into his chest, "You'd better go and make that phone call, Tom, or it will be too late."

He sighed in acceptance. There was no way out. It was Walter's twenty-first birthday, and the least he could do was to phone him. As for Tom's reasons for not returning home, he would tell Walter later - in a letter. He was good at writing letters.

The Commanding Officer had given special permission for Tom to call home. *'Seeing it's such an important occasion,'* he'd said, aware that Tom would be departing with Lucy to America when discharged from duty. It was clear that Tom was held in great esteem by all who knew him, especially those he'd fought alongside. However, Tom knew his family might not feel the same.

After taking fifteen minutes, changing operators and connections, Tom finally spoke with Walter.

"Hello? Hello? Walter, my son! Happy twenty-first birthday, mate. What did you get for your birthday?" He asked, trying hard to inject some enthusiasm into the conversation.

"I haven't got it yet."

"Well, ah…what *do* you want? It's a big occasion, y'know. You're a man, now!"

"I want *you* to c…come home, Dad," Walter said bluntly. "We need to t…talk - man to man."

Grace had confided in Walter about what she'd suspected was going on. *'I'm not positive,'* Grace had said. *'But you had better prepare yourself, Walter. Though if Dad does come home, then all should be well and good.'*

Tom sighed deeply, drawing in the breath that would carry his words to his son, on the other side of the world.

"I'm sorry, Walter, I can't come home. One day, you may understand why. We don't have time to talk about it now. Just know that I love you, Walter, and I'm so proud of you. I'll write. Have a great birthday, son." Tom, choking on these last words, hung up the phone, filled with guilt and remorse. He'd fully intended to use the remaining minute or so to speak with Grace and perhaps Nelly, but the rawness of his emotions had made it impossible.

Lucy had followed Tom and listened to his conversation. She felt Tom's heartache and grappled with guilt. Each admitted they felt compelled to do the right thing for their family, and what they wanted to do, was neither right nor just.

She threw her arms around him, her lips against his neck and her words muffled. "Tom, I want you to go home. I need you to face your family, and I need to face mine. We have to decide where our hearts truly rest." Lucy held Tom's face in her hands, her eyes demanding the truth.

121

"You know it will be impossible for our love to survive if we don't both do this."

Tom nodded, remembering the day he'd left home, leaving only a letter of goodbye. That in itself had been cowardly. He knew now he wasn't a coward; he'd fought and killed the enemy for six bloody years. Lucy was right. He had to go home and face up to his family.

*

Despite her protests, Lucy's father had insisted she stay in Cairo until the fighting between America and Japan came to an end. '*There's too many Jap subs and planes out there, Darlin. I'm orderin' you, for once in your life. Do what I tell you. Stay put!*'

And Tom wasn't going anywhere until the Australian Defence Force said so. They were stranded there until further notice.

*

Grace waited patiently outside the Army Office for Johnno to be officially discharged from service.

Although Johnno had visions about remaining in the Army, he'd risen to the rank of Lieutenant, and this alone gave him great satisfaction. *Not a bad life,* he pondered. However, he was sure that Grace would hate being an Army wife. It would not fit into her *horse world*. So Johnno conceded that Grace held the reins to their future. He didn't mind, as long as his future was with her.

"Congratulations, Johnno. You're free!" Grace kissed his cheek, noting a measure of uncertainty in his smile. She was aware his war experiences had changed him; for the better, she thought. The boyishness had gone from his features, and he had matured into a good-looking young man, his face now sculpted by his strong character. She knew she would never tire of looking at him.

"Yep, I'm free to do whatever I want, Grace. The trouble is, I don't know what I want. I'd like to be like you, determined to be *something*."

"You'll come up with a plan, Johnno. Besides, I always thought you'd make a good teacher. like your dad."

He laughed. "That's the last thing I want, Grace, unless I'm training someone. Like in a profession." He wrinkled his brow, "I've always liked mucking around with cars. Maybe I'll be a mechanic. Not much money, though, not until I have my own business."

"I think you should do whatever you want, Johnno. Even stay in

122

the Army if you want to. You could train young soldiers, just like you've been doing." Her eyes searched his, her head tilted in question. "Why didn't you? What made you leave? You love the Army."

Johnno shook his head in dismay. "Yes, I do like it, Grace. But you wouldn't. We'd have to travel around Australia, maybe overseas. And where would that leave you and your dream?"

"I see. So, you left the Army for me, without even discussing it." Grace's anger rose. "That's not the way to start our future together, Johnno. We have to be honest with each other, or it will never work." Grace clutched his hand and walked him briskly away. "Come on. We're old enough for a beer. Let's talk about it in the pub."

What could Johnno do but laugh?

*

To help take her mind off the inevitable, Nelly began organizing a small party for Walter, cooking casseroles, making sweets, polishing the wine glasses, and ironing the table linen.

Edward had taken Walter to inspect second-hand cars, and Nelly thought they were jumping the gun because Walter had yet to pass his driving test. But still, *boys will be boys*, she mused. The phone rang, and Nelly took the opportunity to sit down and talk.

"Oh, hello, Emma. How are you?"

Their conversation was all about Walter's party - what Emma could make, what she could bring, and if Nelly needed any help with anything. Emma said she could come in the morning to help set up the backyard with tables and chairs. The Melbourne weather forecast promised a day in the low twenties, no wind, and full sunshine. A rare occurrence. Maybe an Angel was looking after Walter? Tom's parents, no doubt. Nelly felt sure they would be looking down on their special grandson.

"That would be lovely, Emma. We do have a spare room, so if you wish, you could come and stay tonight, and we could get an early start. I know it's a luncheon party, but I'm sure the younger people will turn it into a late-night event. Edward and I will leave you to it after we clean up. There will be plenty of sausages to cook on the barbeque for later. No, we won't stay. We will be next door unless I can talk Edward into going to see a movie."

Nelly froze when hearing Emma ask, '*By the way, Mrs Nobel. Have you heard when Mr Nobel will be home?*'

Her immediate thought was, *I don't want to see Tom ever again. I'd rather he write me a farewell like he did when he left for war.* "No – ah, no, I haven't, Emma. But it shouldn't be long."

'It's such a shame he couldn't make it home for Walter's birthday party.'

"Yes, it is Emma. Now I must get back to my baking. I'll see you when I see you."

'If it's okay with you Mrs Nobel, I'd like to come now. I need the driving practice. Not that I'm bad, I just need more confidence.'

"Of course, Emma, but we're only having takeaway fish and chips tonight."

'Yum! I love fish and chips!'

Nelly tried to remember the days when she had been as happy and carefree as Emma.

*

The friends Walter had made at university and many of his childhood mates began arriving. He was utterly chuffed to have Emma standing affectionately at his side as he greeted them. Nelly had excelled with her cuisine. Everything was perfectly cooked, beautifully presented, and appreciated by all. Even her usually over-cooked cakes were delicious, thanks to Emma's improved timing skills.

The only thing missing was Tom. *As long as he comes home eventually,* Walter prayed. *It would mean he's chosen us above that other woman.*

Errol Blake and Gillian arrived, each driving a car. They came in through the side gate, announcing themselves as the bearer of a rather large gift for Walter. "It's too big for the backyard," Errol said, trying to contain his smile. "You had better come and look, Walter."

With lunch almost finished, only the speeches and the blowing out of the birthday candles remained. Grace whispered, "I'll help you with the candles, Walter. I still don't trust your *spit* not to land on the icing.

"The cake *and* my *spit* can wait, Grace," Walter said, feigning insult. He walked out to the street and immediately teared up at the sight of a second-hand 1942 Model, General Motors EX Hydra-Matic Sedan. Walter inspected the car as closely as a fighter pilot would his aircraft, and he was pleased that the boot was plenty big enough to hold his wheelchair.

"Well, what do you think, Walter?" Errol Blake asked.

"It's incredible, but it must have c…cost a pretty penny. How m…much do I owe you, Mr Blake?"

"Nothing at all, Walter. Besides, all of us here today," Errol swung his arm around, "put money towards the car. You may have wondered why no birthday presents had been wrapped in paper and ribbons?"

"Well, I didn't th…think about that. I was just glad to see my friends," Walter said, spreading his hands out to them all.

Errol laughed. "I must say, it took a bit of doing, Walter. There are not many Hydra- Matics around these days. But I have friends in high places. It pays off sometimes," Errol said with a wink.

"I don't know wh…what to say. I think I'll certainly owe you all a lift or two. I'll be the local taxi service!"

"Not until you get your licence, Walter," Edward reminded him. "We all thought you'd have an easier time driving an automatic car. No clutch. You simply need your hand to put it in gear. Now all you have to do is pass your driving test!"

A loud cheer arose, and the party continued well into the night.

*

After several days of serious discussions, Grace and Johnno decided each should follow their own path, mainly to see how they fit into each other's lives. Not that their unofficial engagement would alter, and their plan to marry, one day, was carved in stone.

After her six months ban and the Army had welcomed Johnno's return, Grace resumed her place in the racetrack broadcast box, alongside Cyril. He had remained an avid fan and was a fellow crusader in her fight for equality. "Why, if a girl can call races as good as or better than a bloke, why isn't she allowed to be a bloody paid race caller?"

Many of the old stalwarts on the racing committees around Victoria shuddered when told that Grace Nobel was back on course. *Would she dare to call another race - uninvited?*

At the next Healesville Race Committee meeting, Errol Blake decided to take a stand on Grace's behalf.

"Gentlemen, I fail to see your reasoning. Grace Nobel has proven her ability to call a race as well as any of her male counterparts. Of course, that is *my* opinion. However, I put it to you. Give her a chance to prove herself. Allow Grace Nobel one race call each meeting for a month, and then judge for yourself how well she does. This suggestion, I think, should be put to the vote. However, before you do, may I remind you, gentlemen, the entire world has relied on women for the past six years to take up jobs that were initially male-dominated. And they excelled!"

Errol gazed at the faces he knew so well and felt confident he may have swung even the most critical committee member to his side.

CHAPTER 14

Tom had finally written Nelly the truth. As much as he'd tried, he couldn't bring himself to write to Grace and Walter. Nelly read them the letter he had sent to her. Tom had detailed what they suspected. Ending with, *If you want me to come home and explain further, I will, but please know it will not change my decision to go to America with Lucy.* However, what he hadn't told Nelly, Lucy was pregnant.

"L…let him go, Mum. We've done alright w…without him. He's not *my* father anymore!" Walter hadn't meant what he'd said, but the hurt he felt at his father's refusal to come home was so powerful, he needed to strikeout.

Grace felt sick to her stomach. Fleeing the lounge room, she threw herself on her bed and sobbed uncontrollably, her prayers and hopes demolished with a few words.

Nelly sat speechless; there were no words left to explain how she felt. Maybe injured beyond repair, maybe heartbroken. But then again, she'd been heartbroken throughout their entire marriage.

"I need a stiff drink!" Nelly said defiantly.

For the first time, she unlocked Tom's whisky cabinet and poured a generous measure of Chivas Regal from the bottle she was saving for his return. Nelly preferred champagne but thought it hardly appropriate on this occasion. There was nothing to celebrate here. She virtually poured the whisky down her slender throat and passed a similarly filled tumbler to Walter. "Here, Walter, take a swig. I think we both need it."

Walter couldn't help but smile. The transformation of his mother during the past five years amazed him. "Thanks, Mum."

The amber fluid slid down his throat, spreading a delightfully warm, calmness throughout him. "I need another one, Mum."

Walter handed Nelly the glass and sat back, remembering all the times when Tom had stood up for him, had given him confidence, had loved him, and had been proud of him - no matter what. *What the fuck has happened to my father?*

Grace was inconsolable, and soon her pillow was saturated. How could one person cry so many tears? She was exhausted, and her body grew limp. She could not lift herself off the bed, even when she tried. She stayed there for two nights and two days, along with Nelly and Walter's alternating encouragement.

Nothing had changed within Grace's heart. No matter what she'd said to Nelly about getting strict with Tom and demanding he come home and love her mother. Grace couldn't deny it. She loved her father unconditionally and needed to admit this before she could move on, despite feeling betrayed at her father's decision to abandon them. It took days until Grace regained some composure. Even Johnno, having secured special leave from the Army, and Edward's efforts to console Grace brought her only more tears and suffering.

Nelly was at a loss as to what she should do. *I'm confused about how I should answer Tom's letter. Should I remain emotionally distant, treat him the same way he's treated me most of his life? Or should I try and telephone him? Would it help resolve things more quickly? Ought I tell him about Grace's emotional state or leave it until Grace has recovered enough to speak with him?*

Four days passed, and still, Grace had barely eaten. Nelly was worried and so made an appointment to see their local doctor, as she couldn't negotiate with Grace at the moment.

Doctor Cartwright sat behind his desk, dipped his head, and looked searchingly over the top of his reading glasses.

"So, Grace, it would appear you have had bad news?" The doctor smiled sympathetically and waited for Grace's reply. None came, and she appeared almost catatonic.

"Grace, please talk to Doctor Cartwright. He can help you, I'm sure. You just need to tell him how you feel. Please talk, Grace." Nelly pleaded, wiping away tears.

"Okay, I will!" Grace said fiercely. "I'll *never* see my father again! The father I loved and admired *all* my life has gone to live on the *other* side of the world, and he's *already* forgotten us. Like we never existed. I'd rather he was *dead*! Then I could remember him the way he was, my hero. I *hate* him now! *I hate him!*"

Nelly wrapped her arms around Grace.

"Oh, Gracie, *please* don't say that. Your father will always love

128

you. He'll want you to go to America and stay with him for a while. My heart is broken too, but we must go on. You have your whole life ahead of you. And you should remember, Tom fought alongside other brave men for your freedom. Many lost their life doing so. The world's a small place now. You can travel and experience wonderful adventures."

Doctor Cartwright was so astonished at Nelly's reformed behaviour and attitude that he flung his body back in his chair and gripped the arms so as not to be shocked from its embrace. He'd known her since she was a little girl, and he'd watched the frightened child turn into an unhappy, neurotic woman. He knew why, but he'd never imagined a woman with her tested upbringing, followed by an almost loveless marriage, could give such sensible and compassionate counselling. He shook his head.

"Nelly, I must say, I could not have said it better. I don't know why you needed me."

"My mother doesn't need *anyone*. She's strong. She's fought her own wars and won! We don't need *you*! We don't need *anyone*, not even *my stupid bloody father!*" Grace hung her head, hiding tears she thought she'd cried out of existence.

"That's enough, Grace. I know you're angry, but please don't take it out on Doctor Cartwright. Apologise now," Nelly ordered before she softened. "Please, Grace."

Grace lifted her eyes. "I'm sorry, Doctor."

"It's all right, Grace. Your behaviour is understandable, and I accept your apology. Would you like some sleeping tablets? Just to get you back to a routine? Your Mother said you haven't slept for many nights."

Grace shook her head. *No.* And Nelly nodded. *Yes.*

Doctor Cartwright wrote the prescription in a hand to challenge a cryptic genius.

"There you are, Nelly." He handed it to her and turned to Grace. "Would you mind if I spoke to your mother alone?"

"No, I'm fine," said Grace. " I'll just wait outside in the fresh air, Mum."

*

Something had shifted in Grace. Her, *'She'll be right, mate!'* attitude had changed. Her anger, combined with resentment, was now directed at her father. Plus, those who did not take her race calling seriously. She

129

was sick and tired of trying to prove herself and fighting everyone all the time. *There's no point anymore - I'll give up my stupid dream and marry Johnno. He will never let me down.*

Back home, Walter answered a phone call from Errol Blake. After the usual pleasantries, he asked to speak with Grace.

"I have good news for her," Errol told Walter.

"I'm sorry, Mr Blake, but Grace has t...taken it hard about Dad not coming home. She's g...gone to see the Doctor with Mum."

Walter went on to explain what had happened.

"Oh, I am sorry, Walter. I didn't know. I understand. You all must be terribly upset."

"Yes, we are. However, I'm the m...man of the house now, Mr Blake. I won't ever l...let Mum and Gracie down."

"Spoken like a true gentleman, Walter. And I must say, I hope this situation will not interfere with your legal studies. You are coming along famously, Edward tells me. You couldn't have a better tutor or friend. Oh, by the way, when do you sit your Driver's Test, Walter?"

"Next Monday. I thought if it were all right with you, Mr Blake, I, could dr...drive my new car to Ferntree Gully t...tomorrow and say hello to Emma. Of course, Edward would be with me."

"I'm sure she would be delighted. Should I let her know?"

"No, thank you. I'll ph...phone Emma. I do every Friday because she takes shorthand for me, then ph...phones through my tips and notes on the races."

"Oh, yes, of course. Well, good luck, Walter, or should I say good punting! And do you want me to tell Grace about her permission to call the last race at Healesville? Or will you speak with her, Walter?"

"I'll tell Grace, but I'll also ask her to ph...phone you. Thank you so much Mr Blake. That news will ch...cheer her up, I reckon."

Later, when Walter told Grace the news, she looked at him blank before phoning Errol Blake to decline the race offer. It left Errol speechless. Grace then called Johnno with her proposition.

*

While not able to make it home for the Kentucky Derby, Tom and Lucy felt blessed to hear the call of what was commonly known as *'The Run for the Roses,'* delivered in splendid style by Lucy's father. Due to the war, it was feared the race would not be run at all. However, with the end of America's conflict in sight, the race, usually held in May, was postponed, not cancelled, and scheduled to run on the ninth of June. Tom imagined calling the Derby one day. *Would that make Grace and Walter proud?*

Tom had heard from Edward about Walter's Racing Tips column, and it generated enormous pride in his son, who, by rights, he should have been with, *don't waste your time feeling guilty*, Tom, he chided himself. *It won't work with Lucy if you do.*

"Wasn't that fantastic, Tom! *Hoop Jr*, hey? I think I would have backed him if I'd been there," Lucy said with a wink.

"Of course, you would have, Lucy, and I would have, too. Being a mud runner, a dirt track specialist, *and* a front runner, he stood the best chance by far. We'd be silly if we didn't back him."

Lucy looked a little surprised. "You really do know your stuff, Honeybun, " Lucy said before planting a lingering kiss on his generous mouth.

Matron coughed pointedly, interrupting them before it could build up to something more intimate.

"Oh! Hello, Matron. Tom and I just listened to the Kentucky Derby. My daddy called the race."

"Yes, I do know that Nurse. However, I'm here to inform you. There is an English charter boat that will take you to Greece - tomorrow. And from there, on to England. Several British officers will also be on board, going home, of course. From England, you *should* be able to travel back to America in some manner. But *my* advice is that you remain here until the Yanks and the Japs finish up. It is still far too dangerous to be travelling *anywhere* at the moment."

"Thank you, Matron, but I think we'll take our chances. I need to get home." Lucy gently rubbed her belly.

"I see. Well, it's up to you, Lucy." Matron smiled and held Lucy close. She was like the daughter Matron had always wanted, and with her only two sons killed in the war, she had a very soft spot for this nurse. "You are a wonderful nurse and a good woman, Lucy. I understand and accept your close friendship with Tom." The matron looked directly at Lucy, then at Tom. "War changes us all, and sometimes we lose the people we love most. Sometimes, the separation from home makes us reassess what is important to us. I wish both of you every happiness. We all must learn to take the chance on love if we are lucky enough to find it."

131

"Thanks, Matron, that sort of feels like a blessing, I reckon." Tom looked towards Lucy, who simply smiled.

"Well then, I'll leave the decision up to you two. Good luck, and may God bless you both." Matron turned and left in her business-like way, but her heart was fearful for their journey home.

"It *is* like Matron said. I never thought I would ever love anyone but Sam, and then I lost him. Lucky for me, *you* were there, just when I needed you the most."

Tom smiled. "If it weren't for this war, I would never have met you. And you know I only married Nelly out of a sense of duty. Though I miss Walter and Grace terribly, they have grown up now and will be making their way in the world. I couldn't take the chance of losing you, Lucy." He placed his hand gently on her swelling stomach. He gave her a cheeky grin. "And remember, I have to marry *you* for the same reason."

Lucy laughed, delivering a hard whack to Tom's shoulder for good measure.

*

The charter boat rocked so severely the morning sickness, which so far, Lucy had avoided, rose like a tidal wave, causing her to heave over the rail until she felt her stomach lining shift. Tom could only soothe Lucy by rubbing her back and making her cups of tea that inevitably ended up over the rail, too.

Some of the British officers on board were in the company of female military personnel, who had become the Officers' wives during the Middle East campaign. These couples, along with many others, celebrated continuously during their crossing of the Mediterranean.

Lucy wished she could join the party, but her nausea made it impossible. However, she insisted Tom take time out from ministering to her to join the others occasionally. This he did reluctantly, as Lucy's welfare and comfort were paramount.

"Five days, it's been. They said it would only take four." Lucy wiped her brow with the damp cloth that Tom kept continuously wet.

"Won't be long, Lucy, we should be docked in Lemnos by six tonight, and then I'll find us the best hotel to stay until morning. Hang in there, my darling." Tom kissed her cheek and whispered, "I love you."

Once they had disembarked and Lucy was on steady ground, she felt her nausea slowly drift away. The charter company had already arranged the hotel and no other options were available. "You're lucky to have a place to sleep," they were told.

The bedsprings had popped, and the mattress was hard and lumpy, but somehow, Lucy slept like a baby. Tom slept in the room across the hallway to avoid raising suspicions about the extent of their familiarity.

The morning had long arrived before Tom woke. He yawned, stretched, then braved a cold shower to wake him up properly. His First port of call was Lucy's room. He knocked and received no answer. He knocked harder. "Lucy?" he called and, opening the door, saw her things strewn about the room. *This doesn't seem right*, Tom thought.

He dashed down the sandstone steps, entered the dining room, and noticed a few fellow travellers sipping the last dregs of their coffee.

"Has anyone seen Lucy?" Tom asked, trying not to appear too anxious.

"No. Sorry, Sergeant."

Tom hurried away, talking to himself, "Don't overreact – don't worry."

He searched through narrow streets and old buildings. Not many were left undamaged after the Germans' parting gesture. While the Allies were advancing to liberate the island, a retreating German ferry armed with mortars shelled the town, making a horrendous mess. It would take years to rebuild, and many island men were still hard at work almost a year after the liberation. Tom asked them about Lucy, but none spoke English. *Surely a blonde woman here would stand out like a diamond on black velvet?*

The boat was due to depart at noon. Tom looked at his watch, five minutes to ten, not much time. Maybe he should return to the hotel, pack their bags, and wait. "No, I'll go to the police and report her missing," he said aloud.

The constable in charge laughed when Tom told him Lucy had been missing for an hour. "Kýrie, please! Your friend is probably shopping. Go back to your hotel. She will return." He nodded his head toward the door.

It was not like Lucy to take off and not tell him. Then again, how well *did* he know Lucy? Tom ran back to the hotel, where almost all passengers sat ready, waiting to be escorted to the ferry, taking them to Piraeus. He addressed the group breathlessly. "Have any of you seen Lucy?"

133

"No," came the unanimous reply amongst puzzled looks.

"Sorry old chap," offered one of the English officers. "Maybe she's done a runner with a dark, handsome stranger!" A number of them laughed good-naturedly, failing to notice the desperation which had tinged Tom's words.

Tom turned on his heel and charged up the stairs to find Lucy's clothes untouched. His heart beat even faster and sweat-drenched his shirt. "What can I do?" he asked himself. "Calm down, that's what I can do. Pack her bags. Yes, I'll pack Lucy's bag, then mine and wait in the lobby. There has to be a reasonable explanation for this."

Trying to reassure himself, Tom imagined Lucy in a daydream, strolling around the town's streets, gazing at what was left of the architecture and no doubt finding many things of interest. *Yes, we may never come here again, so the place would intrigue Lucy. Under different circumstances, it would be a charming place to spend a relaxing holiday. One day maybe,* he mused as he closed the lid on her suitcase, then sat and waited impatiently in Lucy's room.

All other passengers had left for the ferry. Twenty minutes remained until departure, and it would take them five minutes in a mule-drawn taxi if he could find one. He became frantic when he heard the ferry blow her final boarding whistle. A further ten minutes passed. Tom sat with his head in his hands, imaging all of the terrible things that might have befallen Lucy.

"Oh, there you are, Tom. I had a lovely time. I met an old lady who makes the most wonderful lace booties and monogrammed baby blankets. She spins angora goat hair and mixes it with silk. She has silkworms by the hundreds. Fancy that, hey?" Lucy held the delicate items up to the light. "Aren't they adorable?"

Tom was furious. "Lucy! I can't *believe* you took off without letting me know. I've been *frantic. And* we've missed the ferry."

Lucy pouted. "Don't be angry, Tom. I couldn't help it; I don't have a watch. I lost it, remember? And besides, I thought the ferry wasn't leaving until one o'clock. There's plenty of time." She kissed him, which did little to alleviate his anger.

"*No*, Lucy, it left at *noon*!" He looked at his watch. "It's twelve-thirty!"

"Oh, shoot! Well, we'll just have to stay another night, Tom." Lucy wrapped her arms around him, and all was forgiven as his anger dissolved; he knew it always would be like this with Lucy.

It turned out that the next departure was not for three days as the ferry, the only one travelling to the mainland, was scheduled to have some maintenance done, and due to a shortage of parts in the region, it would have to be fixed once it docked in the Piraeus.

"I'm sure we can think of something to do while we wait, Tom," Lucy said with a suggestive wink. Tom smiled, thinking that missing the ferry was the best thing he could have hoped for.

*

Grace, no matter how hard everyone tried, would not budge from her decision. Her refusal to call races at Healesville stood firm, even after Errol Blake told her sternly, "It took a lot of convincing to persuade both committees, Grace. Firstly, my own and then the VRC members who, I must add, reluctantly agreed to the proposal by a majority of one vote in your favour, Grace."

The meetings had made Errol more aware of how deeply the chauvinistic attitudes of his fellow committee men were entrenched. Errol had felt sure the war years, which encouraged women to participate in a whole range of occupations previously unavailable to them, would have righted a lot of wrongs with the attitudes towards women as *inferior*. However, it seemed the old ways were deemed never to change. Maybe the male population of Australia needed to reassert its masculinity after having been replaced, albeit temporarily for the most part, by women? *Yes*, Errol thought, *THE 'We need to put women back in their place' school of thought was the consensus.*

After her conversation with Errol, Grace had phoned Johnno. "I've thought seriously about our relationship," she said, almost harshly. His heart plummeted like a shot pigeon but then rose like a lark when Grace said, "I want to marry you, Johnno, and as soon as possible. My race-calling dream is over. I promise to make you a doting and dutiful wife. It's all I want."

Johnno dreamed every day about marrying Grace. The time that would have to elapse before they could live together passed too slowly for his liking, which frustrated him. Nevertheless, he knew what he needed to do.

"Grace, you know how much I love you, and that's why I won't marry you. Not right now. We agreed, remember. Besides, I've got a posting to New South Wales, and at this stage, it could be for six months

135

or longer."

Grace drew an audible breath.

"Grace, *listen* to me. I *know* you, and I know you won't be happy until you've followed every possible avenue to become a race caller. *Please*, for your own sake and mine, *follow your dream.*"

Grace slammed the receiver down hard. The anger she felt towards herself and everyone else was channeled into that piece of moulded black Bakelite. The severity it copped when smashed into its cradle defied its construction.

Nelly had pleaded with Grace. Since the visit to the doctor, she had become moody and angry, even more so after speaking with Johnno. Nelly was worried Grace might be damaged beyond repair because she now seemed defeated. Nelly wanted and needed the old Grace back. Nelly realised how much she had come to rely on Grace's strength and humour to put everything into perspective.

Walter was also feeling miserable, not for himself but Nelly. Even though his parents' relationship had been strained, Nelly had lost a mate and a husband. If Tom did return, they would at least have the opportunity to put their differences behind them and start afresh. But of course, that was never going to happen. Nelly had been left alone, and Tom loved another woman. Poor Nelly. Suddenly, another thought struck Walter. *Edward! Yes, he's been a great help to Mum. I wonder if anything deeper than friendship will eventuate now that Tom is off on a mission to find happiness?. Nelly deserves the same. Is Edward a bit old for her, perhaps? No, he's young in his ways, except for his bung knee. He should have that fixed!*

Walter had made it a point lately of walking unaided and unaccompanied into Edward's home to study. It was quieter. Particularly when Grace was in a mood, slamming doors, or Nelly was yelling at Grace to get up off her bed and do *something, anything*, rather than lie around moping. "*Please*, Grace," Nelly would beg. Walter was tired of the doom and gloom. He, too, was disappointed in his father, heartbroken in fact. But life had to go on, and Walter wasn't going to let his father's infidelity ruin *his* life.

"Hello, Walter," Edward said as he opened the door. "Come in, mate. I just put the kettle on. Do you want a cuppa?"

"Yes, thanks, Edward."

Walter's demeanour told Edward he was troubled. And

considering what was going on, it was no real surprise.

"Anything wrong, Walter? You seem a little subdued. Is Nelly okay?"

Ah! There we go! Usually, Edward would ask about Grace first. That's a glimmer of hope.

"Well, now you m…mention it, Edward. I *am* w…worried about Mum. She hasn't been able to grieve the loss of Dad b…because she spends all her time trying to lift Gracie out of her d…doldrums. I think Mum could do with a night out on the town." Walter studied Edward's expression. *Yes, he'd taken the bait!* Walter continued, "I've got some money saved, but it would be a bit b…boring if I took her out. What say, if I g…give you the money, Edward, then you t…take her out to dinner and a show."

Edward nearly doubled up laughing. "If I didn't know you better, Walter, I'd say you were trying to bribe me!"

"No I'm not! It's j…just that you look after us all the t…time, so it's about time I looked after you. And Mum."

Edward placed a compassionate hand on his shoulder. "You don't have to pay me, Walter. It would be my pleasure to take Nelly out. *Alone*, without you and Grace tagging along for a change."

Walter relayed his relief in an energetic handshake with Edward. He then tried, inconspicuously, to wipe away the tear in his eye before they settled into the study, sipping their hot tea.

Grace had finally decided to leave her bedroom and took a walk the long route to the park where she sat, reflecting under her faithful willow tree. *At least it never changes*, she thought morosely.

Her head flooded with choices. But her heart still ached. She was sick of being a loyal sister, a dutiful daughter, and a loving girlfriend and considered leaving everyone and everything behind and going her own way.

Yes, reinvent herself. Grace's entire life, it seemed, had been helping Walter, in addition to worrying about her mother and trying to prove her talent to her father and everyone else who'd listen. Why bother?

Now, Johnno had left her behind. He seemed happy to leave and go to New South Wales. *Jesus, that's a mouthful! I wonder why they didn't just call it Wales*, she thought crankily, then smiled, feeling a glimmer of the old Grace returning. Hadn't her sense of humour helped her through

137

all the ups and downs of life? Where had it gone lately?

Could she possibly see the funny side of Tom leaving? *No. But Nelly would be much happier without him*, Grace realized, *especially now that she's changed.* Suddenly the thought of Edward came to mind. *Yes, of course, Edward!* Grace, at first, had been angry when seeing Edward consoling Nelly with a cuddle, but now she was thinking about it…*Doesn't Nelly deserve some affection? Yes, she does! Mum needs a man to love her genuinely. I understand that now. Not that I'm a romantic like Nelly. I probably never will be*, Grace thought wryly, *except about champion racehorses.* She smiled at the thought, sprang to her feet, and ran the entire way home—the physical effort doing wonders, freeing her from unwanted thoughts and frustrations. *Life is to be lived to the full,* she thought, *and, of course, to help others. Jeez, Church has done me some good!* Grace felt her mouth break into a broad smile, the first in weeks.

Nelly had received a phone call from Cyril and was deep in conversation when Grace entered the lounge room. Breathless, she stood before Nelly and listened. *Oh, good. She's talking to Cyril. Dear Cyril, he's stood beside me all the way, albeit five inches lower.* She giggled inwardly at her quip and waited.

Grace then threw a brilliant smile at Nelly when seeing the worried look on her pretty face and watched the sadness leave Nelly's eyes as she handed Grace the receiver.

"All right. I've never been to Ballarat, Cyril. It should be fun." Grace winked at her mother.

'My old Aunty will put us up for the night, Grace. She can't wait to meet you. She would have loved to have been a race caller in her day. And now she refuses to depart this earth until you are a paid regular on the wireless."

Grace laughed for the first time in ages, and Nelly teared up. *Thank God! Gracie's back.*

Edward and Walter entered just in time to hear Grace laugh again and thought it might be Tom telling her he was coming home. But not this time.

"See you then, Cyril." Grace hung up the phone and winked at Walter. It appeared things were almost back to normal in the Nobel household. However, Edward put the cherry on top when he approached Nelly and asked, "Would you like to go out to dinner and see a show,

Nelly? Alone?"

Nelly, a little shocked by this proposal, looked hopefully to Grace and Walter. Seeing their smiles and nods of approval, she accepted with pleasure. "I would be delighted, Edward."

*

In the soft flicker of candlelight, Nelly cast a long, analytical look at Edward. His grey hair swept away from his temples looked most distinguished. His blue eyes, soft and were full of compassion and intelligence. His physique was naturally trim and athletic, kept that way by his early morning exercise routine, which he refused to give up, despite his complaining knee. Nelly jumped when he leaned in and whispered, "A young lady should know better than to stare."

Why in the bloody hell did I say that? Edward thought instantly. *Do I want to break the spell?* "I'm only joking, Nelly," he assured her. "Will you tell me what you were thinking? By the way, did I tell you how beautiful you look this evening?"

Nelly didn't even blink. "Yes, you did. Thank you, Edward. Actually, I was thinking how handsome and distinguished *you* look." Nelly grinned. "You have been my guiding light." Suddenly shy, she dipped her head, and her auburn waves fell free from the diamanté clip. Looking up, she smiled warmly before refastening her coiffure.

Edward sat stunned, not only with how lovely Nelly looked but how their dynamic had shifted dramatically. He coughed. "Thank you, Nelly. Now we have established how nice we both look, or beautiful in your case, shall we order?"

Nelly laughed; it was a good feeling. *Maybe, with a little more help from Edward, I will survive Tom's final rejection?*

CHAPTER 15

Grace's spirit rose to the occasion. Ballarat Racecourse welcomed its patrons with professional proficiency. No one could fault the effort that went into this special day of celebrating. Not only was there fine horse flesh on display and fabulous catering provided, but also the feeling of rejoicing after the long war had been fought and won. A jam-packed buoyant group of well over ten thousand racegoers were in attendance. Grace's eyes widened as she took in her favourite scene, and her heart sang with the possibilities of the day before her. How had she ever thought she could leave this all behind and become a boring housewife, even if it meant losing Johnno?

Cyril was overcome with relief when Grace appeared to be her old self. He'd spoken many times with Edward about Grace's 'depression,' as they named it. Now, it seemed she had survived the drought and, ready to bloom again, leaping back into life like a rosebud under Spring rain. He smiled up at her. Grace was now five feet and ten inches tall, and Cyril worried that he'd shrunk when standing alongside her.

"Now, Grace. No unofficial calls today, I'm sorry. But take your time and think about the Healesville offer. Mr Blake is a great bloke, and he went to a lot of trouble on your behalf."

Grace's nod, accompanied with a smile, was all Cyril required.

The excitement of watching magnificent horses gallop past the Announcers' Box was the medicine Grace needed to confirm her passion for calling races professionally. After all, she was a lot closer now to her ambition than during the years she'd spent watching from *the wrong side of the fence*. The day continued to inspire and deliver.

Later, when meeting and staying with Cyril's Aunt, it too became another highlight of Grace's time away. Aunt Maude proved to be a real character and a true champion of women's rights. She stoked the fires of Grace's ambition with a passion, to the point where Cyril threw his hands in the air and bid them goodnight, leaving them to change the world in one evening.

"You had better watch out," he cautioned Grace as he took his leave. "Aunt Maude will have you picketing down Swanston Street for more than just the right of women to call races!"

"Not a bad idea," Grace said with a dry smile as his Aunt shooed him out the door.

Grace returned home excited. Telling her story with animation un- spared, entertaining Nelly and Walter for a good thirty minutes. Grace had them laughing as she related what a character Aunt Maude was and how, if she weren't careful, she would have Grace marching like Joan of Arc and leading 'The Cause.'

"Oh, please don't do that, Grace," cautioned Nelly. "Gentle as you go. Otherwise, you may find yourself taking a backward step rather than slowly but surely wearing the establishment down."

"Don't worry, Mum. I know my dream is before my time, and anyway, I don't know too many women who want to be race callers. I'll just chip away and hope my talent takes me to the next level. I'm not out to change the world," Grace assured her, before adding under her breath, "Just the VRC."

Then it was time for her family to tell their news, and, in a roundabout way, Nelly's conversation put out the feelers to see how Walter and Grace felt about her officially dating Edward.

"You deserve happiness, Mum," Walter said simply, and Grace nodded her agreement. She loved the way her mum said most things so calmly these days. Did being loved by a wonderful man do this for her? Grace hoped so. She looked toward Walter.

"So, Walter, when do you sit your next exam? Or should I ask, are you nervous about going for your Driver's Licence tomorrow?"

"Yes, I'm a little nervous, Gracie," Walter confessed. I hope I get it b…because it will be much easier driving to Uni. Though good old Joe looks after me. He always drives the b…bus that bit nearer to where I need to go. Still, I'd like to drive Emma out on a date."

Walter smiled guiltily, remembering the last time he and Emma had ventured out in public and the trouble they'd caused. They still laughed about it. He knew then Emma was genuine in her affection, but with their studies keeping them busy, they'd only kept company within their own homes. It would be lovely to go out together, just the two of them – alone.

"Yep, good idea, Walter. Maybe you could take Emma on a picnic, or a scenic drive, instead of the pictures. That way, you wouldn't get into any trouble."

"I know wh…what you're saying Gracie, and I didn't th…think you'd say such a thing." Walter looked genuinely hurt.

"Oh, I'm sorry, Walter! I didn't mean it that way. It's just I can't bear to think of you having to fight your way through life, just to be respected." Grace jumped up and threw her arms around her brother, and he laughed.

"I know, Gracie. But think of it this way, whatever doesn't k… kill you makes you stronger. And when I'm d…dealing with The Law, I'll have to be strong." He flashed Nelly and Grace a captivating smile. "As well as handsome, highly intelligent, and ch…charming!"

"Absolutely, Walter." Grace gave him a friendly punch.

"Oh, Grace, I meant to ask you - how is Charlie Norman?" Nelly asked. "Did he understand about you not coming to work because you were upset about Dad?" Nelly felt genuinely concerned for Charlie. He was getting older, and she'd heard talk about the Race Club finding another Clerk of the Course.

"Charlie's fine, Mum, though I think he's ready for retirement, same as his old horses, Charger and Freddy. He's found them a good paddock on a farm near Cranbourne. I told Charlie I'd visit the old darlings and make sure they're doing well and have warm rugs in the winter. Grace smiled wistfully. "I'll miss those funny old horses, and Charlie too, of course, although I did offer Carrot for him to ride on race days, but he said he'd have to paint him white." Grace shook her head, feigning concern. "Somehow, I don't think Carrot would like that. The paint, I mean."

Grace smiled at her mother and brother, thinking that finally, everything seemed to be falling into place.

*

Despite it being early December in Kentucky, Tom wiped the sheen of sweat from his brow. He paused and took a steadying breath to prepare himself to meet the man he hoped to call his father-in-law finally.

Formidable stone pillars flanked the vast front entrance to the stately plantation house, and Tom's heart pounded as if he'd been running a race. He gazed along the wide veranda which surrounded the whole building. *'Old money,'* Tom whispered and suddenly felt the weight of his unworthiness. His resolve faltered, and he turned to leave.

In the months before, he had waited while Lucy gradually broke the news to her parents, firstly about their affair, then about the baby which she'd carried without a trace until the final two months. Not for a moment had Tom thought that Lucy would be reluctant to disclose her love for him. He had assumed it would be, as she had said on their journey home, 'A laydown case, honey.' Her parents only ever wanted her to be happy, and, of course, she was thrilled with Tom and the baby. Wasn't she?

However, Lucy had felt it best, *'At this stage hon,'* to set Tom up in a modest flat near the Churchill Downs Racetrack and introduce him to her family and friends as an Australian friend who wanted to remain in America, hopefully, to become a race caller. Tom accepted Lucy's excuse and played the game of simply being a close friend. It was difficult, as all he wanted to do was hold Lucy tight and tell the whole world how much he loved her. Fortunately, Tom's expertise as an accountant allowed him to pick up casual work at the racetrack until he secured a permanent position in the accounting department.

Months had flown by, and although he had, of course, been introduced to Lucy's father, Brian Forrester, Tom's interactions with him had always been brief and informal. It appeared that Mr. Forrester, a widely known, popular member of the racing fraternity and well-respected race caller, seemed not to want to take his relationship with Tom beyond that of an acquaintance. Brian would hurry by and say, *'Hello, Tom. How ya doin'?'* without waiting for Tom's response, Brian would smack him on the back and say, *'That's good, that's good, Tom'* and he'd walk away.

Tom had pressed Lucy to tell her parents the truth, but Lucy had insisted, *'These things take time, honey bun.'* But when their son had been born, Tom gathered his nerve! The time had come for him to declare he was the father.

He was now, standing outside the door of the Granddaddy and Grandmama of his seven-pound, twenty-inch son. Who Lucy, without any discussion with Tom, had named Tyson. He wondered why he had continued to go along with the pretence. Tom had never known, or maybe he did. *'You're a coward when it comes to women, Tom,'* he admitted to himself. He was halfway down the flight of stone steps when Brian swung open the massive door.

143

"Why Tom, hang on there. Where ya goin'?" He called out in his broad Southern drawl.

"Oh, I'm sorry Mr Forr - " Tom turned a little sheepish.

"Never mind, come on in! Violet and I need to talk to ya, son."

Violet sat primly in a Georgian chair upholstered in a dusky pink velvet. She graced Tom with her well-practised, sweet smile and proffered her diamond-encrusted fingers. Tom recalled the Hollywood movies he'd seen, set in the Deep South. When a gentleman was introduced to a lady, he'd kiss her hand - is this what he should do?

"Pleased to meet you, Mrs Forrester." Tom duly kissed Violet's hand.

"Indeed, sir. The pleasure's all mine, I assure you. Please sit, and I'll have Nellie bring refreshments." Violet rang a bell. Tom swallowed hard. *Oh, shit! Why did their maid have to be called Nelly?*

As big and bluff as Texas, Brian paced the floor puffing on a Cuban cigar, smoke billowing behind until engulfed in a haze. He stopped and looked directly at Tom, pointing his cigar.

"So, tell me, Tom. When *exactly* did you meet m'daughter?"

"*Our* daughter, dear." Violet smiled at Tom.

"Yes, well, of course, *our* daughter. That goes without saying, Violet m'dear."

"Well, Brian. All I'm sayin' – "

The banter between Brian and Violet seemed set to continue until Tom coughed tactically and nodded his head toward Nellie, who had entered and stood patiently with a tray of Mint Juleps.

"Oh, thank y', Nellie. Just in time. I think this conversation's goin' t'be a vera long one," said Violet, accepting a tall crystal glass from the silver tray.

Tom smiled at Nellie as she handed him his Julep then he summoned his strength. *They need to understand what I've given up to be here in America with Lucy. Not to forget the time I've had to wait for her to gain the courage to introduce me as the man she loves. And wants to be with for the rest of her life; she owes me that. Bloody oath she does!* It wasn't the first time Tom felt anger at how Lucy had handled their situation. *I know Lucy loves me, though sometimes she makes me feel second best.* Tom cleared his throat.

"You asked when and where I met Lucy, Sir. Well, allow me to tell you what happened, truthfully, from the beginning until now," Tom said, determined to tell them both exactly how it was.

Tom relayed his family history for the next hour, admitted his faults, spoke the truth, and declared his love for their daughter. Brian and Violet seemed to be taking it all in and, in the end, acknowledged Tom's honesty. Whether they were happy to welcome him into their family was hard to judge. Violet maintained a carefully neutral expression on her delicate features, while Brian nodded consideringly at whatever Tom had to say.

"Well, Tom," Brian said finally, standing to his full height of six foot two. "I must say, I feel you've been honest with Violet and me, as I'm sure you have with Lucy. And that's all we ask." Brian slapped Tom on the back. "So why don't we go to the hospital and say hello - or what do you Aussies say? *'G'day, mate,'* to our new Heir Apparent!"
Tom smiled, breathing a sigh of relief.

Lucy, a picture of serene beauty lay in her private room, winter sunlight softly beaming through a large window. Baby Tyson slept peacefully in an antique bassinet that had held the previous four Forrester generations. Tom's emotions were in turmoil and no wonder. He'd just fought a difficult battle simply to see his son, let alone be part of his life. Guilt at abandoning his first family had never left Tom, and now it swamped him. He fought hard to keep it at bay and carry on, regardless. He kissed Lucy tenderly and then his son with a silent promise to love and cherish. Now, he hoped, their future was about to change because Tom, it appeared, had been accepted into Lucy's family. Although he had the suspicion, he'd need to go on proving himself worthy of being part of the Forrester Dynasty.

*

Walter sat behind the wheel of his car, hoping he'd receive his Driver's Licence. The baby-faced policeman, Ralph, tried hard not to be condescending, especially to a young man whom he was sure had had many battles to overcome. He gave the next instruction.

"Now, park your car between the flags, Walter."

Walter had achieved all tests so far, including the oral examination on the road rules, his capability banishing all the misconceptions Ralph had previously held about people with Cerebral Palsy.

Sometimes Walter, especially when nervous, had trouble turning his head, and at the same time, stopping it from wobbling. The flags representing the parked cars seemed to shift when Walter tried to focus.

Subsequently, he knocked two flags over.

"Have another go, mate," said Ralph. "It's not the same as parking between two cars, I know. At least you can *see* them." He thought about what he'd just said. "Stop! I've got an idea. You stay here, mate. I'm going to park two cars far enough apart so you can park in between." Ralph frowned and shook his head. "I reckon using flags is a stupid way to do a parking test."

He then proceeded to park two police cars far enough apart to accommodate a semi-trailer.

"Now, that should do it. Have another go, Walter." And Walter, with precision, parked his car.

Ralph shook his hand. "Congratulations! You have secured your licence to drive an automatic car, Walter Nobel! And, I have to say, it's a bloody ripper! You're a lucky fellow. " Ralph winced inwardly. *Oh shit, I hope that didn't sound too condescending?*

The following day, Walter drove himself and Emma to university, where Walter needed to sit a crucial exam leading to the Bar Exam, allowing him to be a Barrister if he were successful. After deciding she needed to be close, Emma had stayed at Walter's home the night before, offering her support and positive thoughts for this important occasion. She now waited in the park opposite the university, focusing on his success.

Her telepathy worked. Two hours later, Walter knew instinctively; he'd passed the exam and was now even more determined to become the lawyer Edward had set him on course to be. However, wanting to make Edward happy and proud was secondary to what Walter needed to achieve for himself - a life of his own, a family of his own, and Emma beside him all the way. He simply had to do this for his own sake.

After his exam and on his way to the park, Walter spotted Emma laughing with Peter, her *old flame*, as Walter called him in jest. They hadn't noticed Walter's approach, and soon their laughter turned to a kiss. Walter's heart sank at the picture. Then adding to his anguish, they walked away hand in hand—the energy to move one foot in front of the other disappeared. Walter stood, immobile, as he watched Emma and Peter drift amongst the trees to the other side of the park. Peter then leaped into his red MG sports car, and Emma waved him goodbye. Walter wanted desperately to walk to his car but was inert. To his surprise, Emma then turned and, smiling, ran towards him. Her smile soon vanished when she saw the emptiness in Walter's blue eyes. Immediately she knew he'd been watching her and Peter.

"Walter, please don't do this." Emma sighed with a frustrated edge and placed her hand on his shoulder. "Peter just told me he was engaged to be married. I kissed him and wished him good luck. He wants *us* to come to his wedding." Emma had to force Walter to move, so emotionally overwrought he was. He nodded and smiled, trying to suppress the jealousy he'd felt.

"Sorry, Em, I promise I won't be jealous. If you promise to tell me the m...moment you meet s...someone else."

Emma rolled her eyes theatrically and gave his arm a shake. "I *promise*, Walter. But there will never *be* anyone else. Now, tell me about your test. Better still, let's talk over a milkshake. I don't know why, but I've been craving milkshakes and sardine sandwiches lately." Emma's pretty face creased with perplexity.

Walter kissed her cheek and took her arm as they made their way to a local milk bar. Suddenly, his blood ran cold. *Shit, I hope she's not pregnant.* Walter knew he had to address the subject. *Best to do it when we're seated. I feel a bit wobbly.*

Emma felt the tension in Walter's hand. She gave him a sidelong look. "I know what you're thinking, Walter, and I thought the same." Emma gave him a sly smile. "But no, I'm not pregnant. My dad doesn't have to get the shotgun out." She giggled, then added thoughtfully, "Though I wouldn't mind if I were." Emma stopped and looked searchingly at Walter. "How about you, Walter? You *do* want children - don't you?"

Walter's thoughts instantly travelled back to the only time they'd made love. Initially, Emma's motivation for consummating their relationship had dampened the carnal desire flowing between them. He'd been taken back by the matter-of-fact way she had approached the issue. *'We'd best see if we are sexually compatible, Walter. Otherwise, we won't be suitable marriage partners,'* Emma had said. It had been on the only night they'd been left alone and unchaperoned at Emma's home. After her blunt deliberation, Walter had become a nervous ruin until Emma realized her mistake in being so forward. She then cajoled, flattered, and teased Walter until his inhibitions were replaced with a hungry yearning. Yes, thanks to whatever god plans, love matches, they were indeed compatible. Lying in each other's arms afterward, they declared

147

their love for each other and talked of their future. When Walter had finished his law degree, they would be married, and Emma would be his secretary. After that night, although the heat between them rose often, they refrained from further seduction. In front of family and friends, they kept their interactions to a level of respectability. Kissing chastely and holding hands became the norm.

Emma squeezed his hand, breaking his reverie. "Of course, I do! But not now, Em. We have a lot to accomplish before we take on the responsibility of raising ch…children."

Emma laughed. "I know, and you're right, Walter. But I wouldn't take back our special night for anything. If I were pregnant, I'd think it was a wonderful price to pay. I can't wait until we're married." She kissed him tenderly. "Come on. I'm dying for a milkshake!"

If Walter's heart had been wounded, it healed within moments of hearing Emma's assurance. *She truly loves me. So why do I always find it so hard to believe?*

CHAPTER 16

Johnno was on holiday, and Grace had been thrilled when he asked
her to spend time at Rosebud with his family, where every year they
booked the same campsite and enjoyed a relaxing time on the beach,
cooled by the ocean breeze. But Grace had received a better offer. She
had been invited to call the fourth race at Hanging Rock, and she knew the
New Year Day meeting drew a huge crowd. The first day of 1947 would
mark her debut into official race calling, and she was going to make the
most of this fantastic opportunity. No, nothing would stop Grace from
taking another step closer to her dream - not even Johnno and the serene
shores of Rosebud.

Cyril, of course, had been the instigator of her Hanging Rock
engagement. Grace owed him so much. She only wished the powers-
that-be would agree with Cyril's progressive attitude and cast off their
prejudices and employ her as a race caller – and not for just the odd race
here and there, but full-time.

In the meantime, Nelly and Edward continued along their
path into a satisfying relationship. Although efforts had been made to
consummate their relationship physically, Edward could not banish the
thought of Nelly being Tom's wife. In short, Edward found it difficult to
rise to the occasion.

Nelly had gently reassured him. "It doesn't change the way I
feel about you, Edward. Your affection and support, at this stage, is all I
need." Edward was grateful for Nelly's understanding. He felt incredibly
relieved and immeasurably happier.

New Year's Day at Hanging Rock dawned fine and sunny, with a
gentle north-easterly breeze to cool the projected maximum temperature
of eighty-five degrees. As she was there to call only the one race, instead
of her usual trousers, Grace chose to wear a sun-frock and a smart
straw hat; she'd enjoy the majority of the day feeling a lot cooler. If
the truth were to be told, nerves had flustered her into forgetting her

trousers. *'Never mind,'* Grace muttered at her reflection as she wiped the perspiration from her brow, *'I'm sure no one will notice what I'm wearing, anyway!'*

"What did you say, Grace?" asked Nelly, looking gorgeous decked in a pale blue floral dress, with her hat trimmed to match.

"Oh, I was just thinking out loud, Mum. It was silly of me not to bring a pair of trousers to climb up to the broadcast box."

Nelly laughed, "Don't worry, Grace, just hold your skirt down as you climb. You'll manage." Nelly took a long and appraising look at her tall, stunningly beautiful daughter. *Will she ever marry Johnno, or will she be determined to pursue this dream? I hope it doesn't change her and won't make her bitter if she doesn't reach her goal.*

At the racecourse, the crowd was building, and the temperature was rising to the point where Grace felt claustrophobic and a little dizzy, which Grace put down to a mixture of pre-race nerves and anticipation. Nelly stood between her and Edward while Emma and Walter sat nearby on a rug, sipping cool lemonade under the shade of a stately gumtree.

"I'm going for a walk, Nelly. I feel a bit overcome with all this heat," Grace said and wandered away before Nelly could offer her a cool drink.

Nelly turned to Edward. "Do you think Grace is alright, Edward? I've never seen her like this. Surely she can't be that nervous, excited, yes, but I've never known Grace to be *nervous.*"

"Don't read too much into it, Nelly. I'm sure Grace simply wanted to be alone to gather her thoughts. The fourth race is an hour away. She'll be fine."

Grace found a shady spot under a tree away from the crowd. She lay down on the dry grass, closed her eyes, and soon dappled visions appeared. Her father stood alongside Lucy, laughing at their toddling baby. Then the scene shifted. Tom raised a pair of binoculars to his eyes, and his voice rang out, calling the field of American thoroughbreds racing in the Kentucky Derby. It sent tremors through Grace and sparked a longing so intense. She willed herself to be there. Even though she knew it wasn't real, Grace refused to leave the dream. *Don't wake up, Grace.* But she knew she had to - she heard her name called. *No, I don't want to!* Someone was shaking her.

"Let me go, let me go!" Grace cried as she struggled under the grip on her arm.

"It's me, Grace. It's Edward. Wake up, darling, your race is on in fifteen minutes. Quick hurry!" Edward helped her to her feet.

Grace stood awkwardly and brushed her dress down. She gathered her long auburn hair into a ponytail and sighed in recognition of the task ahead. She hurried as best she could to the broadcast box, and each rung up the ladder felt like she'd climbed a mountain. When she reached the top and stepped unsteadily inside, her head and heart were pounding. Cyril took one look at Grace and realized she was ill; he felt her forehead.

"Jesus, Grace, you're burning up. Here, drink this. I'll tell the crowd you're not well. Sit down over here, love, take it easy." Cyril guided her to a chair and brushed a strand of hair away from her eyes. "You'll be okay. I'm sorry, but I need to call your race, Gracie, and then I'll get the doctor. Okay, love?"

Grace sat oblivious of her surroundings, even when Cyril's voice bellowed excitedly through the microphone, calling the last seconds of a close finish. When the race was over, he called over the loudspeaker for the course doctor to come immediately to the broadcast box.

A worried Nelly, followed by Edward, Emma, and Walter, were already waiting at the bottom of the ladder. They had all arrived there when it became clear to them that Grace was not calling the race. Nelly had kicked off her high heels and was about to climb the steps when the doctor arrived.

"Stand aside! Please, stand aside!" ordered Doctor Forbes.

"Grace is my daughter. She's ill. Please, Doctor, allow me to come up with you."

The doctor studied the woman's pretty face, pleading with him, and smiled, placing a reassuring hand on her shoulder. "I'm sorry, madam, but there's not much room up there. I will let you know as soon as I can what the problem is. Stay calm. I'm here to help," he told her before he laboriously climbed up to the box.

Grace had collapsed on the floor, and Cyril didn't know what to do. He could never have imagined Grace in this state. She was always so strong and determined, so full of life. Grace now looked like a discarded rag doll. Cyril wrung his hands helplessly. He'd heard some strange bugs were going around, bugs that could be life-threatening!

Doctor Forbes knelt next to a barely conscious Grace and proceeded to examine her. Her pulse was weak and erratic, and she was burning up with a fever.

"I'll need your loudspeaker, Cyril. We need the ambulance here, quick smart. If it's what I think it is, we have to move quickly." His manner toward Grace was professional, but this didn't prevent him from noticing not only her beauty but the strength in Grace's face; it depicted a depth of character not often found in one so young.

"Will she be alright, Doc?" Cyril asked, choking back emotion.

"I hope so. But to become this ill, so quickly...if it's what I think it is, well, it's not good. If you're a religious man, Cyril, I suggest you start praying - and don't stop!"

Blaring sirens announced the ambulance's speedy arrival, which had been diverted from another much less serious call a few miles away. The Ambulance Officers placed Grace on a stretcher then carefully lowered her from the broadcast box into the ambulance, with Dr. Forbes at her side.

The Emergency Department of the Royal Melbourne Hospital, situated at Parkville, opened its doors to Grace. The blood tests and x-rays ordered by Doctor Forbes began at lightning speed. He had attended to Grace in the ambulance, with Nelly and company driving close at the rear.

"At least we know she's getting the best of care, Edward," Nelly said, trying hard to keep her voice steady. She squeezed his hand, which had been tightly grasped in her own since their arrival at the hospital.

"Yes, I know. Now, all we can do is wait." Edward sighed deeply. "I should have noticed Grace wasn't herself. I'm sorry, Nelly. "

"Please don't blame yourself, Edward. You came back to us as soon as you'd woken Grace. It wouldn't have made any difference. She's here now, and we were lucky to have had the ambulance not far away and a good doctor on hand." George Forbes's skill was acknowledged by all who knew him.

Edward embraced Nelly then turned to Walter. " How are you feeling, Walter?"

" I think I'm in sh...shock, and I'm so worried. I h...hate seeing Gracie so sick." Walter leaned into Emma, and she kissed his fair hair.

"We'll pray, Walter," Emma said. "I'm sure Gracie will pull through this, whatever it is. She's the toughest person I know. Nothing can beat Grace. It might knock her around a bit, but she'll fight and win!"

*

Hours turned into days, and still, Grace remained gravely ill. Doctor Forbes, along with the specialists, had established that Grace was suffering from Tubercular Meningitis. Gracie was to receive a course of the antibiotic Streptomycin, found to be effective in most cases. All they could do was pray that it would help Grace.

Johnno arrived at the hospital within hours of Grace's being admitted. Only one family member was permitted to be with Grace at any time, and Johnno took his turn at the bedside vigil. He was still on leave for a few more days, though he would apply for an extension on compassionate grounds, if necessary.

Nelly had sent Tom a telegram to inform him of Grace's condition, and he was on his way to reach her as soon as possible, although it would be several days before he would arrive.

Tom's fare had been paid for by his father-in-law, Brian, who'd been an overbearing presence in the life Tom shared with Lucy and their son. Upon hearing the sad news, Brian immediately took control, making all necessary arrangements. Tom was grateful for his help, but it made him feel even more indebted to Brian, who'd already helped Tom with his ambitions to be a race caller. However, after being cautiously welcomed into the racing fraternity through his connections with Brian, Tom had only called two races as a guest caller. 'Not bad for an Aussie,' was the accord.

Brian had also managed Tom's divorce, his lawyers arranging all the necessary paperwork. Tom had wanted to write personally to Nelly, but Brian advised against it. "Leave it to me, Tom," he'd told him.
Nelly felt hurt Tom had not written to her himself and was overwhelmed by all the documents and the intimidating tone of the letter she had received from the lawyers.

However, she simply took a deep breath, accepted, and signed the terms outlined in the documents. It granted her complete ownership of their family home, in which Tom's parents had lived for twenty-five years before transferring the title to their son as a wedding present. After the wedding, his parents said farewell and set off for an extended period traveling around Australia before settling on the Mornington Peninsula. Their trip was cut short after a terrible road accident in which they were both killed.

Tom had carried a burden of guilt for their deaths, even though he knew he was not responsible. With news of Grace's illness, his torment renewed. *Why Grace? Why not me?* He felt he deserved to be the one struck down for what he'd done to his family. *I can't call myself a man - I'm a bloody poor excuse for one. Why in the hell can't I stand up for myself? I should tell Brian where to go, and while I'm at it, I'll tell Lucy enough is enough! It's time we moved away from her parents and set our own rules on how our son should be raised. Her parents spoil him rotten with every bloody thing that opens and shuts and runs on wheels! Oh, Christ!*

I'll shoot myself if Gracie dies or ends up with brain damage or crippled by this Godforsaken illness! I'm no good to anyone - I can't even work out my own life. It's a bloody joke! What did I always teach Grace and Walter? Be empowered, yes, that's what I'd preach and now look at me, a piss-weak groveler, accepting charity from a condescending prick who thinks he's the best race caller God ever put breath into! Well, he's not! Gracie is - and she will survive to show the world she is! Dear God, please let her live.

*

Grace's tragic situation captured the racing public's imagination and was widely reported by the metropolitan radio stations, with newspapers giving similar accounts.

Young Grace Noble, who had her heart set on calling the fourth race at The Hanging Rock picnic races on New Year's Day, was rushed to The Royal Melbourne Hospital after collapsing only minutes before the race. Dr. George Forbes attended to her before Grace was transferred to The Royal Melbourne Hospital with suspected Meningitis. She is in a serious condition and is undergoing treatment, her family by her side. Indeed, the Victorian racing fraternity and the general public send their thoughts and prayers for her full recovery and look forward to the day when Grace Nobel will return to the commentator's box.

For several days Grace had been drifting in and out of consciousness, unaware of all the commotion. Nelly was struggling to deal with the enormous numbers of flowers and cards coming from strangers. It appeared Grace, if not famous, was at least widely known for her talent at calling horse races. The sentiment shown by the followers of Grace's fight for equality touched Nelly and Walter deeply.

"Hey, I wonder if anything happened to me, would my fans send me fl…flowers?" Walter mused, hoping a little humour might help.

"*Of course* they would, Walter! Don't worry, they all know

154

Grace is the sister of the famous racing tipster, Walter Noble," Nelly said, appreciative of Walter's efforts to lift her spirits.

"I'm only joking, Mum."

Nelly smiled and said quietly, "I know, Walter. I suppose we have to do what we can to stay positive. And I know Grace would laugh at what you said."

Nelly hugged him, suddenly realizing how tall he had become, and he'd never stood as much or as straight as he had lately. He even paced the waiting room with scarcely a wobble. *He's trying to be strong for Grace – and me*, Nelly thought.

"But also, Walter, Grace wouldn't want you to neglect your studies because of her. I know I shouldn't tell you what to do, but you're doing so well, and your efforts would have all been a waste of time if you stopped studying now. Do it for Grace. Please, Walter." Nelly held him close again, and Emma, Walter's constant companion during Grace's hospitalisation, beamed.

"I have my car here, Mrs Noble," Emma said. "I also have to study, so I'll drive Walter home if he wants."

Nelly kissed Emma on the cheek. "Thank you, Emma. You have been an absolute angel to us all. Bless you."

"I think we should go with them, Nelly," Edward said, his hand on her shoulder. "I think it's about time we all went home, had a decent meal, a bath, and a good night's sleep in our beds." Edward raised his hands in the air when Nelly threw him a challenging look. "I'm not telling you what to do, Nelly, but there's nothing you can do for Grace at the moment, and Johnno's with her tonight." Edward put his arm around her shoulders. "Come on, what do you say?"

Nelly sighed, suddenly feeling very tired. She leaned into Edward's embrace. "Yes, you're right, Edward. I'll come back first thing in the morning."

*

The following morning Nelly sat alone in the waiting room down the corridor from Grace, nursing the cup of tea a nurse had brought her, her mind drifting. *Tom's been gone nearly seven years - it seems like a lifetime. I didn't mean to push him away, but he could never have loved me the way I wanted, and I punished him for that. I realize now my life was mine alone to live. I can't expect anyone else to make me happy, and I don't have to change from who I truly am for anyone else, either. Not my parents, my spouse, or my children, oh, my dear children. They have been so loving and supportive even in my darkest days and moods. I know now they love me unconditionally, as I do them. Dear God, please save my darling Grace.* Tears of grief, self-pity, anger, and sadness for love lost coursed down her cheeks.

Hearing footsteps, she quickly dried her eyes and looked up at Tom. The years of separation disappeared. Nelly immediately was taken back to when she first saw Tom. It was at a mutual friend's birthday party, her heart had skipped a beat, and she knew it was love, a love that had not wavered. She felt transformed into the teenage girl who'd fallen in love with the handsome man who stood before her—no anger, no regrets - just acceptance.

"Tom. You've arrived safely. Thank heavens." Nelly stood up and kissed him on the cheek. "I'm sorry you needed to come home in such dire circumstances, but I am so glad you are here." Nelly lowered her gaze, lest Tom sees the raw emotion in her eyes.

"How are you, Nelly?" Tom asked tiredly.

"I'm holding up. But you look exhausted. Let's go and see Grace. Then we'd better find you a bed."

Nelly took his arm and guided him to the nurses' station and explained who Tom was and that he'd just arrived, "*all the way* from America." Nelly said with embellishment.

The Head Nurse sympathized. " I'll arrange a bed for you, Mr Noble when you're ready. Only one visitor at a time, though, and you will have to wear a mask and a gown. I'll go and tell Johnno he's to come out and let you in. And I must warn you, the antibiotic treatment Grace has undergone has resulted in quite a degree of bruising on her arms, but don't be alarmed. It looks worse than it actually is. " She gave Tom a reassuring smile.

*

Almost four weeks had passed before Grace showed any outward sign of recovery. Tom squeezed her hand, his hope soaring when she croaked, "Is the race over?" The prayers which had filled his sleepless nights were now answered. He'd not been sure if God would listen to him, but perhaps the fact he was praying for Grace had made the difference.

Grace's eyes strained to try and make out the masked face hovering above. "Dad, is that you?" Grace whispered, not expecting an answer. *Surely not. Why would dad come home? What's happened to me?*

156

Where am I?

Grace attempted to sit up, but her body refused to cooperate.

"Yes, it's me Gracie. You've been very ill, darling." Tom took a deep breath, trying to control his feelings. "I got here almost a month ago, and while you've been sleeping, one of us - your Mum, Walter, Johnno, Emma, Edward, or I - has been by your side, talking to you, praying for you. And it's worked, my darling Grace." He smiled into her beautiful emerald eyes.

"What's wrong with me, Dad? I can't move," Grace said anxiously.

"It will take time, Grace, but the doctors say, with perseverance, you *should* make a full recovery. Now, I must go and tell the nurse you're awake. You've slept for the past twenty-five days, just like Sleeping Beauty, my darling." Tom kissed her before he left to spread the good news, believing he'd been blessed to be the one beside Grace when she woke.

Grace's muscles had wasted away, and she had lost so much weight she looked like a bag of bones. Her skin was unnaturally pale, except for the bruises marking her body. Her condition was still considered potentially contagious, but now Grace had regained consciousness, she would be moved out of intensive care into another section of the hospital expressly set up for patients with infectious diseases. The doctors would take no chances, and Grace had a lot of rehabilitation ahead to regain her strength and mobility. "It may take you six months," Doctor George Forbes had predicted, "but it could be sooner if you do as you're told, Grace."

Things had been emotionally difficult for Nelly, especially with Tom living under the same roof for the past few weeks. She had struggled with her feelings when close to him. Walter had also felt the strain and made excuses with his study to avoid talking to Tom too often. Edward also avoided Tom as best he could. As for Tom himself, nothing had gone unnoticed, so he had a lot of thinking to do. The word *lost* could not even come close to describing how Tom felt.

He thought about being away from Lucy and Tyson for another six months after he'd left their marriage on shaky grounds. Even though Lucy gave her all to Tom, it was in the comfort and security of her parents' Southern mansion, being waited on, hand and foot by the maid Nellie. Oh, how Tom wished that woman would change her name! He felt sure it was just to taunt him.

Actually, the whole situation of living under the same roof as her parents were frustrating. He was hearing his mother-in-law's Southern drawl all day. And to eat at the same table and listen to Lucy and her Daddy swap memories and laugh about shared experiences before the war. Tom's excuses to leave the table became increasingly feeble. Could he return to that? Would Lucy leave the family home and allow Tom to be his own person, not a puppet to her father? Lucy had put her father on such a high pedestal Tom knew it would need a stick of dynamite to remove him.

Meanwhile, Tom had to admit he felt jealous of how close Edward and Nelly had become. Not that they showed their mutual affection in front of him. Tom knew they didn't have to; he knew it bubbled beneath the layers of their friendship, and he didn't like it, especially now that he was aware of how much Nelly had changed - for the better. In fact, part of him found Nelly's newfound confidence, her empowerment, hard to believe. Now, there was a word Tom had tried to live by, as well as teach his children, and yet here he was admiring Nelly for achieving it for herself. Yes, she'd owned up to how she was before Tom had left, and she'd since righted the terrible wrongs within her own family, with her mother in particular. And then, there was Walter…it broke Tom's heart that he hadn't been there to help Walter grow into the man Edward had guided him to be. And to see Nelly encouraging Walter instead of putting him down and stripping him of his pride and self-assurance - by God, Nelly had changed! Tom now felt love and admiration for the new Nelly that he'd been unable to do when he became caught up in his own unhappiness and had to marry Nelly? Well, yes, Tom had been resentful and held her accountable for his misery to the point of her feeling totally unloved. He had desired her, on occasion - but had never loved her. Tom saw now how cruel he had been, abandoning them the way he had, not returning to his family home after the war where, if he had shown a little more respect and affection to Nelly, the marriage could probably have worked. He knew it now. Was it too late to make amends? *This whole fucking mess is my fault.* He berated himself. His sense of duty appeared to have deserted him. *Should I return to Lucy or try to make another go of it with Nelly?* His thoughts felt like nails driven into his brain. *I have to make a decision.*

Tom visited Grace, stayed for an hour, and tried to appear happy.

However, Grace sensed a change in her father, especially when he set a tear-stained kiss on her forehead before leaving. Tom wiped his eyes, then walked out of the hospital and hailed a taxi.

The following day when it was clear that Tom wouldn't be returning, Nelly made some feeble excuses before telling an outright lie. "Your father had to go back to America, Grace. You must understand, your recovery will be slow, and he could not possibly stay for the months it is going to take…"

"Why didn't he tell me? Why didn't he even say goodbye?" Grace cried, her tears falling unheeded down her cheeks. "He's run away - *again!*"

"I'm sorry, Grace, though you should know what your father's like with goodbyes." Nelly was shocked by her brutality. "I'm sorry, Grace, I should not have said that. I know there's no excuse for him not saying goodbye. I'm sure he will send you a letter once he's home in America." *He's good at writing letters.*

"Oh, Mum, I hate it when you say *home*, as in *America*. I thought….well, I thought he might change his mind and stay here." Grace fussed fretfully with her blankets before gazing out of the window. "I didn't hear him talking about Lucy and Tyson much." She then looked squarely at Nelly. "He seemed…I don't know… *lost*. Is that how Dad seemed to you, Mum?"

"I think you've hit the nail on the head, Grace. That's exactly how he appeared. And when someone becomes lost, they're the only ones who can find themselves again if that makes sense." Nelly kissed Grace's tears away, thinking it would not be possible to love her daughter more than she did at that moment.

Nelly never told Grace her father had simply disappeared, least of all when Grace was struggling to recover. However, Nelly had reported him missing to the police then to Lucy. Every day after, Nelly had handled Lucy's increasing and frantic telephone calls with compassion, all the while her own heart was breaking once again, but not solely over Tom's betrayal of them *all* this time. It was the worry of whether he'd done something foolish, or if he'd been murdered, or was he simply *lost*, as Grace had said? The burden of Tom's disappearance and the worry of Grace regaining her health and mobility was getting the better of Nelly. Thank God she had Edward, who'd put off having his painful knee operation so he could always be there for them, even though

Walter had assumed the role as man of the house. Whether he'd truly disengaged from Tom, or he was putting on a brave face, Walter stood firm in the face of disaster, and Nelly was thankful for that.

"I know, Mum," Grace had said later. "I suppose for Dad; it's like it was for *me* when *he* went to America instead of coming home to us. I felt lost for a while, and I remember pulling myself out of it. So yes, I know what you mean." Grace held her mother's shoulder and slowly struggled to swing her legs off the bed. "Help me stand, Mum. I want to walk, so I can climb up the steps and call races." Nelly sniffed back a tear.

"That's my girl. You'll do it! And by the way, how does it make you feel having fans writing to you, Grace?"

"That's why I'm doing my best to get better, Mum. And I'm slowly writing back to everyone who's sent cards and flowers. Johnno's helping me." Grace gasped when her feet made contact with the cold lino. "Slippers, please, Mum."

Nelly placed them on her feet then hesitated. "Grace, have you and Johnno thought any more about when you might get married?" Nelly's words jolted Grace upright.

"No, Mum. Nothing's changed. We've decided to wait and see. That's all I can say, except we *do* love each other – very much." Concentrating, and with her slippers firmly on her feet, Grace took a couple of steps, then stood shakily before taking another two steps. Finally, leaning against the wall, Grace began to laugh. "Now I know how Walter feels!"

"Be sure to tell him that when he comes in later, Grace. He'll no doubt see the funny side of that!"

"I know he will. And you know what, Nelly? I reckon he and Emma will be married before me."

"You may be right Grace. Although I only hope Emma doesn't change her mind."

"Why on earth would you say *that*, Mum?"

"Oh, I don't know. Please don't take any notice of me Grace. It's silly of me to think that way. I suppose it's because of Walter - he confides in me and says he still can't believe his luck at having a beautiful girl like Emma who loves and want to marry him. Silly, I know. Why wouldn't any girl want to marry such a beautiful soul like Walter? No, Walter is an absolute gentleman, and he would never hurt Emma."

CHAPTER 17

Tom paid the taxi driver once they reached the city's western outskirts and began to hitch rides towards Adelaide, where he hoped nobody would know him. Not even during the war had he known more than two South Australians, who later were killed in action. Adelaide would not be Tom's final destination, the Red Centre called him - he didn't know why. *Time to think, time to find me in the outback, maybe? Then whoever wants me can have me. The real me - whoever that might turn out to be,* he thought wryly.

Tom's last ride out of Victoria luckily took him to Mount Gambier. It was a place he'd heard about and was as good a place as any to break his journey. *One night in a pub won't break the bank,* he told himself. When strolling down the main street, the Victorian architecture struck Tom as a try-hard attempt to revisit the Mother Country. Maybe South Australia being a free settler state, had something to do with it. Was it all those Pommies yearning for Home? But the proliferation of iron-laced verandas gave a sympathetic nod to the Australian climate. He smiled at his observations, then signed into the Royal Hotel. He'd freshen up, have dinner, a good night's sleep, and go to see the renowned Blue Lake before pushing on.

Early the following morning, he stood alone to view the spectacular expanse of water. The limestone volcanic crater that formed the lake gave it its deep, iridescent blue colour. "Alice Springs might be the *heart* of Australia, but this lake is definitely the *eye*," Tom said, duly impressed. Once back in town, be bought a bus ticket to Adelaide. As the miles passed by, Tom hatched a plan to reinvent himself.

Not far from the Adelaide bus terminus, he found a second-hand store and purchased a battered Akubra hat, a pair of moleskin trousers, a couple of blue shirts, some riding boots, and a moth-eaten tweed jacket. He stopped at a barbershop a few doors down and bought a razor. Tom Noble made his way back to the public toilets at the bus station, and

161

thirty minutes later, Norm Hawkins emerged - a cattleman with a shaved head. Tom's story had ended, and Norms had begun. With a practised limp from an imaginary droving accident, Norm would make his excuses for not riding. However, he planned to add, in a convincing Aussie drawl, "But I'm pretty bloody good with figures, if y'need a bloke to do y'books."

That was the plan as he kept moving towards the vast expanse of the outback. Once there, he was hopeful he would blend in enough to find work in exchange for some much-needed money; his supply was running low.

Tom stayed one night in a guesthouse, run by a meddlesome older woman, whose hair seemed permanently affixed to hair rollers. Even with the older woman's scolding, he spoke little but ate much, kept his head low, and hat on, "you should know better! A gentleman never wears a hat inside!" she chastised Tom while slamming the serving dishes down on the table in front of him. He'd been up against worse enemies, and Tom merely shrugged and kept his hat on. Little did he know that real cattlemen mainly were well mannered.

In the morning, after breakfast, he was glad to leave the older woman behind. Tom hot-footed it towards the Princes Highway. Before too long, he'd hitched a ride with a lorry driver named Archie.

"On me way to Broome," Archie told him. "Goin' across the Nullarbor. I Gotta drop a load off in Perth. Take a while. Okay with you?"

"Perfect," Tom said, looking at a face that appeared to have gone ten rounds with Tommy Burns and lost every one.

"So what's y'name, and where are y'from, mate?" Archie asked, sporting a friendly grin.

Norm, aka Tom, told a few lies, which sounded feasible.

"I hail from Broome. Born there," said Archie. "I'm on m'way home to the missus and five kids."

Archie soon had Tom belly laughing with stories about the years he'd spent behind the wheel.

"Yep, and I'll tell ya another one! It's about a character named Dawson. He had a horse called Hungry. Well, I reckon Hungry could've won the Melbourne Cup! And if they reran the Cup on the same day, I'd lay me house, Hungry' d win it again!" Archie said with a firm nod.

"Fair dinkum, Archie? I like horse racin'," Tom said, using his new Aussie drawl."

"Yep, I do too, mate! That's why I followed old Dawson around the bush races when I could. Dawson called his horse, Hungry Dawson, because every time they needed a feed, he'd have a stern talk with Hungry, tellin' him he needed to win the next race otherwise they'd both go hungry!" Archie laughed at the story he'd told a thousand times before.

"So, was he *that* good, Archie? The horse, I mean. Did Dawson ever run him in the city races?" Tom asked, intrigued.

"Nup, they reckoned Dawson hated the city. He and Hungry spent their life camped out under the stars. Dawson and Hungry walked between race meetin's, he said that was enough exercise for both of 'em. From memory, I think Hungry ran fifty-five races, near all of them back-to-back. A couple of times, he got beat, and the horses who beat him went on to win big city races. Even the ones who ran second t'Hungry, ended up winnin' in the city. Bloody stupid I reckon, not takin' that horse to the big smoke. Dawson coulda made a bloody fortune!"

"Are there any race meetings in Broome?" Tom asked.

"Camel races along the beach, mainly, but sometimes we round up stray horses and have a race or two. The locals love a bet, they'd bet on two flies climbing up a bloody wall!" Archie guffawed shaking his head. "Y'know, Norm, when y'get ta Broome - " he turned sideways to look at Tom. "Y'say y'never been ta Broome?" Tom shook his head. "Well, I'm tellin ya, y'won't wanta leave. It's the best place on bloody earth. The locals are a mixture of Chinese, Japanese, Malaysian, and God knows what else, but it seems ta work. We all get along well and call ourselves, Aussie Brooms." His laughter vibrated when his hands hit the steering wheel hard. Suddenly, a huge red kangaroo had bounced in front of the truck. Wham, smack! went the carcass. Archie didn't blink, but Tom had raised his arms to cover his head. Archie grinned. "Don't worry, Norm, dead meat that one, mate!"

About four hours into their trip, Archie pulled into a truck stop. Tom jumped down from the cabin, stretched and found his way to the toilet. Archie undid his fly and watered the tyres wondering why Tom needed the dunny. "Must need to do a bog," he muttered.

They met in the café after Archie had filled the truck up on juice, as he called petrol. Tom, kept his head down and his hat on, searching the menu.

"Y'got somethin ta hide mate?" Archie said and meant it. "I

163

always take me hat off when I go inside ta eat. The Missus'ud tar and feather me if I didn't." Archie yanked Tom's hat off. "There y'go, that's better. Christ! A shaved head! Didja 'ave nits, mate?"

Tom blushed, "Yep. Gone now."

Archie's laughter drowned the clatter of knives and forks against the background hum of deep voices. He took a look around at the faces in the café, now looking their way. "Don't worry fellas. This one's a clean pick-up. De-liced and all!" Nods of approval greeted this remark. Tom felt like disappearing.

After eating a substantial mixed grill, Tom needed a nap and hoped Archie had run out of stories. They strolled toward the truck, and Archie turned to Tom.

"Hey Norm, can you drive a truck? Two reasons - if we take it in turns, we'll make Perth in two ta three days instead of five, then Broom in another three. Pushin' it, that is. I'm hankerin' ta see the missus, if y'know what I mean." Archie winked and jabbed an elbow into Tom's ribs.

"I don't have a truck license, Archie," Tom said, holding his bruised ribs.

"Oh shit, that don't matter! I only gotta teach y'the gears, mate. You'll be right. Nothin' but a straight road ahead. I just need a coupla hour's kip and I'll be right for another ten."

Tom's swift aptitude for learning anything new had always been valuable. He immediately took to truck driving like a pro and enjoyed the feeling of being in control of such a powerful machine. Archie had spread his copious body out in the back of the cab and didn't stop snoring until he began choking on a fly that had hitched a ride back at the truck stop. Just as well, Tom thought as the initial excitement of learning then driving the truck had worn off after six long hours, and Tom was more than ready to 'tap the mat.'

"Jesus! Bloody fly! Where the fuck did he come from?" Archie sputtered, looking at his watch. "Christ, I've been sleepin' for six hours! Stop the truck, Norm. I need a pee."

Tom pulled over, relieved and grateful for the pesky fly.

By swapping drivers, they made Perth ahead of schedule. "In record bloody time, Norm. You're a bloody beauty, mate! Hey y'don't want a job, do ya?"

Tom smiled, shaking his head. "Sorry mate, not my cuppa tea.

164

On my way to Alice. Gotta a mate there."

"Oh, y'do, do ya? Well, I know a heap of blokes there. What's his name?" Archie said, head tilted.

Oh, shit! Tom had to think. "Ah, Eddy Burns. Know 'im?"

Archie scratched his head. "Now, let me think. Would he be the only son of old Buster Burns? Great bloke Buster. Died two years back."

"Nup, Eddy's old man's still alive, as far as I know."

Archie slapped Tom on the back. "Well then, let's get this cargo off loaded, and I'll shout y'a feed and a bed for the night. In the truck, that is!" he chuckled.

Three more days of continuously changing drivers saw them roll into Broome late afternoon.

"Home sweet home. This is as far as we go, Norm, but if y'ever change your mind about being a truckie, give me a call, mate."
Tom smiled and shook Archie's hand. "Thanks again for the lift, Archie."

"No, Norm, thank you! I'm home three days early - couldna done it without ya. Come in and have a feed with the family."

"No, thanks, if it's all the same, Archie. It's been a pleasure to meet ya but I best be on me way."

Tom swung his knapsack over his shoulder and strolled towards the small township of Broome. He gazed toward the impressive pearling luggers, the setting sun outlining their dark shapes against the distant horizon. White seagulls soared, black against the fading pink sky. Tom raised a hand, shading his eyes, captivated by the scene before him. *What would it be like living in Broome for a while, learning how to dive for pearls*, he thought wistfully. *The divers make good money, I've heard. Maybe - maybe not.* He walked on, boots stirring the dust on the road that ran parallel to the foreshore; it went for miles and miles underneath imposing red cliffs. No headlands to add interest, just pale sand and flamingo sky meeting the ink blue Indian Sea at the horizon. It would all change again in the morning, and Tom decided he may sleep the night on the beach, witness the sunrise, and then head for the Alice. But first, he needed to eat.

Twilight softened the creamy corrugated building that held produce, farm gear, and anything else the inhabitants of Broome needed to survive. Tom opened the glass panelled door, hearing a conversation between two men, one of Asian appearance and the other, more European, possibly a half-caste. He waited patiently.

"Okay, Sam, I'll tell her next time she's in, or you could go and tell her yourself."

"No, no! Happy you tell. My face not welcome by husband in home. Me just for business. Savvy?"

Tom was intrigued. He remembered Archie saying they all got along well, 'No prejudice in Broome, mate,' he'd said. And yet Tom heard it right here. He waited until the thank yous and goodbyes were complete, then nodded a smile at the departing, Sam Su, who was, in fact, a well-known and respected pearl seller.

Tom approached the counter. "G'day, mate. I need somethin' ta eat. Stayin' overnight on the beach. On me way to Alice. S'pose you don't know anyone travellin' that way?" Tom asked in his best Aussie drawl.

"I can help you with a meat pie or two. The wife makes them, and they're delicious. But I don't know anyone heading for Alice, not anytime soon. Are you looking for work, mate?"

The storekeeper, Joe, only had to look at the tattered state of Tom to guess his predicament.

"All depends. I fell off m' horse and broke m' leg in three places. Gives me hell. But I'm good with numbers. Can do a bit of book work." Tom rubbed his leg. "Just until the leg heals proper."

Joe said a silent prayer of thanks. "Well, you've come to the right place. What's y'name?"

"Norm, Norm Hawkins."

"Well Norm, I have a pile of paperwork a bloody mile high. Buggered if I know when I'll get the time and the missus hasn't been too well so it's piling up. Between you and me she's never been real good at figures and such. So, you've got a job if you want one, Norm!" Joe said, walking from behind the counter, proffering his hand.

"Right you are, Joe. Though I can only stay for a short while. I've planned to meet up with me mate in Alice."

They shook hands, and Joe handed over two hot meat pies and escorted Tom to a room out the back. "You're welcome to sleep here, Norm. At least there's a bed and a blanket, not that you'll need a blanket here in Broome."

Tom stayed for three weeks, keeping to himself, using his work as an excuse for anyone who'd ask him to join them in a drink. "No thanks, mate. I need to get on with Joe's bookwork before I head off."

And get on with it he did, with ease. It was one role Tom could play without having to think too hard. His prowess at numbers, he assumed, ran in his blood. His Grandpa had been a good number cruncher in his day.

Upon completing the final tally, Tom gratefully accepted his pay. Joe had been most generous in his appreciation of Tom's precise bookwork. Joe waved Tom goodbye with an offer. "If you're ever back here, Norm, please drop in. I'm sure I'll have work for you and a bed to kip in; thanks, mate!"

Word of Tom's ability with accounts had become known around town. And the woman to whom Sam Su had been referring when Tom first entered the general store, one Naomi Black, had tracked down Tom two days before his planned departure. She made him a lucrative offer. Naomi was an astute pearl dealer who travelled to Perth whenever her supply warranted the trip. She mainly bought pearls from Sam Su, then set them in rings, necklaces, bracelets, and brooches, all beautifully designed by her jeweller, who resided above Naomi's exclusive jewellery shop in Fremantle.

Tom didn't have to think too hard and long about taking Naomi's job offer. He weighed up his current financial situation, comparing it to where it could be if he worked for Naomi for six months. She seemed like a straight-shooter, was clearly very good at what she did and her direct offer of a very generous wage made it an easy decision to accept her proposition. She was also quite a beauty for a town like Broome – not that he had the slightest interest.

Wasn't I heading for Alice? Oh well, what're six months in the big scheme of things?

The drive back down south proved interesting, although a little uncomfortable when Tom was subtly offered duties of a more physical nature, in addition to those of bookkeeper. Tom smiled wryly, remembering the other women he'd met like Naomi. She struck him at first as a genuine business-all-the-way type. Otherwise, he would never have taken the job. Now. On closer examination, he was able to see what he had missed at first. Her coiffured blond hair sat strategically to one side, almost covering her right eye, a la Veronica Lake - most seductive, as was the heady perfume she wore. Naomi chain-smoked, using a long, elegant cigarette holder. She wore deep red lipstick, which she would reapply now and then, using the rear vision mirror to do so, despite the vehicle swerving dangerously whenever the touch-up was needed.

The contrast between his lack of style and her overabundance of it made Tom smile. Surely Naomi wasn't genuinely making a play for him? He'd purposely disguised himself as a down-and-out character, to the point of not showering as often as he should, to ward off approaches from any woman, let alone one like her. The more she spoke about her life and her business, the more Tom recognised what type of woman she was - narcissistic and ruthless where money was concerned. She reminded him of his mother-in-law. He would be glad to reach Perth, though if Naomi put too much pressure on him, he'd make an excuse and bolt.

Tom had never thought himself handsome, though he'd had no trouble attracting women. Tom thought about his teenage years when he used to wish he had a twin brother so that he could share all the 'giggling girts,' his mother used to call the girls who, for the flimsiest excuse, came knocking on their door. Suddenly it hit him – he was alone. No siblings, no parents; he was utterly alone. Except for the two families he'd deserted. *No, don't go there, Tom. You're Norm Hawkins now.*

"Penny, for your thoughts, Norm?" Naomi asked with a sideways smile. "Are you thinking about being on board my boat? Not only will you make good money, but you'll receive a lot of fringe benefits." She raised her skirt over her knee, slowly rubbing her upper thigh. "Mmm, it must be a bug. Can you see anything on my leg, Norm?" she asked coquettishly.

The transparency of her true intentions was enough for Tom, and he intended to bail out at the next stop, which couldn't come quickly enough as far as he was concerned. When Naomi slowed up and pulled into a petrol station, Tom grabbed his knapsack from the back seat, got out, and before shutting the door, said, "Thanks for the lift, Naomi. I'm sorry, I won't be taking up your offer. I just remembered gotta mate who lives nearby. See ya!" Tom turned before she could reply and hurried into the men's toilets. At least he was only halfway to Perth. Every so often, he'd peek out the door to see if she'd gone. It took her a while.

Naomi had waited, feeling annoyed and trying to work him out, hoping maybe he might change his mind. *What sort of bloody dill would knock back my offer?* "Oh, well." She gave a philosophical sigh, slid into the driver's seat of her silver Mercedes, and pulled out onto the highway. Tom slumped with relief when he heard her car take off. He emerged from his hiding place, drank deeply from the water tap nearby and proceeded to hitch a ride back towards Broome or, if he was lucky, he might get someone going on further to Katherine, or maybe to Alice Springs.

Tom had been walking for a good hour before a truck pulled over. He gratefully climbed up into the cabin. "Thanks, mate. The name's Norm," Tom said.

"Dave," the driver replied through a mouth full of potato chips. He was a giant of a man, and Tom wondered how he managed to squeeze his enormous bulk behind the steering wheel. Wedged between the seats was a box filled with soft drink bottles, packets of chips, bars of chocolates and bags of lollies, among other things vaguely resembling food. The cabin floor was littered with greasy paper bags that contained the smeared remains of hamburgers and steak sandwiches. Dave spoke little but ate a lot; his hands were like a conveyor belt to his mouth. *No wonder he's enormous,* Tom thought. Obesity wasn't Dave's only problem. They were only about ten miles down the track when a hideous smell invaded the cabin, and Tom had to lean his head out the window to avoid the poisonous gas emanating from Dave's ample rear end. Tom calculated that windburn was preferable to suffocation.

With night falling, the truck's brakes finally screeched to a grinding halt at the first set of traffic lights they'd encountered, and Tom made a quick exit. Choking on his words, he called, "Thanks for the lift, mate!"

"No worries!" Dave mumbled, mouth around a sausage roll. The truck pulled away, and Tom left with the lingering smell of a farewell fart.

Loneliness sledgehammered Tom as he signed into cheap lodgings at a place he'd never heard of. He felt a world away from everyone and everything familiar. Still, this was what he'd chosen, to use a new palette to paint the picture of the man he hoped to find.

CHAPTER 18

"I'm sorry, Mrs Nobel, we've had no further news about your husband."

Nelly hesitated but chose not to correct the Police Sergeant in charge of missing persons; she always considered Tom her 'husband.'

"Thank you, Sergeant. I apologise for phoning you so often. It's just my daughter – well, as you know, she's recovering from tubercular meningitis. It would help lift her spirits if she were to hear some good news." *Apart from the fact that Lucy's been irritatingly insistent. She's phoned me every damned day since Tom's disappearance.*

The phone rang again the moment Nelly hung up.

"Hello, Lucy." Nelly cursed silently before continuing. "I just spoke to the police, and there's still no news."

"I know Tom's out there somewhere, Nelly," Lucy said, just as she had, time and time again in her broad Southern accent. "He's not dead. I can feel him." Today, she confided in more personal information. "We did have problems, and I realized, only when he left, that we should have made it on our own from the beginning. We shouldn't have allowed Daddy to interfere as he did. I was going to surprise Tom when he came home. I'd found a place to live, near New York. Daddy had spoken to a friend who calls harness racing there, and he was going to give Tom a chance. I knew that's what Tom really wanted. I hope it's not too late. I hope he comes to his senses and comes home to Tyson and me. I'm sorry, Nelly, we never meant to hurt you. But I love him so much."

Nelly, after hearing Lucy's arrangements, nearly dropped the phone. What chance did she have now with Lucy recognising the difficulties which had caused a rift in their marriage? And now Lucy would change everything to suit Tom?

"I have to go, Lucy," Nelly cut her off. "I promise I'll phone you if there's any news. Goodbye." Nelly hung up the receiver and wept.

*

Grace had spent three months in hospital, at first fighting for her life and then, after a long-time recuperating, she was ready to be discharged. "In record time," Doctor Forbes had said, "and it will be on the day you can walk the entire length of the ground floor corridor, Grace."

George was not Grace's specialist, but he had maintained a personal and professional interest in her case. His quick and accurate diagnosis was noted as the main factor in Grace's survival, and he was delighted to have saved this young, vibrant woman. George would have liked a family of his own, but unfortunately, he and his wife were childless. Now, he felt he had found a surrogate daughter in Grace.

*

"Are you ready Grace? You have to agree that you have come far in such a short time. And now, I'm pleased to say. It's time for you to go home. Walter's downstairs with Emma. They're standing at the far end of the corridor waiting for you." George took Grace by the shoulders and looked at her resolute expression. "Are you ready?"

Grace took a deep breath and looked squarely at George.

"Yes, I'm ready. Let's do this, Doc."

Grace waved and smiled at her beloved brother and dearest friend Emma as they emerged from the elevator. She called to them excitedly. "Hello, you two!! Now, stay right there. I'll walk to you and give you both the biggest bear hug ever. Ready?"

"Yep! You can do it, Gracie," Walter replied.

"Here I go. One step...and another step…and a little tap-dance," Grace said and did a little jig, making them all laugh before walking slowly along the corridor and into their welcoming arms. In their warm embrace, she felt she had returned home and that she was like her old self - albeit a little deaf in her right ear and in need of more muscle-building exercises.

Johnno had assured Grace he would take three months' leave and help her regain fitness. She couldn't wait to begin.

Grace's release from the hospital had made the news. Once again, cards offering support flooded their letterbox, and the doorbell often rang when flowers were delivered.

"Oh, my goodness," was all Grace could say and the feeling of being loved and respected helped to both buoy her recovery and dull, a little, the pain of her father's disappearance.

Edward sat in what had become *his* armchair in Nelly's lounge room, his leg elevated on a new 'pouf,' as she called it, to help the

171

throbbing pain in his knee. "Let me help you write some of those cards, Grace. It'll take you a month of Sundays if I don't."

"Thanks, Edward." Grace handed him the cards then studied his features; he was so kind and distinguished. Grace took a moment to think how fortunate they all were to have him as their loyal and caring friend. "I love you, Edward. You have been a wonderful role model for both Walter and me. And I don't know which way Nelly would have turned if you hadn't been here to guide her." With a little less effort than a week ago, Grace rose and embraced an emotional Edward.

"I love you too, Grace, and I'm proud to be your friend. You will make a full recovery, and that dream of yours will become a reality - I know it will. Just never give up." They held each other for a moment longer. "Now," said Edward briskly, trying to hide the emotion in his voice, "we'd better get to work, Grace."

*

Nelly found her long-held receptionist position at CJ Brown both a pleasure and a necessary distraction from her worries. As always, she enjoyed dressing up for work and was even happier when her efforts with her couture were noticed and appreciated by fellow employees. Today, looking her very best and knowing Walter was at university, sitting yet another exam, and Grace was at home spending time with Edward. Nelly felt a sense of excitement as if something good was about to happen.

Maybe Tom will phone to say he's alive and he'll be home soon? Perhaps I'll get a pay rise? Who knows? I just feel happy.

The work phone rang, as it did every few minutes, though this time, unfortunately, it was not Tom.

"Good afternoon. CJ Brown Accountants, Nelly speaking."

"Hello, Nelly, It's Doctor George. May I call you Nelly?"

"Yes, yes, of course, George. May I call you George?" She giggled. "How are you, George, and to what do I owe the pleasure?" Nelly held undying gratitude for Doctor George; his care for Grace had been far above the call of duty.

"Well, I suppose I could have phoned Edward, but I thought I'd let you know first. A fellow doctor, actually a friend of mine, is an orthopedic surgeon, has agreed to operate on Edward's knee –at 'mate's rates, as they say. I know Edward has put up with crippling pain for far too long. Would you rather I phone Edward, Nelly, or would you be happy to pass on the message."

Nelly started to answer but had hardly uttered a word before he interrupted her. " Wait, Nelly. I have another favour to ask you. It's a bit awkward. I hope you don't mind me asking ..."

Nelly was intrigued. "Please, George, ask away! There's nothing I wouldn't do for you. I so appreciate everything you have done for Grace."

"Well, then. As you may know, my wife and I have long separated and are waiting for our divorce to be finalised. The thing is, I need to attend the annual Medical Practitioners Ball, and I'd feel a bit, well, a bit alone without a lady to accompany me. Would you do me the honour of being my partner for the evening?"

Nelly's jaw literally dropped; she sat speechless for a long moment.

"Are you there? Nelly, can you hear me?"

"Oh, I am sorry, George, I wasn't expecting such a wonderful invitation. Why I haven't been to a ball since...since I can't remember when, I'd be delighted to accompany you, George." Nelly felt her cheeks flushing as her romantic imagination leaped into action.

"Good, thank you, Nelly. The ball is in two weeks. I'll be talking to you before then if that is all right with you?"

"Yes, of course – anytime, George. Oh, and I will pass your message on to Edward. I'll tell him to phone you. Goodbye." She hung up the receiver. "Well! I'll be a monkey's uncle!" Nelly said aloud.

"You don't look like one," said her boss with a warm smile as he hurried past into his office.

But how will I approach Edward? A wave of guilt washed over Nelly. *Oh, it's nothing. It's simply the right thing to do, especially after all George has done for Grace. He deserves to enjoy a night out. Yes, that's how I'll explain the situation to Edward, and he'll understand. Of course, he will!*

*

"I'm home, " Nelly called, shutting the front door behind her.

Grace yelled, "We're in the kitchen, Mum!"

The aroma of something delectable came wafting along the hallway, and Nelly inhaled deeply as she followed it into the kitchen. When passing the dining room, she noticed the table had been set. *Have I forgotten a special occasion?* She wondered.

"Hello, everyone!"

"Hi Mum, we have good news, so we thought we'd celebrate. Edward bought two bottles of champagne, they're on the ice, and I've cooked a special recipe from the 'Woman's Weekly.' I just have to cook the rice, and it'll be ready," said Grace loudly – a side effect of her deafness. Nelly didn't have the heart to ask Grace to turn the volume down, and neither did anyone else at this early stage.

"Well, don't keep me in suspense, Grace. What is it?" Nelly unpinned her hat and peeled off her gloves. "I must say, it smells amazing, Grace!"

"Yep, that's what they call me - Amazing Grace!"
Laughter filled the room as Walter stood to make an announcement. "Emma has p…passed her final exam. She's a fully-fledged l…legal secretary and I have p…passed The Bar exam! In record time, I may add. I am a lawyer!"

Applause and cheers broke out. Walter and Emma each took a bow. "And if that's n…not enough to celebrate. Emma and I have made a d…date to get married."

Nelly flopped on the kitchen chair, "My goodness, such wonderful news - and all at once. I don't know who to congratulate first." Nelly held her hands over her heart as tears welled. "I am so proud of you, Walter - and you too, Emma. Does your dad know about all of this?"

"Yes, as a matter of fact, he should be here any mo..." The doorbell rang. "I'll get it," said Emma.

As she opened the front door, Errol Blake stood a moment, smiling, then hugged his daughter. "Congratulations, darling." He proffered two cold bottles of champagne and a bunch of flowers. "No, give the flowers back. They're for Nelly. Is she home yet?"

"Yes, Nelly's here. We all are, Dad."

Nelly accepted the bouquet graciously, though was a little surprised to see Errol come alone – again. Gillian seemed to have faded away from family gatherings.

After a delicious dinner for which Grace was deservedly complimented, they sat in comfortable silence in the lounge room, sipping on a fine port, each reflecting on recent events.

Errol was the first to break their reverie. "I feel so privileged and happy to see my daughter marry into such a close, caring family. Unfortunately, Emma's missed much of that, with her mother dying so young. I know now I was too busy dealing with my own pain; I perhaps was a little neglectful of Emma. I think…" Errol paused and looked lovingly at Grace. "You Grace, I'm sure, were sent to Emma from above. And, of course, you Walter. How could I be any happier for my daughter? You, young man, are an inspiration, and I hope one day that you can find time to travel around schools and Repatriation Hospitals to talk to others about what can be achieved with hope and determination. Would you consider that, Walter?"

"I have already, Mr Blake. It w…would appear you and Emma think alike." Walter raised his port glass. "Here's to our future. All of us!"

Nelly hadn't had time to tell Edward about the offer of the knee operation or her invitation to the ball with Doctor George. It could all wait until tomorrow.

Nelly rarely took a 'sickie,' but the next day her head throbbed so savagely she felt it would explode. She asked Grace to phone her boss to say she was ill. Grace obliged then went on her daily exercise routine with Johnno.

After drinking copious amounts of water and having a Bex Powder and a good lay down, as the commercial recommended, Nelly felt almost human. "Self-inflicted," she admitted to Edward, who'd come to help with the clean-up. He felt no better than Nelly. Together, they carefully dumped the empty bottles in the bin; six champagne, two-port, and six beers. "Any wonder we have headaches, Edward!" Nelly smiled, and they laughed together - quietly.

Nelly saw reflected in Edward's blue eyes the love and respect he harboured for her. *How could she even think of going out with George*, she thought guiltily.

After their toils, the house gleamed and smelt like gardenias. Nelly took a deep, rewarding breath. She surveyed their efforts before sitting at her kitchen table to share a pot of tea with Edward.

"I'm sorry, Edward, I have some news. It was remiss of me not to let you know sooner, although I'm sure you will forgive me after all that happened last night."

"Tell me now, Nelly."

"Well, it seems you're in luck, Edward. Doctor George phoned me at work yesterday and said to let you know, a friend of his, an orthopedic surgeon, is willing to operate on your knee. At mate's rates, I may add." Nelly raised her cup of tea in the air.

"I'll think about it. Thanks for telling me, Nelly."

Edward gulped his tea, looking despondent.

Nelly was perplexed. "I thought you'd be happy to be rid of the pain Edward. I know I would."

"I'd like to wait until after the wedding. Walter's asked me to be his Best Man, and I'd like to walk, even if I'm in pain. They say getting over a knee operation can take months."

"But they're not being married until late September. That's almost three months away."

"No, I'll wait if it's alright with you Nelly." And with that Edward rose. "I need to make some phone calls. I'll see you later."

Nelly sat cradling her cup of tea, trying to fathom his attitude. Suddenly, it dawned on her, *Sylvia had an operation and never came out of the hospital. I wonder if that's it? As a matter of fact, he's always been hesitant. Maybe it is because of Sylvia?*

Edward's hurried departure gave her no time to discuss her invitation from George. Should she just phone George and make her excuses? She knew she would never deliberately hurt Edward's feelings.

CHAPTER 19

The following day Tom hitchhiked along the Great Northern Highway and received another lift which ended in a seaside town called Port Hedland. Tom soon tracked down a guest house where he hoped he could stay. The owner, Flo Goodall, was a joyful lady who made Tom think that this was how his mother would be if she were still alive. She sat behind her reception desk, talking on the phone with a friend. Tom stood waiting and heard her decline a day out. "Sorry, I would love to come, Betty, but I need to do a load of bookwork." She placed her hand over the receiver and smiled at Tom. " Sorry, I'll be with you in a jiffy."

Why Tom offered to help Flo, he didn't know, but as soon as she had hung up the phone, he heard himself saying, "Look, I couldn't help but overhear, and I reckon I could give you a hand. I'm an accountant." *Buggar, me, and my kind heart.*

Delightedly, Flo immediately took him up on his suggestion. "You're on!" she said and smartly phoned Betty back. Then Tom, aka Norm Hawkins, signed into Flo's beautifully clean and polished two-story home.

Two days later, with his bookwork completed, and just as Tom was about to leave, Karma delivered a gift in return for his succour. A well-spoken, dapper gentleman in his fifties walked through the front door and made his way to the desk. He placed his hands firmly on the reception desk, next to where Tom stood with his packed bags, waiting for Flo to pay him before he departed.

"Hello there, my good man. I'm exhausted. I need a bath, a good home-cooked meal, and a clean, comfortable bed for the night. Can you help me?"

Tom hesitated before replying. He was sure he recognised something familiar about the man's voice. "I'm sorry, mate, I've only been 'ere a couple of days meself. I've been doing some bookwork for the owner, Mrs Goodall. If you just wait ere, I'll see if I can find 'er;

I think she's out back hangin' some clothes on the line. Can I ask yer name?"

"It's Gollan, Ken Gollan. And you are?"

Tom flushed, suddenly nervous as he realised he spoke with the most prominent race caller in Western Australia.

"Tom, ah, I... I mean *Norm* Hawkins." He dropped his affected drawl and said in his normal voice. "Pleased to meet you, Mr Gollan." Tom proffered his hand; it was accepted and shaken firmly. "I'll just go out back and get Mrs Goodall. I'm sure there won't be a problem." Tom walked towards the yard, turning back to smile at Ken. *He must think I'm a bloody idiot! Pull yourself together, Tom!*

Mrs, Goodall promptly threw her wet nightgown back in the wicker basket. "Are you sure, Norm? Jesus, Mary, and Joseph!" Flo said, crossing her chest while waddling at speed back inside to the reception desk. "Mr Gollan! What an honour and a pleasure it is to have you here in my humble abode." Flo clapped her well-worn hands together. "So, you'll be wanting a nice clean bed, a hot bath, and a proper dinner? Would that be right, sir?"

"Yes, indeed, Mrs Goodall, that would be correct." Ken nodded solemnly.

"Well, sir, you have certainly come to the right place. I'll show you to your room." She turned to Tom, standing a polite distance behind her. "Can you wait a moment longer, Norm, and I'll fix your pay up. Then you can be on your way."

"Ahh, I was thinking of staying a couple more days, Mrs Goodall, if that's alright with you. I'd like to look around town a bit more." Tom smiled disarmingly, and Flo raised her eyebrows speculatively. Ken Gollan also caught Tom's drift and smiled wryly.

"You can stay as long as you like, Norm. But there's not much to see in this one-horse town." She laughed. "Now that's funny, seeing we have a famous race caller staying with us. A *one-horse* town, yes, one horse, indeed." Flo grabbed a key off one of the several hooks behind her desk. "Mustn't keep you waiting, Mr Gollan. Now follow me."

Later the same evening, Tom entered the dining room, decked in a new suit that he'd bought in *the only* clothing shop in the one-horse town. Noticing Ken sitting alone at a table, he thought he might as well stop wasting time. *In for a penny, in for a pound.* He walked straight up to where he was sitting.

178

Tom cleared his throat a little nervously. "Mr Gollan? Would you, ah, mind if I joined you?"

"Not at all, Norm. Please, take a seat - and call me Ken. I don't know about you, but I feel brand new after my bath and a kip. Bloody long way up to Port Hedland from Perth." He noticed Tom's interest. "Been to a funeral. An uncle of mine. My favourite uncle, in fact. He was the one who gave me the confidence and the encouragement to see how far I could take a career calling races."

At that moment, Jane, the attractive young woman employed by Mrs Goodall to serve meals and wash up, arrived bearing their meals. She'd worked for Flo over the past year, secretly hoping a wealthy gentleman might come to stay and sweep her off her feet and deliver her to wonderland. She smiled dreamily at Ken and said, " Your meals, gentlemen."

Without looking at Jane, Tom simply murmured "Thank you" and sat back as she delivered his plate.

However, Ken looked directly into her eyes, smiled, and said in his most dulcet tones, "Thank you so much, Jane. It's always such a pleasure to be served by a beautiful young woman." He took her hand gently and kissed the back of it as she blushed furiously. "You have the most alluring eyes, by the way." As she turned to leave, Ken gave her perky rear end a deft pat and watched her hips sway as she departed to the kitchen.

Ken turned his attention away from Jane's charms and back to Tom. "As I was saying, Norm..." he began but paused to inhale the aroma of roast lamb. He sprinkled it with homemade mint sauce, took a mouthful, and sighed contentedly. "Now, this is why I stay at Bed and Breakfasts. Just like Mum used to cook, hey? You tell me, Norm, what's better than a perfectly cooked lamb roast?" Ken took another mouthful, savouring it before he swallowed. "Mrs Goodall's place was recommended to me by my friend Charlie. He said she cooked the best roast dinners anywhere, and the place was clean and organised but homely. That's what I like. What about you, Norm?"

"Yes, I'm the same, Ken."

"Then we have something in common." Ken grinned.

There was not a race caller in either Australia or America that Tom hadn't heard of. He admired them all and had forever dreamed of joining their ranks. And now meeting Ken, it might just provide him with

179

an opportunity to realise his dream. Am I leaving my run a bit late? *Am I a little too long in the tooth at forty-two, maybe? Tom wondered. Well, nothing ventured, nothing gained!*

"Tell me, what's your story, Norm? I like to hear about other people's lives. It's better than reading books - doesn't strain the eyes." He ate another mouthful and chewed reflectively. "That is if it's interesting." Ken, with fork poised in mid-air, studied Tom for a moment. "And from the look of you, Norm, I think you have a tale to tell. So go ahead, I'm happy to eat and listen. Especially with a voice like yours, good timbre - yep good to listen to."

Tom smiled. "Thanks."

Once again, Tom created an interesting and plausible story that substantially covered his tracks, though he chose to provide a vein of truth. "So, you see, Ken, I've studied race fields and practised calling races since I was very young – always have and always will, I reckon. Sounds stupid, I know, and I mean, where would it ever get me?" He gave Ken a self-deprecating smile.

Ken gave him a measured look. "You know, I was just thinking, Norm, with that voice, you might easily be a radio announcer. But hey! A race caller? Well, I suppose so - if you have the aptitude. It's a bloody tough business, Norm. And there are not too many callers needed. So those of us in the game hold onto our jobs like a dog with a bone."

"Yes, I can understand that," said Tom, feeling any chance of his dream disappearing.

"Where were you headed before you changed your plans and stayed to get some inside information from me, Norm?" Ken grinned, a knowing twinkle in his eye.

"Caught me out, hey?" Tom gave a sheepish smile. "I was on my way to Alice Springs. I have a mate there - that is if he's still there. He travels around a bit. I thought I'd get a job at a cattle station. Or," he said, eyebrows raised, "I could see if they needed a radio announcer in town." Tom laughed at his own retort, and Ken joined in.

"I'll tell you what, Norm, I've got a few weeks off, and a young, would-be-if-he-could-be race caller is supposed to be filling in for me. He's not going to do me out of a job, that's for sure. He tends to get all tongue-tied, but he's giving me a well-needed break, so that's good. I have a mate in Alice. He's the boss of the ABC Radio Station there. I reckon he might be able to give you an early morning or late-night spot.

You know, a talk show, play some music. What do you reckon, Norm, would you like a lift to Alice?"

"Would I? Bloody oath I would! But were you planning to go there, or were you heading back to Perth?"

"Doesn't matter, I can easily turn around in Alice and head back home to Perth. Anyway, I have a new car that needs to do some miles; let's call it an adventure!"

"It's a deal, then. When do we leave?" Tom asked, completely re-energized.

Ken proffered his hand, "How about first thing in the morning? You'll have to put up with my bad driving, Norm. Better still, if you're willing to do the driving, I assure you, you'll feel a lot safer. I'm sure you have a yarn or two you can tell me to pass the time."

The following morning outside the guest house, Tom kissed Flo on the cheek, "Thanks Mrs Goodall. I enjoyed my stay. You run a tight ship and serve better meals than any flash city hotel, I reckon."

"I enjoyed having you stay, Norm, and I appreciate your help with the bookwork. It's the only thing I hate about running a business. The government wants to know everything these days, which makes it hard. Never mind. You take care now and come back and see us again."

Tom stood admiring Ken's four-door black Ford Anglia. The latest model, no doubt.

Ken sat behind the wheel, waving through the open window. "See you next time, Mrs Goodall! Great place to stay. I'll spread the word! Come on, Norm. We've got a big drive ahead." Ken blew a kiss to Jane, who had suddenly appeared, looking slightly dishevelled and sad. She gave Ken a sad little smile.

Tom sat back, luxuriating in the Anglia's leather upholstery, taking a moment to reflect on the characters he'd left behind and would most likely never meet again. *It seems I've made a few new friends, but no one relies on me to stay, not like... oh shit, there you go again Tom! Focus on what's ahead, it may be the chance of a lifetime and you will accomplish it on your own. No wealthy, superior father-in-law, no woman holding you back - it's up to you.* He then thought about Jane and the one-night fling she had clearly had with Ken. *He's obviously a ladies' man. I hope Jane finds her man. Poor Jane, she deserves someone nice.*

"Tell you what Norm, I'll drive for a few hours and you can take over until we reach Fitzroy Crossing."

"Here I go again." Tom smiled at Ken, who looked puzzled.

Tom explained about his truck driving stint and Ken laughed. They talked nonstop as they drove, covering a wide range of topics mostly in agreement. The vast empty landscape flew by, with only the occasional vehicle breaking the vision of the road ahead. Over the next day and a half, they drove in shifts until dark, then stayed in outback hotels, sleeping soundly and rising early to continue their journey

By twilight on their third night, they were pulling into Tanami. "How're you feeling, Norm? Not too tired, are you?"

Despite having done the lion's share behind the wheel, Tom was feeling good. "No, Ken. I'm looking forward to reaching Alice. I don't know why. It's just a feeling I have about the place."

The following morning, Tom slid behind the wheel and took time to study the red dirt road that lay before them. He'd heard about it. "You know, Ken, some parts are graded, but mostly it's an unsealed surface all the way. It's a bloody rough trip. Are you sure you want to do this? I mean, let me drive your new car on this dirt track all the way to Alice?" Tom shook his head. "If it were me, I'd have second thoughts."

Ken laughed, "Easy come, easy go, Norm. The car I bought with the money left me by my uncle from Port Hedland. And when I get back to Perth, I could buy another one, as well as a new home and anything else I want – or need. Got it, Norm?" He drew amusement from the surprised look on Tom's face. "Besides, I'm a spiritual man. I know- I know! I don't look like I am! But I'm inclined to think Uncle Bill put you in my path. And if anyone needed a hand, Bill was always there to lend one. Got it, Norm?"

"I can't believe my luck. That's all I can say." Tom placed the car into gear and rolled smoothly towards their first stop, Rabbit Flat. Where they would refuel and press on.

Several times throughout the journey, Tom, especially after a few beers in various pubs along the way, had had the urge to tell Ken the truth. Not all of it, but a lot of it.

One evening, Tom had confessed to his years fighting in the Middle East, for which Ken had shown great respect. As for Tom's family saga, well, he was not yet sure how Ken might judge him. So Tom steered the conversation away from any touchy topics.

"I don't know how you blokes did it, living in those terrible conditions and having to kill another man perhaps," Ken had commented.

"I don't know if I could have. Lucky for me I have two flat feet and without my specs, I'm short-sighted to buggery – I'm lucky if I can even see the horses." Ken's offering had made them both laugh to the point where they found it hard to stop. Eventually, with a gut full of grog, they had staggered off to their basic rooms in the tiny run-down pub in the middle of nowhere.

And now, the journey was nearly over. The next day would see them in Alice. The Ford Anglia hadn't complained, although it looked a lot worse after the harsh conditions that had been thrown at it. Tom, Ken, the car, and everything in it arrived in Alice covered with red dust.

After buying some new clothes, their first task was to find a decent hotel to stay in so they could scrub up, get their clothes washed, and search for someone looking for a bob to clean the car. All of this was accomplished within a couple of hours. The car would never look the same, but after the wash, just like the two men, it passed muster.

Then, they decided, it was high time for a drink or two, in an unusual bar recommended by the manager of the hotel where they were staying.

"Unique is all I can say. Best you go see for yourselves, fellas," the manager said with a cheeky grin.

Walking through the half swinging doors and into a bar styled on the American West, Tom grinned broadly.

"Surely they're not trying to copy the Yanks, Ken?"

"Yep, why not? After all, we are in the Wild West!"

Tom slapped Ken on the back, and as he did, a pretty young barmaid dressed as a dance-hall girl glided towards them carrying a tray of drinks.. Ken took a long appreciative glance at the vision of loveliness. A feather boa lay loose around her slender shoulders, and her low-cut corset displayed her ample cleavage. An ostrich plume decorated her elaborately coiffured blonde hair. She winked saucily at Ken as she brushed past. Ken winked back.

"I reckon yer right, pardner. Everything's wild out here!" Tom said in a broad cowboy accent, nodding towards the barmaid. He then walked up to the bar with an exaggerated, bow-legged gait.. "Set 'em up, bartender! Two whiskeys on the rocks!"

The bartender shook his head amused, thinking, *Just as well none of these truckies have noticed his show - they'd have him for breakfast!*

"A real cowboy has his whiskey straight–*pardner*," the bartender

183

replied.

Tom and Ken both laughed. "Listen, mate. It's so bloody hot in here; just pour our whiskey over ice, thanks. Chivas Regal, if you have it," said Tom.

Pantomime over, the two men sat conversing about whatever came to mind, which eventually led to a discussion about horse racing, including the great Australian trainers and their champion horses.

"Who won the first Melbourne Cup?" Asked Tom.

"Archer!" answered a slightly inebriated Ken.

"Right,"

"Who won it in 1946?" Asked Ken.

"That's easy, Russia!" Tom hung his head, running his finger around the rim of his whiskey glass. "It's a wonder they let a horse named 'Russia' win the Cup. Bloody brutal bastards, those Russian Soldiers. Still, he's a home-bred horse and the best stayer in the land."

The mood turned a little melancholy after six, maybe seven straight whiskeys followed by the same number of beer chasers.

"You know, Norm, I don't like to pry, but I think there's more to your story than you've told me."

Slouching over the table, Tom lowered his nose to his whiskey glass and drew a deep breath.

Ken continued. "It's the little things, Norm. Like when you picked up your first Chivas Regal, I could see memories flooding back. Whether they were sad war memories, I don't know, but something triggered a solemn recollection. It's none of my business, and if you don't want to share your real past with me, that's fine. Though I must say, it'll do wonders if you could shake the load off. Same as getting rid of a heavy backpack after a ten-mile mountain hike, I reckon."

"You're observant. I'll give you that, Ken."

"Have to be in my game, Norm."

Tom gave a deep and meaningful sigh and lifted his head.

"Why not? It's about time I shed some weight off my shoulders." He gave Ken a steadying look. "You'll have to give me your word, Ken, that you won't tell another soul."

"I lay a solemn oath - not a word to anyone, Norm."

And so, the entire sorry story of Tom's life was placed on the table in front of Ken, who could then make a judgment, laugh, cry, or do whatever he liked.

"Shit, Tom, that is one *helluva* story! You could write a book. Ah - should I call you Tom from now on?"

"No, I'd rather you didn't. I'd like to keep things undercover for a while longer."

"Fair enough. So, if you get your act together, have you thought about which way you'll swing? America, back to the arrogant father-in-law and a wife who can't get by without her parents? Or stay? Maybe Nelly will take you back? And just before you answer that, I've heard about your daughter Grace Nobel. I haven't heard her call a race yet, but the word is she's pretty damn good. It beats me why they don't give her a fair go down South. I'd be more than interested in hearing her call a race." Ken proffered his hand. "Pleased to meet you, Tom Nobel." He smiled to see the relief in Tom's eyes, but he also saw the sadness at the mention of Grace's name.

"Thanks, Ken. I don't know about you, mate, but I'm ready for a good night's sleep."

"I'm with you, *Norm!* But before we go, think about letting Nelly or Grace know you're okay. It's the least you can do."

The following morning, Tom woke with a splitting headache.

"Arghh! A man should know when to stop drinking," he criticized himself while stretching his limbs. "No more booze for me," he declared, making his way to the bathroom. His mouth felt like the bottom of a cocky's cage.

After his ablutions and cleaning his teeth, Tom felt slightly more human. He ventured slowly to the breakfast room and met a bright-eyed and seemingly unscathed Ken tucking into a farmer's breakfast.

Ken looked up, grinning. "Good morning, Norm."

"Why so happy, Ken? I thought you'd be the worse for wear, like me. I feel like shit."

Tom approached the self-serve buffet and walked away with an entire jug of freshly squeezed orange juice, then sat next to Ken, who was still beaming like the Cheshire Cat. Tom shook his head, but not too hard; it hurt.

"You'll buck up in a minute To - I mean, Norm, when Freddie Sanderson joins us for a coffee."

"Who's Freddie Sanderson?" Tom asked before gulping down a glass of juice.

"He's the mate I was telling you about, remember? You know, he manages the ABC Radio here in Alice. He also owns shares in stations all over WA. I told him you had a quality voice – deep – well timbered, which he likes on the radio. Comes across *soothing*, he says. Plus, the races are on Saturday."

"Where?" asked Tom.

"Here, mate! Here! I told Freddie I'd do a call, but if you're up to it, Norm, maybe he'd let you call one, too. As my apprentice, of course," he added with mock superiority. "So, what do you think, Norm?"

Tom shrugged his shoulders, and Ken bristled. "Well, if you're not interested, I'll phone Freddie and call off the meeting. Then you can go camp with the blacks at the river. They'll have you if you keep them in smokes."

Ken's smile vanished, and he finished his breakfast in silence, wondering how he could have misjudged another man so quickly. *Jesus, I went all out for…for whoever he is – and this is the thanks I get!*

Tom ran his fingers through his thick hair, sat back, his head up, and studied a fly crawling around the ceiling. *This is your chance, you bloody idiot, and you're acting like you don't care. God stone the bloody crows! It's is what you've been looking for, someone to give you a break so you can lay your talent on the line and see how far it gets you.* He sighed deeply and smiled apologetically at Ken.

"Nerves, mate. That's all it is. I'll be right after a few more of these." Tom held up another glass of juice. "I *am* incredibly grateful, Ken. Don't get me wrong. It's just I feel so bloody crook. It's hard to get excited when you'd rather lie down and die," he grinned sheepishly, "or at least sleep it off."

"Would you rather meet Freddie *tomorrow* morning, Norm? You do look bloody awful." Ken said before he took a long gulp of his now tepid coffee. He caught the attention of the waitress. "Would you mind bringing us a pot of coffee, Miss? Oh yes, and a full breakfast for my friend here." Ken gave the pretty little waitress a charming smile which she returned before throwing a furious look at Tom and grabbing the empty juice jug. *It took me half a fucking hour to squeeze those oranges!*

Ken was correct; Tom did feel better after a full breakfast, and now, with his nerves soothed, he listened to Ken.

"Be confident, Norm! With a speaking voice like yours, well, it could take you anywhere." Ken shook his head. "Fancy that Yank thinking he could call races better than us Aussies. Bloody boring, that's

186

what their calls are! At least we create drama and excitement, and every horse gets a mention. Just imagine if you owned a horse in America, and the race caller didn't even remark on how he was going in the race? How's an owner supposed to know if his horse even started? I tell you, Norm, I reckon they're scared. If the Yanks gave us Aussies ago, the public wouldn't be bothered listening to the Yanks' lackluster calls. Did you get any praise from anyone over there? I mean, from the public, after you'd called a race?"

" I did - and you're right. They loved my calls, few as they were. But Big Daddy kept a tight rein on where and when I was allowed to call a race, usually in the back blocks of the bayou." Tom laughed but remembered all too well how that had hurt.!

"Well, Norm, here you are again in the back blocks, only this time it's the desert!" Ken laughed, then sprang up from his chair when Freddie Sanderson's frame loomed into view. "Thanks for coming, Freddie. We could have come to your office." Ken shook Freddie's hand.

"No, I like to get out of the joint, and the coffee's good here." Freddie then proffered his hand to Tom, "You must be the 'velvet voice' Ken told me about, Norm, is it?"

"Yes, sir, Norm Hawkins."

"No sirs with me, Norm, just Freddie."

Tom immediately liked Freddie. *Laid back, honest, and straight to the point, Tom guessed.*

A good-humoured conversation took place for well over an hour before Freddie looked at his watch. "Oh shit, I gotta get going." He hesitated, studying Tom, then said, "Why don't you come with me, Norm? We can do a sound test, though I'm sure it'll be a waste of time. I like your voice - deep, cultured, and you don't talk too damn fast. I swear some of the announcers I've hired think they get paid by the word! A hundred miles an hour, they babble. Hate it!" Freddie smiled, shaking his head. "It's hard to find any radio stars way out here. Let's hope I've found one." Freddie shook Ken's hand. "Thanks, Ken. You coming with us, mate?"

"Wouldn't miss it for quids!"

CHAPTER 20

Edward stood facing Nelly and listened patiently to her stumbling explanation. When she'd finished, she looked up at him, her eyes shining with unshed tears.

"Nelly, please. Why on earth would you think I'd be jealous of you going to a ball with Doctor George? I'm sure he meant what he said. He and his wife are estranged, so he needs a glamorous woman to accompany him. He probably doesn't know many single women; I'd say he'd be a workaholic. Well, that's how it appears. Go with him, Nelly, with my blessing. Don't feel bad or guilty - enjoy yourself. You deserve it."

Nelly held Edward close.

"Thank you for being so understanding, Edward. I don't care if I go to the ball or not. It's just I wouldn't like to let George down, not after all he's done for us." She kissed Edward on the cheek then looked him in the eye. "And," Nelly added in her no-nonsense tone as she took hold of his lapels and shook him gently, "about your knee, Edward! I saw you limping so badly this morning. I *know* you're in terrible pain. You *must* take up the offer to have it operated on. Please, Edward. I hate seeing you in so much pain!"

Edward laughed. "You don't miss much, Nelly. All right, I'll do as I'm told and make an appointment soon, I promise."

*

On the evening of the ball, Edward beamed when Nelly appeared smiling in a twirl. She raised her eyebrows in a silent question. "You look out of this world," Edward said sincerely. There was a knock at the door, and he went along the passage and opened it. "George! Good evening! Nelly won't be a minute."

"Thanks for allowing Nelly to accompany me, Edward," he said, fiddling with a beautiful gardenia corsage.

"Not up to me, George. Nelly is her own boss. I hope you both have a lovely evening."

Nelly strolled down the hallway, noticing the appreciative glances of both men. "Hello, George. Oh, how beautiful! Thank you," she said as George presented the corsage. She turned and held it out to Edward. "Would you, please?" Edward smiled and expertly pinned the corsage to the shoulder strap of Nelly's gown.

"All right, Cinderella, your Pumpkin Coach awaits! Off you go, you two!" He watched as George opened the rear door of his chauffeur-driven Mercedes and helped Nelly inside. George walked around the other side and gave Edward a friendly wave, then he got in himself.

Before the car moved off, Edward went back inside and closed the front door very carefully and quietly.

*

Nelly felt lightheaded, not only from the crowd's energy in the stately ballroom, which encompassed them in a glittering fantasy world but also from the showering of compliments she'd received from George's many friends and colleagues to whom Nelly was introduced. They were so attentive, offering her champagne and canapes, that she suspected they knew something that she didn't. Both the distinguished medicos and their beautiful wives fired questions at her. Some, so personal they were to the point of almost being rude. So welcoming and curious were they? She thought George might have told them that she and he were 'an item.' It was the last thing she wanted them to feel. She pointedly referred to George as a 'family friend' to set them straight, but the men continued to give her appraising looks, and the women took in every minute detail of her outfit. Poor Nelly felt like an exotic specimen brought out on display for the pleasure and scrutiny of a bunch of butterfly collectors. *How am I going to get out of this? I don't feel right being here.* She bantered with George and pretended to enjoy the dancing, but her heart was not in it. *I wish Edward were here.* She found herself thinking. After a while, Nelly wanted to go home, and she needed to find an excuse for her subdued behaviour.

"I'm so sorry, George. I hate to spoil your evening, but I just don't seem to be able to shake my headache, and I think it's getting worse."

George, suitably sympathetic, plus a little intoxicated, called for his chauffeur to drive them home. The traffic was light at that time of night, so speed was encouraged, but not fast enough for Nelly, as once they were travelling in the privacy of the car, George's hands were everywhere. Nelly fended off his advances as politely as she could.

"Please, George, behave yourself," she repeated, with increasing desperation, but to no avail. In the rear-view mirror, she saw the chauffeur's gaze on them. *Help!* she mouthed silently as George attempted to execute a plan that was undoubtedly not on Nelly's agenda. The driver gave a brief nod then tapped the brakes sharply enough to end his passengers' embrace.

"Good lord, Henry! What the devil is going on?" George demanded.

"So sorry, sir. A dog ran out in front of the car." Only Nelly saw the driver's conspiratorial wink. Fortunately, the incident was enough to cool George's ardour, and the last five minutes of the drive, George conducted with decorum.

As they pulled up out the front, Nelly wondered why, at eleven o'clock, every light in her house was on.

"Let me escort you to the front door, Nelly." George had also noticed the lights.

"No, thank you, I'll be fine. I just need to take another Bex and go to bed. Thank you for a lovely evening, George." She leaned over, intending to give him a chaste kiss, but George had a different idea. Nelly placed her hands on his chest and forcefully pushed him away. "Thank you, *Doctor Forbes!*" Nelly snapped and made her escape from the car as quickly as her long gown and high heels would allow. She slammed the door and, without looking back, hurried up the path to the front door. *Whew! That was a lucky escape!* she thought ruefully. *Once bitten, twice shy.*

The front door opened as she fumbled for her keys.

"Edward, what are you doing here? You weren't -"

"Come inside, Nelly. I have sad news." Nelly followed him into the living room. "I think you should sit down."

"Oh, no! It's not Tom, is it?" Nelly sat on the couch, and Edward joined her, placing a comforting arm around her shoulders.

"No, it's not Tom - it's your parents. A fire started somehow, and their house has burnt down. Apparently, they were asleep and overcome with smoke, so the police said. They would have known nothing. I'm deeply sorry, Nelly."

She leaned back, her hands over her face, trying to remember if there were any good times she'd shared with her parents. Her father, yes, there were happy memories with him, but not her mother. *Poor Mum, what an unhappy, troubled soul she was. Oh, what a terrible way to die!* The last phone call Nelly had received from her mother had struck her as unusual. Yes, her mother had changed her ways for the better, but Nelly still knew instinctively something was troubling her. Nelly had tried to talk to her, sitting face to face over a pot of tea and then again by the phone. That was less than two weeks ago now, and all her mother could say was, "I know I'm not long for this earth, Nelly. But I strongly believe God will forgive me all my sins." Morose, to say the least, Nelly had thought. She knew it would have been a fruitless exercise to pursue the reason for her mother's state of mind but had hoped and prayed that she would let go of what was bothering her. *Nelly believed some rivers run too deep*, and she had no intention of giving in to those sad depths. Suddenly, another thought occurred. *Would Mum have burnt the house down intentionally?* She imagined her mother giving her husband and herself a sleeping drug, adding it to their hot chocolate perhaps, then quickly set the ground floor on fire before hurrying up the stairs. *Oh, that's too terrible to think about now. Let it go, Nelly.*

Edward interrupted her chaotic thoughts by handing her a Chivas Regal. "Here, Nelly. Sip this. Is there *anything* I can do or say?" he asked gently.

"No. Not now. Thank you, Edward. I will most probably need your help to track down my brothers, and that may prove difficult." She paused, deep in thought. "And making the funeral arrangements." Nelly looked up into Edward's kind eyes, her own brimming with tears. "You know I love you, Edward, but I need Tom to come home. Do you understand?"

"I've always understood, Nelly."

Grace, Johnno, Walter, and Emma crept into the lounge room from the kitchen.

"Oh, Mum, I'm so sorry," Grace said before she enfolded Nelly in her arms.

"I feel so sad and so very sorry for you, Mrs Nobel." Emma came forward and placed her hand on Nelly's shoulder. Her show of compassion caused Nelly's tears to fall anew. They were tears of hurt and anger, but most of all, regret. *Can I ever truly forgive my mother?*

*

191

As expected, it was not an easy task to locate Nelly's siblings. Nelly, under Edward's advice, had hired a private detective. He'd discovered the two brothers had travelled the entire continent before settling in Western Australia, where they were now partners in a mining operation. A rich deposit of iron ore had been found on a property the brothers had invested in, hoping to find what they'd suspected was a vast amount of the profitable mineral. Tony and Allen, the private detective observed, were wealthy and happily married. They agreed, after his explanations, to attend the funeral.

"For Nelly's sake," said Allen, the younger of the two.

Only family and close members of their parent's church group attended the funeral, a brief and rather unemotional affair. Her brothers later had agreed not to rush back to Western Australia.

"It will give us time to catch up, Nelly since we haven't seen each other for so many years." Said Tony, with a warm smile.

Nelly thought she probably would not have recognized either of them if she passed them in the street, but Allen was so like their mother, shorter and a bit stout, though he was still handsome with his thick dark hair, square chin, and deep blue eyes. Tony and Nelly were more like their father; tall and slim, with auburn hair and green eyes. *We could be twins*, Nelly had thought.

"And we have two well-oiled machines running our business - our wives. They're sisters," Tony continued.

The brothers laughed in unison. It was a welcome tonic for Nelly to see her big brothers again and a bonus to see them successful and happy.

"No children?" Nelly asked.

"Nup. We married too late for that, Sis."

Oh, what a lovely sound, 'Sis'! I remember them both calling me that when I was a little girl. It's sad to think of the time we missed being together.

After the funeral, the brothers spent time around Nelly's kitchen table, sharing a pot of tea and her special apple cake, sharing stories about how each of their lives had panned out. The disappearance of Tom was discussed in length, along with his dream of being a race caller. The brothers suggested various reasons why Tom may have gone *AWOL*. None of which Nelly found convincing. She accepted they were trying to help, but she felt no closer to an answer. Nelly needed to change the subject from Tom's disappearance to a less irritating topic. And to her surprise, she found something they had in common, which brought some excitement into the mix. The brothers loved horseracing.

"With our wives, we own five racehorses between us," Tony said with a wide grin.

"Oh, that is exciting." Nelly looked proudly at Grace, "Grace wants to be a race caller." There was a stunned silence. "Remiss of me not to tell you sooner," Nelly added. The silence continued.

"Well...ah...um...that's..." The words seemed stuck in Allen's throat. Tony glared at Allen, but Grace gave an accepting smile. She was used to this reaction to *a girl* calling races.

"That's fantastic, Grace, and I know you're tough," Tony said enthusiastically. "You've survived meningitis, and a lot haven't. So whatever hurdles you need to jump to be a race caller, I reckon you'll do it if anyone can. Good luck, Grace."

Allen gave an embarrassed cough. *One out of two ain't bad*, Grace thought.

"Thanks, Uncle Tony. Actually, I jumped a few hurdles the other day," Grace said airily. "Johnno's mate's in training for the next Olympic Games in London. He let me have a go at calling a training race, and I did pretty well." It was almost true; her voice was fine, but her motor skills were still a bit out of whack.

"And, of course, if you ever need a lawyer, Walter can help. He'll graduate just before he and Emma marry," Nelly said proudly, studying her brothers' looks of approval mixed with surprise.

What's the problem? Nelly wanted to say. *Don't you think a man with cerebral palsy can be a lawyer? There's nothing wrong with his brain!*

"Western Australia's a l...long way to travel, Mum. It'd be best if our uncles found a good l...lawyer in WA. Besides, I'm sure I'll be booked up for years!" Walter had noticed their surprised looks and chose to make light of it. The tension in the room evaporated as they all laughed.

The following day the brothers checked out of their hotel and came to bid Nelly farewell. The siblings said their goodbyes with a sincere promise to keep in touch.

"Oh, and if there's anything left to us in Mum and Dad's will, we don't want any of it and we certainly don't need it. We want to give it to you, Grace and Walter," Tony said, shaking Walter's hand and giving Grace a kiss and a hug.

Nelly thought again how dreadful their mother must have been for her sons to have disappeared and never contacted her – or Nelly. How sad, especially when their father also bore the heartbreak of his sons' leaving.

Her brothers had insisted on catching a taxi to the airport, and so she stood on the footpath and waved goodbye until the car turned the corner. Nelly sighed sadness at their leaving. But there was also a feeling of hope for a shared future, after all these years apart. Just as she stepped back inside, the phone rang. Nelly hurried to pick up the receiver.

"Long-distance, America calling. Will you accept the call?"

"Yes, of course." *Bloody hell! It's Lucy - again!* This time, Lucy was in tears; she called every few days, and Nelly was getting tired of it all.

"Hello, Lucy. No. There's no word. I'm sorry." Lucy cried even louder. "You must try and control yourself, Lucy, if only for Tyson's sake. He shouldn't see his mother crying all the time." Nelly tried hard not to sound critical.

"He's not with me—Tyson's with Daddy and Mommy. I can't handle him at the moment. I think I'm having a nervous breakdown! You always sound so calm, Nelly. How can you bear it? But then I suppose you've divorced Tom, so that makes all the difference, doesn't it?" Lucy sniffled wetly.

"It was not *my* choice to divorce Tom! I care very much about him, and he is also the father of *my* children, Lucy!" Nelly struggled to keep her temper in check.

"Yes, I know that. But you don't *love* Tom anymore, do you?"

Nelly took a deep breath, then exhaled slowly. "I love Tom with all my heart, and I always will. But you can't *make* someone love you back if they don't. So, when Tom comes to his senses, he'll come home to you, Lucy." Nelly heard a man's voice in the background. "Is your father there?"

Surprisingly, Lucy stopped snivelling and gave a self-conscious laugh. "Oh, no, no. It's just…just a friend - an old friend. He dropped in to say hello. I'd better go Nelly. I'll phone you again soon."

Lucy was gone, and Nelly looked down at her receiver as if she might see Lucy's 'old friend.' *Well,* Nelly thought, *that was interesting.*

194

No sooner did Nelly hang up the telephone when it rang again. "Hello? Oh, hello, Errol."

"I'm sorry for not attending your parents' funeral, Nelly. I was stuck in court. Please accept my apology and my sincere sympathy." Errol coughed a little. "Now, I do have some good news. Hopefully, it will cheer you up a little. I have spoken with the Committee of the Healesville Race Club, where I am still President. They have agreed unanimously to pay Grace a wage to call the last two races at every meeting held there for the next season." Errol waited for Nelly's response. "Nelly? Can you hear me?"

"Yes, I'm sorry, Errol. I'm a bit stressed at the moment. So much has happened." Nelly sniffed back tears. "I cannot thank you enough for all you have done for us, Grace and Walter in particular. I would never have believed how wonderful people could be - "

"Now, now, you don't have to thank me," Errol interrupted her.

Oh, Errol. I do. I don't think you know about my background or my childhood," Nelly took the deep breath she needed to continue. "Don't worry, I won't give my life story, but I will tell you, it was a strange journey, bought up by a mother who never saw the good in anyone, not even herself. I shouldn't speak ill of the dead, but all I can say is that it's people like you, Errol, who have shown me how to live my life. I will be eternally grateful for your friendship, your help, and especially your respect for Walter."

"It is my pleasure to help you, Nelly," Errol told her quietly. "As far as Walter is concerned. I admire him for everything he stands for - and I'm looking forward to the wedding. Emma's fortunate to have Grace and Cookie helping her organize everything, and from what I've heard, it's going to be an extravaganza! All I have to do is foot the bill!" Errol laughed.

"We all need brightness in our lives, particularly at the moment, and to tell you the truth, Errol, I don't know how I've coped. " Nelly thought about it. "Actually, yes, I do know. Wonderful friends surround me. Thank you again, Errol, for everything."

*

It was six months to the day since Grace had fallen ill, so to hear what Nelly had to say to her when she came home from her exercise routine had Grace's heart pumping harder than if she'd done a five-mile jog – which she had.

195

"Seriously, Mum? You're not joking, are you? I will be *paid* for doing what I *love*?" Grace's eyes were wide in disbelief.

"Why would I joke about such a thing, Grace? Anyway, I know you've been studying all the fields, with help from Walter. And Edward told me you're up to your old tricks, calling races from *the wrong side of the fence*, as it were." Nelly laughed; it felt good to laugh.

"I'll never give up, Nelly, ever! At least, not unless I lose my voice. I must ring Mr Blake and thank him. And Cyril, too. He would have had something to do with this." Grace threw her arms around Nelly and hugged her hard. "Oh boy, I just can't wait! And fancy being paid for calling races? I just can't believe it!"

CHAPTER 21

"Good morning, Alice! Wakey, wakey! This is Norm Hawkins coming to you live from 8AL! I'm your new morning host. Please feel free to phone me with your choice of songs or simply trust me to play some great tunes that will start your day on a good note. And if you have anything you want to talk about, the line is now open. But first, here's Bing Crosby with *When the Saints Come Marching In!* Hit it, Bing!"

Tom prayed his smooth, distinctive radio announcing style would last until his first paycheque. He also hoped to lend a compassionate ear when listeners called with their problems. *I've got enough bloody difficulties of my own;* Tom had mused when Freddie gave him the general idea of how the morning show ran.

Tom shouldn't have worried as the word soon spread.

"That new bloke, Norm Hawkins on early morning 8AL Breakfast Radio - have you heard him? He's fantastic!" It was the general consensus.

Freddie had found his 'Radio Star' and felt excited when hearing people talk about Norm Hawkins and his 'velvet voice.' The week after Norm had made his mark, while seated in his favourite café Ken overheard a couple of women discussing the new presenter.

"You should hear him, Jenny. Norm sounds like a dreamboat. And he gives all the right answers. The only trouble is it's hard to get to talk to him because the line's jammed with calls - all morning!" one said.

Her friend replied, " I know. I tune in every morning. I just love his show!"

Freddie left a generous tip and hurried back to the station.

"Norm, you're killing it, mate! The ratings are going through the roof, especially with the sheilas! I should pay you more money. And I will when we have a few more sponsors. The government doesn't fund the lot you know. If they did, we'd only have news bulletins and bloody cattle sales results!"

Freddie whacked Tom on the back, so hard his headphones near fell off.

"I'm glad to be of service, Freddie," Tom sputtered. "What I'd rather do though, is call races. Remember when Ken was here? You said my call was perfect. So how about you give me a go?"

"Yeah, yeah, I know, Norm. But you may have painted yourself into a corner, mate. I mean, the women love you, your voice does things to 'em, I've heard them say it. Fare dinkum, I have. Even the blokes like you. So, let's talk money. I'd rather you stay on morning breakfast, and maybe I'll let you give a race call every so often. I reckon the girls would swoon to the races just to hear you call. What do you reckon, Norm?"

"I reckon I'll give you another month, Freddie. And if you won't give me the racing gig - permanently - then I'm out of here. And remember, I could easily do Breakfast Radio *and* call the races!"

"Oh shit, you'd want me to sack old Charlie? He's a bloody legend! I couldn't get rid of old Charlie."

"Just move him over, let me be his offsider. Charlie does one call and I do the next. Anyway, how old is he?"

Freddie scratched his head. "Jeez, I don't know; he's been around since I wore knee pants."

"Exactly! Everyone has to retire one day, Freddie."

*

A month passed, and within that time, Tom's conscience had finally gotten the better of him. One afternoon, he sent a two-word telegram to Nelly - 'I'm alive.' The telegram would be received in Melbourne later that day but delivered the following morning. However, the relief at ultimately letting his family know he was safe gave Tom an excuse to plan to go out for a drink later that night. *This evening, I'll walk to the nearest pub and drink to the health of my two families. What a bloody lie! If I really cared I'd be home. But where is home?*

*

Nelly heard the doorbell ring and opened the front door to the delivery boy. "Telegram for you, missus."

Nelly felt the blood drain from her face; telegrams were always bad news. With shaking hands, she opened it and scanned its contents. She clutched the flimsy piece of paper to her heart. *Lucy - I must phone her.*

Lucy was not satisfied with knowing her husband was alive and fired many questions at Nelly, who tried hard to maintain her composure.

"Lucy! Listen to me, will you? I don't know any more than you do right now. If you want to find out more, I suggest you get over here and start searching the entire country yourself! I'm too busy with my own family, especially at the moment." *Jesus Christ, deliver me from this bloody woman! She knows what I've been through.*

Nelly took a deep breath and continued in a more conciliatory tone. "Look, Lucy - if I were you, I'd allow Tom to find himself. He's obviously in a bad place and needs to work out his problems. And, as I've said before, eventually, he'll come home to you. It's up to you to decide if you still want him, Lucy." Nelly didn't wait for an answer. She hung up the phone, slamming the receiver into its cradle with an angry grunt.

*

Tom had rented a small cottage on the outskirts of town and kept to himself. He liked it that way; the less people knew about him, the safer his disguise. So far, Ken Gollan had kept Tom's secret. Tom knew because hardly a day passed that Ken wouldn't phone to see how 'Norm' was going, even though he was well aware of the popularity of Tom's morning show. Freddie sang his praises to Ken regularly. Since his arrival in Alice, Tom had avoided socializing, but he definitely would walk to the nearest pub tonight and have a beer.

It took only a few words to the bartender for people to recognize 'the velvet voice,' and soon he was surrounded by fans and well-wishers.

"Thanks. Thank you. I'm pleased you all enjoy my morning show. But I'd rather be calling the races. What do you lot reckon?"

Voices joined, creating a friendly onslaught.

"You could call anything, mate!" A slap on the back.

"Bout time old Charlie retired. Most times he calls the wrong bloody winner!"

"Jeez, I don't reckon Y'should, mate. Me wife would always be at the races!" General laughter.

The accolades continued. Tom had his answer and he would confidently take this knowledge to Freddie in the morning.

*

"All right – all right," said Freddie, smiling, hands in the air to signal his surrender. He chuckled. "You won't believe it, Norm, but old Charlie confided in me last night. Said he was ready to retire whenever I could find a replacement. The Sooner, the better, he said. His wife isn't too well, and she needs his care. And he knows he makes too many mistakes these days. So, Norm, it's all yours!"

After his debut as official race caller, Tom read the newspaper headline announcing, 'Norm Hawkins, Radio Commentator - An Overnight Success!' *What a lot of rot! If they only knew how long I've dreamt, wished, and worked for this chance. Still, who cares? It's happened, and I'm on my way!*

Not letting the public know about his friendship with Tom, Ken Gollan spoke on air after his Perth Racing Broadcast had tuned in to an Alice Springs race. Afterward, he asked his audience, "Where did that magic voice come from? I'm jealous! Rooky Race Caller Norm Hawkins just called that huge field like he was having a picnic in the park! I'm telling you, listeners - I'd better watch my back!"

And Ken meant it.

*

The brothers, Tony and Allen, sat sweating in their Perth office. A fan blowing hot air did nothing but disturb the papers strewn across the large desk. Allen finally scooped those remaining and piled them on the floor out of the way. There was more important business at stake.

"Why don't we sell old Shamrock to Harry in Alice?" asked Allen. "There's nothing wrong with him except a bit of arthritis, and the heat up there would do him a world of good. He'd win on three legs there, and old Harry needs a change of luck – he's helped us out plenty of times in the past. Maybe it'll do the trick, and Shamrock will find his old form? He's hard-pressed to win a race around here."

Tony scratched his head, an old habit that indicated he was giving the proposition some serious thought.

"Maybe you're right, Allen. I wouldn't mind a trip back to Alice. Shame we missed the carnival back in May. Next year we should take a team."

"Yep, for sure, mate. Meantime let's do it, Tony. We'll take Shamrock ourselves. I wouldn't mind catching up with the old crew. And we could look at a few places for sale on the way."

"Agreed! I figure we'll have plenty of time before Walter's wedding. Hey, how excited are Suzie and Kate? They've never been to Melbourne before. S 'pose we'd better give them a free hand with the checkbook that'll keep them happy. They can buy new outfits for the wedding while we're away."

*

The vast MacDonnell Ranges, ragged and majestic, was a magnificent backdrop to the racecourse. This magical land had instilled in Tony and Allen a feeling of being smack bang in the heart of Australia. The brothers had lived there many years ago and had found it difficult to leave when the perfect property closer to Perth had been specked for them by an old mining mate. At the time, the brothers had accumulated a hefty amount of capital, saved explicitly for the reason to mine iron ore on their own land. And it had paid off in spades.

After handing the horse over to Harry, the new owner-trainer, the brothers had taken only a few steps into the Turf Clubhouse before being inundated by old cronies and well-wishers. Why worry? It was a great day to catch up and enjoy reminiscing, standing under a sky so uniquely Australian. Yes, nowhere else on earth was the sky so vividly blue. It provided a stunning contrast to the red earth and sage green scrubby bushes, adding an ideal mix of shades to capture in watercolours, made famous by contemporary Aboriginal artist Albert Namatjira. His prints were becoming increasingly popular and adorned many a suburban wall across the country. Tony was a massive fan of Indigenous art, especially the dot paintings depicting dream time stories. He promised himself to buy several more before he returned to Perth and was deep in discussion about this with Ray, an old friend whose family members produced some beautiful artworks,

Allen arrived on the scene and gave Tony a nod. "Sorry to interrupt, Ray. We need to go. Shamrock's in the first," he said, steering Tony towards the betting ring.

"Got a chance, Tony?" Ray asked. "Worth laying a bob or two each way?"

'You'd better ask old Harry; he owns him now. But between you and me, he's each way all day." After landing a customary farewell slap on the back, Tony and Allen hurried over to the gaggle of bookies, who shuddered upon seeing the brothers make their approach.

Shamrock's confidence rose as he quickly passed weaker rivals in the home straight, running on the dense sandy loam track. Consequently, he won by two lengths, much to the bookmakers' dismay. However, feeling a bit sorry for the local bookies, the brothers had only bet a percentage of what they'd usually layout in Perth.

"Did you listen to that caller, Tony?" Allen asked.

"Yeh, he's bloody good, whoever he is. Wonder where old Charlie is?"

Tony spotted Freddie standing in the payout line at one of the bookies. Tony tapped him on the shoulder, and Freddie spun around.

"Oh, congratulations, Tony! I thought Shamrock would win, seeing he's in much weaker company. The bookies were mad offering even money; he should have been odds-on."

"Thanks, Freddie. Glad you clued in. But we sold him to Harry before the race. Oh, and by the way - who was the bloke that called the race?"

"Damn good isn't he? Well, let me tell you. Norm Hawkins, that's his name. I call him our new 'boom voice.' He does breakfast radio as well. Old Charlie retired, so Norm got his job. It'll be hard to keep him here. You obviously didn't hear about Ken Gollan giving Norm a wrap on Perth radio? Said he had to watch his back, and I reckon Ken could be right. Norm never makes a mistake; he has a voice you could listen to all day long, and he comes up with some great quips to boot. I'd hate to lose him, but I reckon I will when his contract's up."

Tony laughed. "Sounds like you're in love with the guy, Freddie."

"Just about." Freddie gave a hearty laugh. "Our ratings have gone through the roof, but I can't take all the credit. Actually, Ken introduced Norm to me. When Ken had some time off a while ago, he stayed at a bed and breakfast in Port Hedland and met Norm. They got talking, and Ken drove him here to meet me. Good bloke, Ken. Loves the ladies, though, and I reckon he leaves a few broken hearts behind wherever he goes."

"I know he does," said Tony with a wry grin. "Katie, my wife, was one of Ken's conquests, but she's my diamond now. I don't know what I'd do without her." Tony looked squarely at Freddie. "I'd like to meet this Norm Hawkins, Freddie. Where did he come from, and what's his story? Any ideas?"

"I don't ask personal questions, Tony, but I think Ken may have drawn a bit of information out of Norm. Ken's good at that. All I know is, Norm keeps to himself. He's a real loner."

Tony didn't know why, but he had a gut feeling that this mystery man had a significant connection with his life.

"Would you mind introducing us after the races, Freddie?"

"Of course not. Hey, wait a minute! You're not going to poach Norm, are you?"

"No, I'm not. I just think I may know a bit more about this 'mystery man,' Norm Hawkins."

CHAPTER 22

The phone rang, and Nelly cursed. , Reluctantly, she picked up the receiver, "Hello."

"It's Tony. How are you, Nelly?"

"Oh, hello, Tony. I'm battling along, thank you."

"I think you'd better take a seat, Nelly." She immediately dropped heavily into the armchair - not her usual elegant style. "Tom is in Alice Springs, Sis, and he's calling races there."

Nelly gave an audible gasp as a whirlwind of emotions raced through her. Firstly, it was relief Tom had been found, then Nelly smiled, thinking how Tom had always wanted to be a race caller. Then, sadness and regret, remembering the old Nelly who'd been so critical. *You need a steady job, Tom, and we need money to live on!* Finally, she felt joy and a sense of pride. *So, you're finally living your dream - good on you, Tom.*

"How on earth did you find that out, Tony?"

"Well," Tony began, "it's a bit of a long story…" and he proceeded to relate the tale to Nelly, who laughed in all the right places.

"I can't thank you enough, Tony," Nelly said. " And I can't wait to tell Grace and Walter. We'll talk again soon." Nelly sat cradling the receiver for several minutes after her brother had hung up. *Well, this is going to be interesting.*

Later that evening, Nelly summoned everyone to sit around the kitchen table, giving them the news. The relief of Tom being found was palpable – but so was the anger and resentment, particularly from Grace and Walter. They, not unreasonably, harboured some ill-feeling toward their father for abandoning the family for a second time. Edward remained diplomatically silent.

"So, that's what Tony told me earlier today." Nelly looked around the table, determined not to let her own emotions get out of control. "I know this has been a difficult situation for us all, but the best thing we can do is let things unfold." She saw Walter and Grace exchange speculative looks. "Right – now how about a cup of tea, everybody?"

And with that, the wheels of the Nobel household resumed their turning.

*

Emma seemed to be in a constant battle with time. The responsibility of the wedding had her, Grace, Cookie, and sometimes Nelly, in a dither. Wisely, and with Edward's encouragement, to focus on his studies. Walter left all the arrangements up to the women in his life. Now, another problem presented itself; her wedding had to be postponed due to her father's involvement in a high-profile criminal case. Errol was defending the accused against what everyone else assumed was a clear-cut conviction for murder.

However, Errol always looked beyond the obvious and felt strongly that his client was innocent. He could not let this case go. It was a man's life he was fighting for, and if his daughter must wait another month to take her wedding vows, so be it. Hopefully, both his client *and* his daughter would live happily ever after.

He had explained the situation to Emma and given her his sincere apologies, bracing himself for the argument he felt was sure to ensue. Emma had simply smiled and confessed that she was relieved at having more time to make everything perfect. Errol promised come hell or high water. Nothing would prevent the wedding from taking place on the new date – December 20th.

*

Edward had been suffering badly with his knee, and he had not been able to take his early morning run for several months. He'd tried walking the miles, but it also hurt. He was almost living on painkillers, and realising the damaging effects of long-term use, decided to make an appointment and see the surgeon Dr. Forbes had recommended.

If Edward told the truth, he was reluctant to go under the knife. He knew it wasn't major surgery, and he'd probably suffered needlessly. Still, after his wife, Sylvia, had gone in for a simple procedure and had died of complications, he had an irrational fear of any operation. Now it was time to overcome his phobia.

"I've decided to have the knee operation, Nelly. I saw the orthopedic surgeon this morning." He sighed as if accepting a death sentence. "I can't stand the pain any longer, and if I go in next Monday, Doctor Evans said it's a pretty straightforward procedure, and he could

205

do me straight away. I'll only have to stay in hospital for a few days. He said I was lucky to get him as he's taking a holiday the following week. So, there you have it, Nelly – finally!"

"Good for you, Edward. I'm sure you won't regret it. And now the wedding is not until late December you should be walking pain-free, alongside Walter. I'm so happy you've decided to do this." Nelly placed a soft, lingering kiss upon his cheek then hugged him with all the relief and love she felt. She gazed into his blue eyes and saw the gentleness of his soul reflected there. "I'll be able to look after you. I can take a break from work – they owe me at least four weeks' holiday. No buts! I'll arrange for it to start the week after next. It will work out perfectly!"

"You will? Ah, Nelly. What did I do to deserve you?" He gave her a grateful hug.

Nelly wasn't being entirely altruistic. She had felt emotionally drained and run down with everything that had been going on in her life. With her son about to be married, feeling flat was the last thing Nelly needed. Spending a few weeks looking after Edward meant she could return some love and care to the man who had saved her and her children from what may have been a disastrous situation. *I'll have time to rest, put my feet up and reread a few romance novels.* She smiled at the thought.

"It must have been a sign Edward, that *you* needed *me* for a change. So, I'll be here - with bells on!" She laughed and gave him a saucy wink. "And in a nurse's uniform."

Edward held Nelly close. "Thank you, Nelly," he whispered.

The thought of Tom having been found and potentially hovering around on the sidelines caused Edward to feel pangs of jealousy, something he had never thought he would where Tom was concerned. But now, there was a chance Edward could lose the family he'd adopted, and it would break his heart to take a back seat once again.

*

It took Grace a few days to get over her instinctive anger at her father's discovery in Alice after having done another runner, but now, just to think about her dad calling races in Alice Springs, then to be able to hear his call over the radio filled Grace with pride. No matter what Tom had done prior, her admiration and her love for him were ultimately unshakable.

Grace was in her element, having established herself as the official caller of the last two races at Healesville. 'The proof is in the pudding,' as they say, and crowds came flocking to the Healesville

Racecourse closer to the end of the day, just to hear Grace Nobel bring to life all the colour and drama of those two races. One question was on the lips of many racing enthusiasts.

Why doesn't Grace Nobel call all the races? She's just as good, if not better than those blokes.

The more lateral thinking members asked the metropolitan, provincial, and country racing committees the same question. The general public's approval and admiration for Grace's talent, tenacity, and determination to do a job that was only deemed suitable for men were unprecedented. How ridiculous not to have female race callers! No physical strength was needed to call races, merely a trained eye, a sharp intelligence, a quick wit, and, of course, an articulate and mellifluous voice.

No doubt there would always be disgruntled critics. Edward's advice, to Grace, was simply to ignore them, and she took his advice.

The Spring Racing Carnival for 1948 had begun, and Ken Howard listened to Grace's calls at Healesville, noting how much she kept improving. It prompted him to write a letter of congratulations, which Grace received and kept safe along with Ken's get-well cards. He was her idol.

However, Grace knew Joe Brown would be calling the 1948 Melbourne Cup from the Flemington broadcast box - not Ken. Would she be bold enough to ask Joe if she might join him and see another top race caller at work firsthand? Maybe not.

To her surprise, Ken had already intervened and asked the favour of Joe. Grace received the telephone call.

"Mr Brown, I cannot believe it! Is it really you?" Grace was breathless.

Joe laughed. "Yes, Miss Nobel, it's me, Joe Brown. And a good friend to both of us, Ken Howard, has asked if I might allow you to sit in my broadcast box at Flemington on Cup Day -"

Grace thought she was going to scream.

"- and when Ken told me about you, Grace, I took time to listen to your call at Healesville. You, young lady, call like a professional *and* with a great deal of theatre. I would be delighted if you would join me on Cup Day."

Grace opened her mouth, but nothing came out. Joe waited, sensing her shock.

Finally, Grace found her words. "I'm finding this all too hard to believe, Mr Brown. I am *so* grateful, and *of course*, I will be there. Thank you *very* much."

*

Johnno's smile remained fixed while he listened to Grace, who told him her story over the telephone, almost babbling with excitement. He struggled to interject his voice with a suitable level of enthusiasm.

"You're on your way, Grace. I knew the universe would deliver. I couldn't be happier for you!" He drew a deep, melancholy breath and paused. "I love you, and I miss you, Grace," Johnno added softly.

Grace's heart plummeted. Johnno had been her rock through her physical and mental healing. She knew what she was about to ask could be a game-changer; could she risk everything they'd built between them.

"Johnno?"

"Yes, Grace?"

"I love you, too. But…but what if I become a race caller. And all my time, well, most of it, is taken up with my job? You know how hard I study and practice. I may not have time to care for a family." Grace took a deep breath, holding her courage, knowing Johnno's answer before she asked. "Do you want children?" She waited, listening to the silence on the line. "Johnno?"

"Yes, I'm here, Grace, and I'm thinking. I have to be honest; I would love to have a family with you, but we don't have to rush into making a decision either way. What say we let things ride until you're twenty-five? I'll be twenty-nine - it's not too old for either of us. Then we can re-evaluate our situation. What do you think?"

Grace released the breath she hadn't been aware she was holding. "I think you're right, Johnno. That's if you're *sure* you don't mind waiting?"

"Of course, I'm sure, Grace, and by then, I should have received another promotion. So, apart from not seeing you and holding you in my arms whenever I want, I'm happy. All I can say is, *Go get 'em Gracie!*"

*

One hundred and one thousand racegoers gathered at Flemington Racecourse on Tuesday 2nd. November 1948. While bathed in sunshine, the crowd watched disappointedly as one favourite after the other got beaten on what was described as a heavy track. Nevertheless, they remained hopeful that the Cup favourite, Howe, would hold form in the soggy going.

Being an avid student of form and attentive to her instincts, Grace had chosen *Rimfire*, a rank outsider, to run well. For some reason, she felt he was the one to watch in the Cup, or better still, as a long shot to have a bob or two on him each way.

The previous night *Rimfire's* jockey W.A. Smith had pulled out to ride another horse, fearing that *Rimfire* would break down over the distance. The ride was picked up by little-known apprentice Ray Neville, 'the boy from Birchip,' the scribes called him. Little was written about either horse or rider, other than the new kid had ridden only one winner beforehand, and the chestnut horse was notoriously unsound.

Sitting alongside Joe Brown in the tiny broadcast box, watching the races unfold and listening to his impeccable calls, Grace felt it all surreal. Though she dared to dream that one day it would be *her* calling the Melbourne Cup.

"*Silence is golden*," Joe had cautioned Grace. "I cannot afford for *anyone* to hear you in the broadcast box. Just sit, listen and learn, and maybe one day it will be *you* calling the Cup." Grace nodded obediently, too overawed to speak at all, but still hearing the words in her head: *Yes, it will be!*

*

Although happy for Grace, Walter was a tad jealous of her bird's eye view from the commentator's box, even though he was awarded a non-spectator spot for being a well-known tipster - almost a sports journalist, he claimed - and no one argued.

The night before the Cup, Walter had sat opposite Grace at the kitchen table, where they had studied the race fields. He had laughed when Grace claimed, "*Rimfire* has a slim chance, I reckon."

"Grace! The horse is u...unsound – he'll be lucky to finish, let alone win! And this new k...kid they've put on him, he'll probably get *lost* out there!"

"Well, you've *lost* your instinct, Walter! My advice is to *find* it! Remember, horses survive on instinct. Besides, your latest tips show you've also *lost* a bit of insight; you're relying too much on facts and figures, Walter."

Walter, far too intelligent to completely dismiss Grace's observation, then changed his tips for the Cup. He placed the favourite - *Howe*, to win, *Black Marne*, second, and *Rimfire*, third.

The crowd soaked up the magnificent weather on Cup Day, banishing their thoughts of the previous few days of rain and gloom in Melbourne. Ladies adorned in lightweight spring dresses and flower-bedecked hats paraded their fashionable ensembles around the Members' Enclosure in what was becoming *the thing to do* when attending The Grand Frontier of Fashion – The Spring Racing Carnival.

The Cup was due to start in twenty minutes, and the Betting Ring was inundated by eager punters frantically waving pound notes about, placing their final wagers on what they hoped would be the winner of the famous race. The bookmakers were the real winners, happily taking the punters' cash and handing back a dream scratched on a slip of paper.

Although the standout favourite remained *Howe* at 7/4, and despite having a few fans, Ray Neville, who wasn't even told he had the ride until the morning of the race, and Rimfire, with legs as dodgy as his form, remained at 80/1. The few quid the horse's connections might have laid out didn't have any effect on the odds.

The Cup horses were entering the starting gates, and Grace forgot what Tom had said about needing a panoramic view. She wiped her binoculars and focussed. The barriers flew open, and Grace watched *Rimfire* gallop past the post for the first time. He was travelling near last, in nineteenth place. He held his position all the way around before moving to seventh place on the final home turn. As the front runners began to tire, she saw *Rimfire's* young rider urge the chestnut horse forward, and they charged to the front of the field after *Howe*, the crowd favourite had faltered at the three-furlong mark. Grace held her breath as *Rimfire* galloped ahead, alone until challenged by *Black Marne*. Jack Thompson, a top Jockey from Sydney, gave his everything to catch *Rimfire*, this saw the two horses fight out the finish, and they hit the line together. Grace felt her blood pounding and was sure her long shot had pipped *Black Marne* at the post.

As if from a great distance, she heard Joe's voice. "Well, ladies and gentlemen, it's too close to call. What a race! What a finish! The judges have called for the winning photograph. It's the first time this has happened, ladies and gents. Amazing! No more relying on the naked eye! Stand by for the first-ever photo result."

Grace was relieved when the newly installed photo finish camera showed *Rimfire* had won by a nostril, beating *Black Marne*. A distant third went to *Saxony*. The crowd wasn't happy, and we assume Jack Thompson felt the same. Grace could hear the crowd booing as the results were announced.

With the race over and all announcements completed, Joe switched his microphone off and turned to Grace. "Why the tears Grace, I thought you had two bob each way on *Rimfire*?"

Grace had turned her binoculars on *Howe* as the injured horse limped back down the straight. It was the one part of horse racing she hated.

"I hate to see a horse injured." Grace wiped her eyes a little self-consciously. "I hope *Howe* will be okay."

"You are a sweet girl. Though I'm the same, I loathe seeing these magnificent animals injured in any way. Sadly, as they say, *that's racing*." Joe patted Grace on the shoulder, his warm smile showing her he cared, too.

"Thank you, Mr Brown. I appreciate you letting me sit with you. I've learned so much today and hope one day it will come to good use."

"I'm sure it will, Grace, that's if we can change the majority vote against women calling races. I mean, it's not as if you want to be head of the V.R.C., for heaven's sake! I'll keep an ear out for you, and if I can help in any way, I'll be there for you, Grace. Now go and collect your winnings! By the way, how much did you wager?"

"I had a pound saved from helping Mum with the housework. I haven't got a proper job yet, because of my illness," Grace added, a little coyly, "I put it all on *Rimfire* at eighty to one."

"My goodness, Grace! Congratulations! Now, don't spend it all at once." Joe wagged his finger with mock severity.

Grace grinned. "No, I won't. But I'll be buying Walter and Emma a decent wedding present."

"Good on you, Grace, and give Walter by best wishes. He does a damn good job tipping winners. Pity about *Howe* – a lot of punters would have done their dough, although Walter did tip *Rimfire* to run third, so he'll be popular with those who backed him for a place." Joe gave Grace a conspiratorial look. "I reckon you might have had something to do with that."

With a cheeky grin, Grace nodded then left to enjoy her win with Emma and Walter.

Nelly had happily stayed home to look after Edward, whose

operation had been successful. They'd followed Grace's advice and had a small wager on *Rimfire*, then listened nervously until he was announced the winner.

"Thank Heaven for the new photo finish, Nelly," Edward remarked, "otherwise, we wouldn't be celebrating. I can't remember ever backing an 80 to 1 winner before! A clever girl, your Gracie!"

"Yes, you're absolutely right, Edward. This calls for a celebration. I had a feeling we'd be in the money, so I put a bottle of champagne on ice."

"I agree, let's celebrate!" said Edward, feeling deliriously happy, not only about the outcome of the race but surviving his knee operation.

The phone rang just as Nelly rose from her armchair. Happy with her world, she picked up the receiver. And said cheerily, "Hello, Nelly speaking."

Edward noticed the colour leave Nelly's face, and he attempted to stand, thinking something was wrong.

"Tom. Where are you?" Nelly said flatly.

Edward made an effort to get himself up, using his crutches. He made his way toward the kitchen and took his time in the hallway to gaze fondly at the family photos. He smiled, seeing those happy faces. Underneath the smile, a feeling of sadness and loss overcame him.

Tom was on the phone. *He'll come home, and everything will change.* Edward thought. Then suddenly, a pain gripped his chest, so crippling he crashed to the floor. The sound caused Nelly to drop the phone and run.

"Edward! Edward, what's wrong? Please, Edward, answer me!"

Meanwhile, at the end of the phone line, Tom strained to hear what was going on. He could just make out Nelly's panicked voice calling Edward's name. *Oh shit, I'd better get there quick.*

Ambulance sirens cut through the silence of the quiet neighbourhood. Most residents were either attending the races or were inside listening to the broadcast.

Edward's body convulsed again and again under the Ambulance Officer's attempts to shock Edward's heart back to life. Mouth-to-mouth resuscitation was simultaneously applied. Nelly had lost count of how many times the Officers had worked on Edward. And how much time had passed. Eventually, they rested and exchanged looks of hopelessness.

"Please, I beg you! Please keep trying! Please try!" Nelly sobbed, praying as she'd never prayed before.

The two men continued their attempts for another ten minutes before eventually giving up. The younger man put his arms around Nelly, who wept inconsolably.

The Ambulance Officers placed Edward's corpse on a stretcher and covered him with a sheet. Nelly watched miserably as her best friend departed for the final time.

Later, she was given a cup of tea by a kind young policewoman, Sarah, who'd been called to the scene by the ambulance crew.

"There you are, Mrs Nobel." Sarah placed the cup of tea on Nelly's side table. "Now, is there anyone you would like me to call?

"No, not at the moment. Thank you. My children will be home soon, and they will know what to do." A sad smile crossed her lips; she was sure she could hear Edward warning her not to refer to Grace and Walter as *children*.

The passage of time between Edward's death and Grace, Emma and Walter arriving home, was like a dark abyss for Nelly. The three young people burst through the front door, sharing smiles and laughter. So happy were they? They hadn't noticed the police car parked outside. Their joy dissolved upon seeing Nelly sitting slumped in her armchair, consoled by a policewoman.

Nelly peered through swollen eyes, her voice blank.

"It's Edward. He...he had a heart attack." Nelly sobbed into Sarah's shoulder.

"But he'll be okay, won't he, Mum? Which hospital have they taken him to?" Grace rushed to her mother's side.

Sarah stood and moved away, saying gently, "I'm sorry, Grace, Edward died from a massive heart attack. He couldn't be revived, and they –"

"NO!" Grace screamed, "NO! He can't die, not Edward. We need him. We love him. NO, NO, NO!"

Nelly got up slowly and took Grace into her arms. *Once again, I'll have to find strength, but how?* Nelly looked to the ceiling, "Please God, help me," she whispered.

*

Tom had paced from one end of their street to the other. Their modest Californian Bungalow looked precisely the same as he remembered it, but Tom was not the same. Not after spending five years in an intolerably hot desert, firing weapons with the sole aim of killing other human beings. He'd had to face his daemons. But then he had run from everything and everyone he loved. His memories set his thoughts spinning like a top. Abruptly, he remembered the words Edward had once said to him: *Follow your heart, Tom, or you will never be happy.* His thoughts then became calm, and he felt like a summer breeze had suddenly blown his troubles away. Tom realised his heart belonged *here* - in this street, in this home. *Here* -with Walter, Grace, and Nelly. No doubt a piece of him also belonged in America, but tonight his Australian family needed him, and he needed them.

As Tom approached the front door in darkness, the lights inside unexpectedly switched on. Was it an omen? He knocked on the door tentatively, and within seconds Grace opened it. Her expression of sadness and despair hit Tom like a hammer to his heart. Grace held out her arms, and Tom fell into them.

CHAPTER 23

Tom had not left Nelly's side since arriving home. He'd supported her in organizing the funeral, and his respect for and adoration of Nelly was plain for all to see. She was certainly not the woman he'd left back in 1941, nor was he the same man. Grace would always be the same - determined, funny, and talented. And Walter? Well, Tom was so full of pride for his son he could burst. Never would he have envisaged Walter gaining his law degree, let alone becoming a racing tipster. And to see him engaged to such a beautiful, caring young woman gave Tom the most significant gift he could wish for.

Lucy had been phoning Tom every day with the same question. *When are you coming home, Tom?*

He had given her a litany of excuses. *I have to be here to attend the funeral of my best friend, Edward. I couldn't miss my son's wedding in late December. I've had an incredible job offer as a race caller in Western Australia that I really can't turn down.* But he could only keep delaying the inevitable for so long. Yes, Tom had some serious decisions to make and serious questions to ask. The most important was would Lucy agree to come and live in Australia? Tom resolved to put the question to Lucy when she would phone the following day, as promised. But today, giving Edward the best send-off possible was Tom's priority.

The mourners attending Edward's funeral tallied into the hundreds, spilling out the church and onto the street. The service was simple and dignified, and Walter delivered a heartfelt eulogy with nary a stutter. The wake held at the Caulfield Race Club was a sombre affair, though frequent laughter peppered the muted conversations. Edward was being remembered both as a fine lawyer and a thoroughly good man. Who had retained his sense of humour and compassion until the very end.

Errol Blake approached Tom and shook his hand. "Good to see you home, Tom, and please accept my sincere condolences. "

215

Tom accepted Errol's firm handshake. " Thanks so much, Errol. Edward was such a great bloke. And yes, it *is* good to be home. And I want to offer you my sincere thanks for helping with both Walter and Grace," Tom hesitated before adding, "while I was missing." They exchanged a wan smile before their steering the conversation to back to Edward.

Nelly noticed them in discussion and took the opportunity to excuse herself from an overbearing acquaintance of Edward's. Again She smiled to imagine Edward whispering in her ear, *What the hell is he here for? Free drinks and food, no doubt!* Still, Nelly needed to show everyone her gratitude for their attendance and their sympathy. There were no surviving relatives in either Edward's or Sylvia's family, but it was a testament to Edward's position in the community that the place was packed. Nelly walked closer, noting with interest the absence of Errol's long-standing fiancée, Gillian. Nelly had neither seen nor heard of Gillian since Walter's twenty-first birthday. She was sorely tempted to ask Errol what was going on but thought better of it.

"Oh, Nelly, there you are. I've been trying to get your attention," Errol said with an expression of relief. "I must leave now, but before I go, I need to tell you something. Edward appointed me as legal executor of his will, and in that capacity, would it be possible for you - I mean the Nobel family - to grace my chambers tomorrow? I know it's rushed, but the murder trial I'm involved in is taking up most of my time."

"Of course, Errol," Nelly said. "I hadn't thought about Edward's will." She looked at Tom. "Is that alright with you, Tom?"

Tom agreed, then looked at his watch. "I think it's about time we all said our goodbyes. I can see the manager discretely tapping his watch - it's time to go home."

*

The Nobel family, including Emma, sat to attention. Errol positioned himself behind his antique desk and cleared his throat before reading Edward's last will. After a moving prologue handwritten by Edward. The property and monies he possessed had been distributed fairly amongst the people who now gathered in Errol's office. Grace and Walter received the lion's share of Edward's estate, and the rest he divided up between Nelly and Tom per his wishes. Nelly was touched by Edward's generosity, and Tom was surprised that he got anything after misbehaving. *It's more of a reflection of what a good man Edward was than of me,* Tom thought wryly.

Walter squeezed Emma's hand when Errol announced he would be the benefactor of Edward's home. Emma wasn't so sure. *Living next to my mother-in-law! Even though we get along well. I think it's a bit close. I felt a fresh start, maybe in East Melbourne, close to the city where Walter will be working.* Nevertheless, she was grateful to Edward, and she smiled warmly at Walter. *Wherever Walter wants to go, I'll be there.*

Sad as they all were, memories of their time shared with Edward helped keep smiles on faces and warmth in their hearts. Lunch at Pellegrini's, Edward's favourite restaurant, added another memory to share. The owner, Antony, had known Edward for many years, and he provided everything 'on the house' as a tribute. The entire staff joined in the toast, Antony proposed. "We drink in memory to our good friend, Edward. A truly wonderful, generous man!".

*

On arriving back at the family home, Nelly handed Tom the key to unlock the front door. They'd be alone for a night or two as Grace had elected to stay at Ferntree Gully with Walter and Emma. Later, thinking about her decision, Grace confided to Walter. "I think it's a good idea for Mum and Dad to have some time alone. You know, to work out what comes next for each of them."

The two days gave Tom and Nelly time to chat in the uninterrupted privacy of their lounge room. Over and over, they discussed their years of marriage: the whys and wherefores, the woes, the triumphs, and the heartbreak. Emotions rose and subsided, and the passage of time had lent them new perspectives to solve some old issues. Tom shared his torment at having to kill other men, albeit in the arena of war.

Nelly truly felt for him, seeing the raw emotion and regret stamped on his features as he related the events that haunted him. His romance with Lucy came later. Tom knew his confession would be hard for Nelly to hear, so he glossed over the details of his recollections. Finally, he tried to explain the reasons why he felt the need to go outback. This, Nelly understood. Simply put - he had been desperately confused.

"Unfortunately, Tom," Nelly said, trying not to sound too indignant, "I had to stay home *for our family's sake*. So, in between work and dealing with my difficult mother. I also had to cope with my feelings of being *deserted* and *rejected* by you." She sniffed back a tear, and Tom waited for what he knew was coming. "You *left* us, Tom, not to fight in the war but to run away from *me*." Tom knew she was right. She was perfectly entitled to be angry – he had been a coward, and he felt ashamed of himself.

Nelly saw her words had hit home. She took a shuddering breath and continued. "To be perfectly honest, Tom, I don't blame you. I can see now how I had become bitter and twisted. Loving someone who doesn't love you can have that effect." Nelly's eyes welled and distorted her vision of Tom's handsome face. "When love is not returned, well…." Nelly took a deep breath, gazing at their wedding photo that still sat on the mantle. "I've never had anyone love me, not even my mother." Nelly paused. "I suppose that's not entirely true because the only thing that's saved me through all these years is the love and acceptance from our children," she laughed as tears fell. "I mean, Grace and Walter. I'm not allowed to call them children. And Edward, of course. I don't want to think about what would have happened if he hadn't stepped in to take the reins."

Tom rose from his chair and approached her, his arms held wide.

"No, Tom. It's too late. You have a wife and another son, and you must go to them." Nelly forced a smile. "Not until after Walter's wedding, though."

"Of course, Nelly. But you're wrong. I was to blame for your bitterness. Never feel guilty. I'm the guilty one. I can only ask for your forgiveness. Please, forgive me, Nelly."

Nelly stood to embrace Tom. "I forgive you, Tom, and although I will always love you, I can also honestly wish you every happiness with Lucy and Tyson. I give you my blessing."

Ten years ago, had Nelly never thought she would ever be able to forgive Tom, no. But she had changed. She was a different person now, a better person - a person who would never have emerged had Tom stayed.

Grace and Walter returned home to find their parents laughing at old photos, some they'd retrieved from Edward's home. The smiling shots revealed a glimpse into a once happy marriage. Until, for a whole range of reasons now firmly anchored in the past, it had eroded. Now, they both looked forward to enjoying a special friendship based on mutual respect.

Lucy had willingly decided to come to Australia. When Tom had asked her, through her tears, she had said, in a genuinely dreadful attempt at an Aussie accent, "I'll give it a red hot go, mate!"

Tom had taken up the lucrative offer with a new and enterprising radio station in Western Australia. He would be their star presenter of Morning Radio and the only race caller. The station manager had said, "There's positive talk about a new wave of entertainment hitting Australia, Tom. Commercial television – it's the next big thing. Menzies announced licenses would soon be available to everyone who wanted to purchase a television." Tom could only imagine how exciting his life might be if he worked in television. Imagine if they televised race meetings?

Edward's home, they decided, would remain a shrine until well after the wedding. His photos were the only things they took and shared between them, each treasuring their box full of memories.

*

The Saturday before the wedding, Grace received a phone call. Cyril was in the hospital, suffering from a chronic bout of diverticulitis. The entire card of the Healesville Races was hers to call. Never had she imagined being given this responsibility so soon and managing all the announcements between the races. Grace wondered if she was up to it - she'd only ever had to concentrate on the last two races of the day.

Tom couldn't be there to support Grace. He'd gone back to Western Australia, where he told the details of his past to reporters, radio hosts, and anyone else who cared to ask. Alias, Norm had changed his name back to Tom Nobel, and his exploits told a great story and made him quite a celebrity. It seemed he could do no wrong, and everyone within cooee accepted Tom back into the fold. His future was now set. Lucy and Tyson would join Tom in Melbourne next week; when he returned for the wedding. Then together, they would return to Western Australia to live.

Grace felt a little abandoned. The rest of the family had been kept busy with last-minute wedding plans, so when Grace found herself on her own in the broadcast box, she simply stuck to her routine. She took deep breaths to calm her nerves and gave silent thanks to Cyril for all he'd taught her. And now, his invaluable lessons would come in handy. Grace hoped.

The first race approached, and fourteen highly groomed thoroughbreds began one by one to enter the parade ring, their coats gleaming in the warm December sunshine. In her unique and recognisable voice, Grace gave an accurate commentary on each horse's fitness, form, and presentation; her nerves evaporated once she began her delivery. She called the first race, and with her usual flair for the vernacular, Grace brought the challenge to life before naming the winner in a close finish, generating a loud cheer from the crowd.

And so the day went. Grace had finally completed a full day, calling every race on the card - without one mistake. Later, her humorous input and expertise were hailed as a welcome change by punters and officials alike.

Smiling and ruminating on the events of the day, she walked through an almost empty racecourse towards the bus stop, cursing as the bus pulled away when she was still a hundred yards distant.

"Damn! I'll have to wait for the next one."

Grace sat on the seat and pondered her future. Walter and Emma's happiness had her spellbound, and their talk of having children stirred a longing within Grace. It felt ages ago when she'd fought her feelings toward Johnno when he wanted to hold her, kiss her. Grace thought she hadn't been ready. But she had. She just wouldn't admit it. Now, after a magical day doing what she'd dreamt of doing all her life, Grace found her truth. *Yes, I can do it! I can call races as good as, if not better than, anyone else. I can, and I will become a professional race caller.* But suddenly, her resolve faltered, as if a dark shadow loomed, clouding her vision. *But is it worth giving up a family for? Is doing this worth losing Johnno, the only man I'll ever love? He has a career, too. He loves the Army; he loves training young men and women! Yes, women! They're in the mix now.* Jealousy stirred Grace's heartstrings; she imagined Johnno finding another woman, one who shared the same interests, the same lifestyle. *NO!*

"Oh, what's a girl supposed to do?" Grace said aloud.

Her words were overheard by a well-dressed man standing at the stop. He smiled and tipped his hat. "May I sit, Miss Nobel?"

Grace returned the smile, studying a middle-aged man's familiar, character-filled face, maybe in his early forties. His misty blue eyes seemed sad like he'd lost his way. She tapped the seat.

"Of course. Please do."

"I have to congratulate you, Grace. I hope you don't mind me calling you Grace?" His voice also had a listless quality.

"No, not at all. And your name, sir?"

He chuckled. "I'm afraid I am not as well-known as you, Grace. The name is Menzies, Robert Menzies." He laughed more heartily at Grace's double-take.

"I know. It's my cross to bear - I have the same name as our illustrious Prime Minister. And I've been told I even look a bit like the great man, or not, depends on who you ask. All I want to say is, I admire you, Grace Nobel. You show true grit, young lady. If you were a man, you would have been Victoria's number one race caller by now." He studied Grace's beautiful face; she reminded him of his wife - same colour hair, emerald eyes. "You bear a resemblance to my wife, Grace, when she was your age, of course. And like you, she was brave and determined. I lost her during the war."

"How did your wife die, Mr Menzies?" Grace saw him fighting back emotion. "Oh, I am sorry, you don't have to talk about it if you don't want to." She touched his shoulder.

"I hate to think about it, Grace." He paused, looking to the west where the pink glow of sunset was now fading behind the ranges. "If you don't mind listening to a lonely soul, Grace, I'm sure I just heard Maudie telling me to share her story with you." Grace nodded her approval. "Well then, Maudie was a nurse. She loved to help people, to watch them heal under her care. She was an angel. Anyway, the Hospital Ship she was on in the war was sailing to New Guinea when it was torpedoed by a Japanese submarine. Maudie survived the explosion and swam three miles to an island, along with the other survivors. The Japanese soldiers were waiting for them on the beach. One nurse had managed to escape and hid in the jungle, and from there, she watched the massacre. Luckily, she was eventually saved by New Guinea natives. Later, after the war, she told the story about how Maudie tried to stop the slaughter. Maudie attacked the soldier nearest to her." A smile creased the corner of Robert's mouth. "Maudie had six brothers, so she'd learned how to fight. She downed the bastard with a rugby tackle and slit his throat with a scalpel. Another soldier ran up behind her, and Maudie was bayoneted." Robert wiped a tear away, and Grace patted his back. "Now, all I have left is Maudie's Bravery Medal, though it's cold comfort."

"No children?"

"No."

Grace held his hand in a gesture of comfort. They sat silently until the last bus arrived, and together they boarded. They sat, and Grace turned to Robert.

"I'm so sorry for your loss, Robert. Too many people suffered unspeakable cruelty in the war. I can only thank the Lord my Dad survived and my fiancé, Johnno. He was wounded, but not badly. He was sent home just before the war ended. He's fine now. Johnno stayed in the Army. He's training young cadets."

"I'm truly happy for you, Grace. And I thank you for listening - and caring. I don't know why I felt the need to tell you." He smiled. "Maybe I did hear Maudie ordering me." He squeezed her hand. "Tell me, Grace, when I came and sat next to you, you seemed deep in thought, like you were trying to make a decision. Am I right?"

"Yes, you're right, Robert. I knew after today that I could call races and run the show as well as any man. Then I wondered if being consumed by all the work and study it takes to stay on top of the racing game. Would it ruin my chances of having a happy marriage and a family? I thought calling races was everything, but I don't know now." Grace stared out the window, trying to fathom her feelings. "But now, I'm thinking that maybe having someone to love and building a home with them and raising children together is what matters. Do you think that's the most important thing in life, Robert?" He lowered his head. "Oh, that was thoughtless of me. I am sorry."

Robert looked at Grace, tears filling his blue eyes. "Don't ever be sorry, Grace. Be guided by your heart, and I'll pray it never gets broken like mine." Robert turned away to look out the window. "This is my stop, Grace. Good luck with your decision, but just remember, your ambition and your heart may not always agree with each other.

CHAPTER 24

The Church of St John The Baptist opened its humble doors to accommodate everybody wanting to witness the vows taken by beautiful Emma Blake and handsome Walter Nobel. Never mind, he had a disability; he had captured Emma's heart. The local congregation and the guests invited to join the celebrations chatted excitedly about the best wedding to be seen since the war ended. Thankfully, the weather had gifted them a mild sixty-eight degrees with a gentle south-easterly breeze. Perfect!

Tom was Best Man and stood proudly to the right of Walter, where they waited patiently at the altar for his bride, Emma, and Grace, her bridesmaid.

Nelly, Johnno, Cookie, Lucy, and Tyson sat in the front pew until Tyson became uncontrollable, and Lucy thought it best to take him outside until the ceremony ended. Nelly's brothers and their wives sat in the pew behind. Their presence made Nelly completely fulfilled. She kept turning to smile her delight at them coming all the way to Victoria, and she was forever grateful to them for having the good sense to follow their intuition. *They found Tom for us. I wonder if Dad up in Heaven had something to do with that?* Sometimes, like today, she felt his presence.

Emma felt like she was part of a fairy tale. She sensed her mother's presence and spoke silently to her throughout the service. *I have no doubt I am marrying the right man, Mum. Everything we have been through together has only strengthened the bond between us. I know some people only see what Walter can't do. But I see everything he can do. I love him more each day, and I know that you would love him, too.*

Later, as Nelly danced with Errol, she summoned her bravado and asked him what no one else seemed to know. "Where's Gillian these days, Errol?" His body tensed for a moment before leading Nelly off the dance floor. Together, they found a quiet corner of the room.

"I realize I should have told you, Nelly. I apologise. Gillian left me for a younger man." He snorted mockery. "I'm afraid I've been working too hard, and I let her slip away into the arms of *a football player.*" He shrugged and smiled ruefully. "Of all the men I thought Gillian would be attracted to, I never thought it would be a football player. Even if he is the star player for Carlton." Errol raised his eyebrows.

Nelly tried to look appropriately sympathetic before she collapsed into laughter. "I'm so sorry, Errol," she said, dabbing at her eyes. "I'm not laughing at *you*. But - *a football player?* Fancy trading a man like you in for *a football player!*" Realising what she had just said, Nelly blushed furiously.

"Don't worry, Nelly, I'll take that as a compliment. "Actually, Gillian told me she wanted a family – a large one, so I had to tell her I was not planning on having any more children, and that was the end of it."

"Well," said Nelly, having regained her composure, 'it's far better you both found that out before you got married." She smiled wickedly. "I can just see Gillian staying at home to raise a brood of footy players!" She burst out laughing again, and this time Errol joined her.

"I know, Nelly, I can just imagine it." He sighed deeply, with philosophical resignation rather than regret. "However, I must admit I'm rather looking forward to some grandchildren. You get to enjoy them and then hand them back. What do you say, Nelly?"

"I absolutely agree, Errol. I'm looking forward to having our grandchildren running around the garden. Before they go home." Nelly gave a small chuckle, then thought about Tyson's behaviour at the wedding. She felt some fleeting sympathy for Tom, but after all, they were the choices he'd made.

Errol was struck by what Nelly said - *our* grandchildren. He knew he had been attracted to Nelly from the start, but Tom was away at war, and then Nelly became close to Edward. Just how close, Errol didn't know and didn't care to know. And, of course, there was Gillian. There hadn't been an opportunity to let his feelings for Nelly go any further than admiration – but now?

Errol sent a shiver of delight through Nelly as he looked deeply into her eyes, held her tight in his arms, placed a soft kiss on her cheek, and whispered into her ear, "Dance with me, my dear?"

Nelly stepped back and looked at him levelly. "Errol, I'd be happy to dance with you forever." Smiling, he swept her into his arms and onto the dancefloor.

Johnno relished the warmth and softness of Grace as they waltzed effortlessly around the floor. He'd give anything to take her back to Sydney as his wife, not his fiancée. *Do weddings do this? Make you all romantic, so you forget reality and want to make your dreams come true like Grace made her dream come true?*

"Johnno." Grace stopped abruptly when out of the way of the other twirling and laughing couples.

"Jesus, Grace! You nearly tripped me up! I thought I was supposed to lead!"

"That's what I want to talk about." She gave him that determined look he knew so well. "I've been doing a lot of soul-searching, Johnno. I met a man at the bus stop outside the Healesville Racecourse last Saturday, and he told me a pretty harrowing story about his wife, Maudie." Gracie softened and led Johnno away to find a secluded spot where they could sit. Grace gazed searchingly into Johnno's eyes. "Maudie lost her life in the war, Johnno. It got me thinking – with my heart – not my head. I weighed *everything* up, and you are *the* most important thing in my life." Johnno chuckled, and she smacked him over the arm. "I'm serious!"

"I know you are, Gracie, but you just called me a thing! I hope I'm more than a thing."

"Don't get smart with me, Johnno! I'm trying to propose marriage -without any strings. Meaning, I'm ready to be home to cook dinner for you every night and kiss you good morning." With an eyebrow raised, she added, "and to provide anything else you need. You know, like children." His jaw dropped. "I mean it with all my heart, Johnno. I'm ready. Besides, I'm sure even after I've yelled at kids for five years. I'll still have a voice to call races. Studying the fields will remain my hobby while I'm barefoot and pregnant." Johnno's shocked expression made Grace laugh. "Don't worry. I won't let go of my dream. I'll just put it on the back burner to simmer for five years. Besides, I'd like to live in New South Wales or anywhere else you get transferred."

Grace gave Johnno a dazzling smile, stood up, and pulled him to his feet. She was now the same height, five foot eleven, and no longer needed to be on tippy toes to kiss him, as she now did, passionately, with all the love, respect, and adoration she felt for him.

EPILOGUE

Unfortunately, Grace and Johnno were unable to have the family they both longed for, and after three years of marriage, Grace returned to call races. And her struggle began anew. One after another, the men in the racing industry refused to recognise her talent as one of the best race callers the country had seen. Grace remained a popular race caller on the Provincial circuit. Still, no matter how loud the crowd roared, no matter how many accolades she received, the closed-minded brethren of the Metropolitan Race Committees refused to acknowledge her talent.

Tom Nobel experienced great success in radio and television to soon become a household name in Western Australia. He and Lucy had another son, whom they named Edward.

Nelly and Errol were happily married, with Nelly relishing the added status of being his legal secretary. She continued to dress up for work, and Errol, every day. *Some things never change.*

Walter became a successful lawyer and a champion of the rights of people with disabilities. He and Emma had four children, who were doted on by their Grandparents. For short periods.

Their only daughter, Victoria, followed her Aunt Grace's path to become a successful race caller. Victoria's mentor was John Tapp, a receiver of an OAM, plus an enormously admired and well-respected leader in his field.

Grace never gave up her fight for equality, and finally, it paid dividends when she was asked to call the primary race at the 1960 Melbourne Oaks Day meeting - and be paid for it. After all, that particular race day has been and always will be known as 'Ladies Day.' The winning horse, *Lady Sybil*, ran to victory under the perfect call of Grace Nobel, who had placed a decent wager on the filly. The name reminded her of Edward's wife, Sylvia, whom she still loved and missed.

After that day, a colossal petition was mounted for Grace to be given Metropolitan status as a race caller. And she won. All those men who, over the years, had tried to deny Grace her rightful place in racing had lost.

On her retirement from race calling, Grace Nobel was finally rewarded for her trailblazing efforts in the world of race calling and was acknowledged as 'one of the best, ever!'

www.ingramcontent.com/pod-product-compliance
Lightning Source LLC
Chambersburg PA
CBHW070017120726
47909CB00003B/970